NEXT
OF KIN

A. E. LAWRENCE

 FriesenPress

One Printers Way
Altona, MB R0G 0B0
Canada

www.friesenpress.com

Copyright © 2025 by Lawrence Ayliffe
First Edition — 2025

Edited by Diane Young
Jacket art by Carlo Giambarresi
Cover Design by Coni Kennedy

All rights reserved.

This novel is a work of fiction. The thoughts, words, and actions of real or fictionalized characters, and names, events, dialog, and incidents are products of the authors imagination and are not to be construed as real. Some locales and organizations are real but are used fictitiously. E.&O.E.

No part of this publication may be reproduced in any form, or by any means, electronic or mechanical, including photocopying, recording, or any information browsing, storage, or retrieval system, without permission in writing from FriesenPress.

ISBN
978-1-03-832819-9 (Hardcover)
978-1-03-832818-2 (Paperback)
978-1-03-832820-5 (eBook)

1. FICTION, THRILLERS, CRIME

Distributed to the trade by The Ingram Book Company

ACKNOWLEDGMENTS

Thank you for buying this book. Without readers like you, writing is akin to self-flagellation.

I hope you enjoy the story, tell all your friends that it's a pretty good yarn, and implore them to buy a copy.

Also, I hope that you share positive words about the book on social media, and that you'll encourage a groundswell of readers to have *Next of Kin* made into a movie. The only other thing I ask, is that you purchase a copy of *Ghosts of Angels*, the prequel to the book you're now holding.

I am forever indebted to the good-hearted friends who suffered through reading the numerous rewrites and offered honest critiques and unfaltering words of encouragement. In no specific order, they are Brian Nason, Bryan Smith, Michael McEwan, and David Klugsberg. I would also like to thank those who read *Ghosts of Angels* and insisted that I write this sequel.

Finally, I would like to thank Diane Young, who in my humble opinion is the world's best editor, Carlo Giambarresi for yet another amazing cover illustration, Coni Kennedy for her design brilliance, and my wife Vickie for her unwavering love and patience.

My frustration with trying to break into the world of "traditional" publishing led me to publish *Next of Kin* independently, so the book you're holding, or reading on your device, is my commitment to storytelling and a true labor of love. Please enjoy the journey.

For my very own next of kin—Vickie, Adam, Barbara, Emily, and Natalia.

"What is the son but an extension of the father."

—Frank Herbert, "Dune"

CHAPTER ONE

Youthful, sonic-pitched laughter and boisterous chatter ricocheted off the ancient wood-paneled walls of the small bistro in the 7th arrondissement, near Paris's famed Eiffel Tower. The source of this joyful revelry emanated from a group of students from the nearby American University of Paris celebrating the end of the final semester.

Some of the restaurant's other customers smiled, possibly recalling their own earlier days at school. Others were less charitable, scowling and throwing disparaging glances with every morsel of food being shoved into their downturned mouths.

The party broke up at 9:45 p.m. and after many goodbye hugs, handshakes, and cheek-to-cheek kisses, the friends dissipated and wandered off into the darkening night.

Jessica Devlin, a sophomore at the university, loved Paris. It was a far cry from the wide-open spaces of her home in the states and sometimes, mostly at night, the narrow streets and ancient alleyways frightened her. Jessica pulled up the collar of her coat to ward off the early spring chill and misty drizzle that shrouded the shadowy streets. She hesitated, cautiously scanning the streets in front of her, and seeing nothing out of the ordinary, began quickly walking towards the tiny apartment that she shared with Giles, her French boyfriend.

An indiscernible shape stepped out from the shadows in front of her. Jessica froze, her heart pounding like it was going to burst from her chest, and for one short moment she stopped breathing. Then, just as quickly as he had appeared, the apparition passed by, head bent low against the inclement spring weather. Jessica took a deep breath and continued walking. *I'm being crazy*, she thought. *Just calm down. There's nothing to be afraid of.*

She heard the muffled clack of approaching footsteps on the pavement behind her, and the terror that she'd felt just moments earlier returned tenfold. A rancid metallic taste rose from the back of her throat. She quickened her pace then crossed the narrow street, hoping that whoever was behind her would pass by. Instead, the steps grew appreciably faster—and closer.

A sense of impending dread shot up her spine and the imagined claws of terror seized her by the shoulders and dug their stone-hard thumbs into the soft flesh at the back of her neck. Trembling she turned to face her stalkers, and the gut-wrenching fear left her body like a quickly deflating balloon. *Whew, just a couple nuns rushing to get out of the crappy weather.* Jessica smiled at the sisters, breathed a deep sigh of relief, then turned to resume her journey home.

Suddenly, she was grabbed, and a coarse black cloth was thrown over her head. The repugnant odor of chloroform filled her mouth and nostrils. She coughed, just once, tried unsuccessfully to scream, then slumped into unconsciousness. Minutes later, Jessica's shroud-covered body was manhandled into the rear compartment of a nondescript, dark gray Citroën Relay, one of many such delivery vehicles scurrying, like harried little animals, around the streets and boulevards of the French capital.

The van, carrying its anesthetized cargo, sped off into the night toward a preordained destination: a dank chamber where the young life of Jessica Devlin would be sacrificed to appease the insatiable appetite of Quetzalcoatl, the snake god, and the thousands of worshippers of La Orden de las Serpientes de Cristo.

CHAPTER TWO

Claire opened her eyes. The sky was a dull, soapy-water gray, and the early spring rain that had started the previous evening splattered hard against her bedroom windows. She reached over to the young man who was sharing her bed, gently ran her fingers down his chest, and felt the beginnings of an arousal.

"*Bonjour chéri.*"

The man turned, looked toward her, and smiled.

"Good morning, mother."

She rolled over, straddled his torso, and kissed him. A tremor of eagerness ran through her body, and a tiny gasp emanated from her open lips.

Thirty minutes later, the man slipped quietly from the comfort of his mother's bed, showered, dressed, and strolled back into the bedroom. Claire was still seductively sprawled across her unkempt bed he stopped and stared lovingly at her still beautiful body. "I'll be back as soon as I finish our business in Mexico City. Love you."

"Love you too, darling." *But you're very much like your father, and sometimes you scare the living hell out of me*, she thought. Philippe bent over, kissed her gently on the forehead, left the apartment, and ran downstairs to his waiting limousine.

ψ

Philippe and Claire Rodriguez had risen from the ashes of scandal. He'd picked up the pieces of his father's devastated business enterprises and rekindled the fire of La Orden de las Serpientes de Cristo, the Order of the Serpents of Christ. Not that he gave a shit about the quasi-religious global cult that he now headed, but it was a convenient and profitable entity that enabled him to control many of his far-flung business and criminal activities.

To compensate for the inherited shame brought upon him by his father, Philippe had meticulously cultivated an image of respectability. He used his tremendous wealth to support numerous charities and had earned an enviable reputation for integrity and honesty in all his business endeavors—the ones that were public knowledge, that is.

Philippe hated his father but harbored a depraved admiration for the man's accomplishments and acknowledged that without his munificence, he wouldn't be blessed with the lavish lifestyle he now enjoyed. This love-hate relationship was one of the few contradictions in his normally compartmentalized life.

ψ

Inca Gold Investments, the keystone of his father's financial empire, was gone, as was the man's priceless collection of pre-Colombian artifacts. In Philippe's mind, the downfall of his family's fortune and reputation lay at the hands of Nicholas Palmer. His innermost feelings about what the ex-cop from Chicago had done to him and his family often rose like a thick, sour bile in his throat, causing him to lash out in uncontrollable rage at anyone or anything within striking range.

As he jetted across the Atlantic Ocean, he managed to temporarily bury his venomous thoughts of revenge. He had more pressing things occupying his mind, namely his impending meeting with the twelve apostles of La Orden de las Serpientes de Cristo.

Under Philippe's stewardship, the cult had transformed and modernized into an organization virtually unrecognizable from its predecessor. Gone were the dank hidden chambers, wizened old men, crackle-voiced hags, and heinous snake tattoos of his father's rule. Gone was the perverse custom of leaving the martyred victims in a postulating position on the front steps of Catholic cathedrals. Under his rule, it was inconsequential if the young women, so cruelly murdered by the cult's followers, were left on the steps of a church or roughly thrown into a filthy, garbage-strewn alley. The only holdover from Hector Rodriguez's regime related to the selection of the cult's sacrificial victims: they had to be nineteen-year-old women born on November 19.

ψ

Philippe's evening meeting was convened in a sleek boardroom on the nineteenth floor of an ultra-modern tower in Mexico City's upscale Polanco district. The attendees were mostly young, affluent men and women, specialists in various aspects of the cult's business. This new, highly efficient incarnation of the Order had morphed into a multibillion-dollar enterprise with thousands of devoted followers. These sheeplike acolytes made contributions and donations that continually filled the Order's coffers and fueled many of Philippe's heinous business activities.

The darkened boardroom was occupied by this new breed of apostle. All were dressed in black hooded robes with multicolored ropes tied at the waist, one of the few legacies from the Order's past that Philippe decreed be perpetuated.

Philippe was also clothed in a black robe. The only feature distinguishing him from all the others was that his face was hidden behind a dazzling gold mask representing the nightmarish countenance of Quetzalcoatl. This carefully construed disguise imparted a horrific godlike aura and commanded fearful respect from those who knew the man's depraved nature.

Philippe walked slowly around the table. He stopped behind one of the attendees and placed his hand on the woman's right shoulder. This seemingly benign act initiated an inexplicable look of both rapture and anticipation on the face of its recipient.

He completed his rounds, sat at the head of the table, and called the meeting to order. The evening's agenda included financial reports from the Order's far-flung drug-and-arms-trafficking enterprises and sex-trade operations. Following the nuts-and-bolts financial reviews, discussions were tabled regarding a suggested alliance between the Order and a notorious Russian crime syndicate. The proposal was vetoed by Philippe and rejected by the full retinue of apostles. Finally, the name of the sacrificial candidate, chosen earlier for the biannual human offering to Quetzalcoatl, was announced to the elite congregation of apostles.

The gathering lasted well into the night, and when all other items on the agenda had been covered, Philippe adjourned the conclave. Individuals from the assembly stood and walked silently toward his chair. Each apostle stopped, bowed their head in devotion for their master, and kissed the ring on his right hand: a twenty-four-karat gold representation of a serpent coiled ominously around his index finger. The chosen one remained seated, her head bowed in respect for the man god she revered and feared above all others.

Philippe raised his right hand and pointed toward her, and then, in a voice amplified through the mask he wore, gave her the order to initiate the task that she'd been trained for.

"The martyr has been chosen and identified to the apostles."

The woman acknowledged his declaration. "Si, El Cardinal."

He gave her the order to initiate the task that she'd been appointed for.

"Fly to Paris." Philippe paused. "The holiest of rituals must happen tomorrow night."

A smile of sadistic anticipation flashed across the woman's face. She stood, kissed her leader's ring, and left the room.

Philippe remained seated. If the sect's thousands of followers could read his mind, they'd be shocked and horrified by his cold-blooded ruthlessness. *Dumb fuckers would jump off a cliff if I asked them to.* The thought of thousands of lemmings leaping to their deaths made him smile.

CHAPTER THREE

Nick Palmer felt uneasy. Nineteen years had passed since Henri Deneuve had been murdered. Nineteen years since he and Gabriela were instrumental in shattering Hector Rodriguez's brutal cult, and nineteen years since he'd seen or heard the paranormal messages from the sect's ghostly, long-dead victims.

The feeling he was experiencing, the gut sense that a good cop gets when something is about to go wrong, was deeply troubling.

He was standing in front of the living room window of his and Gabriela's apartment on Île Saint-Louis, silently watching the ominously dark waters of the Seine and the endless parade of tour boats and barges gliding by.

"What's up, big boy?"

Gabriela Martinez, Nick's wife, slid behind him and placed her arms gently around his waist. She sensed the tension in his body. It felt like a coiled spring ready to burst free from its tether.

"I don't know, something's bugging me, something I know that I'm not going to like." He lifted his shoulders and clasped his hands together on the back of his neck.

Years earlier, Gabriela had seen the ghostly images of girls in mirrors, just like Nick had. She'd heard them speak about their brutal deaths at the hands of La Orden de las Serpientes de Cristo, and she knew that her husband had an extraordinary sixth sense when it came to impending danger.

She didn't reveal her concern. "Don't worry, honey. You'll figure it out soon enough. C'mon, let's go and grab some lunch." She tossed him his raincoat.

ψ

The Brasserie de l'Isle Saint-Louis, one of Paris's popular lunch spots, was a short walk from their apartment, and because of the unpredictable episodes of heavy spring rain, it was unusually quiet. They sat at a small round table next to the window. A white-aproned waiter who they knew from many past visits strolled over and tried to hand them menus. They smiled and waved him off, it wasn't the kind of day that they wanted to exchange pleasantries. The server shrugged and walked away. He already knew what they would order: cheese omelets made with Brie and four of the heavenly croissants that the restaurant was famous for.

"Figured it out yet, honey?"

Nick was about to respond when he glimpsed a reflection in the restaurant's window. It was the fleeting image of a man. A man who looked familiar. A man that he hadn't seen or heard from in almost two decades. A shock wave, like a storm-born lightning bolt, shot up his spine.

"Henri. I think that I just saw Henri."

He leaped from the table, rushed outside, and frantically scanned the surrounding area, but the street was virtually empty—just a few passerby's running to escape a sudden downpour.

By the time Nick returned to the table, their lunch had arrived. Gabriela reached across the table and gently took his hand.

"Let's just eat and go home."

ψ

When they'd returned to their apartment, Nick went straight into the bathroom and stared into the mirror. It was as if he needed to see and hear from the ghostly images of the long-dead young women who'd originally led him to Hector Rodriguez and the cult that the man once headed. There was nothing. None of the pleading, ashen-colored faces of martyred women he'd seen years earlier. Just his own haggard face staring back at him through his dark, worried eyes.

When he turned to leave, he heard a stifled giggle. It was a voice that brought back a flood of memories, some good and some bad. He spun around and there, reflected in the mirror, was the enigmatic face of Henri Deneuve. The apparition of Nick's elderly friend and benefactor had a mischievous smile on his face, and a tear of joy trickled down his cheek. The apparition of Henri quickly wiped away the offending teardrop with a massive red handkerchief.

"Ah, *mon ami*. That was a good one. *C'est bon*?"

Nick was overjoyed to see his old friend and reached out to try and touch him.

The old professor looked back. His face had suddenly changed into a mask of sadness.

"Would that we could, Nicholas. More than anything, I miss the touch and embrace of old friends."

Gabriela's voice interrupted from outside the door.

"Nick, are you okay in there? Are you talking to your girls in the mirror again?"

Nick smiled. The face that he was looking at was anything but a pretty young woman.

"Tell me, Henri, why are you here? What is it that you want from me?"

The professor's mood darkened. He lowered his eyes and spoke—his words were barely above a whisper.

"The serpent has slithered from out of its lair. It seeks revenge and retribution. Be vigilant, *mon ami*. Be very vigilant."

The old academic's ghostly face grimaced.

"Nineteen years and now it begins again. Once more, innocent young women are being slaughtered and sacrificed to the unholy snake god."

The reflected image of the elderly professor slowly faded and vanished.

Nick stood in front of the mirror for a few minutes longer. His thoughts were spinning out of control. *Fuck, this is just about the last thing I need to hear.*

ψ

Gabriela was standing in the middle of the room, her arms folded across her chest.

"So, what was that all about?"

"Nothing good, I'm afraid."

Nick was about to tell his wife about the chilling conversation he'd had with the ghostly apparition of Henri Deneuve when his cell rang. He didn't recognize the number showing on the screen.

"Hello, Nick Palmer here."

A cryptic digitized voice spoke. It was foreboding, like something from a horror movie or a bad dream.

"Who is this?"

The disjointed voice ignored Nick's question and kept speaking.

"Tomorrow night, homage will be paid to the great god Quetzalcoatl. Tomorrow night is the ceremony of sacrifice, as decreed by the only true faith."

Nick couldn't believe what he was hearing. Everything that Henri had just warned him about was becoming a horrifying reality, and he was being dragged right into the middle of it—again.

"Where? When?"

"Paris. Tomorrow. Number nineteen."

There was an ominous *click,* and the line went dead.

CHAPTER FOUR

"Number nineteen? What the hell does that mean?" Nick buried his head in his hands. "Is it an address? An age? A date? How in God's name am I supposed to figure it out?"

Gabriela stepped up behind him and placed her hand on his shoulder. "Who was on the phone? And what's with the number nineteen?"

Nick told his wife about how he'd seen Henri in their bathroom mirror and about the ominous call he'd just received from an unknown person. Gabriela repeated his words verbatim. "Tomorrow? Paris? Number nineteen? Tomorrow's the nineteenth—could that be the nineteen? Or does it refer to something else? We'd better start thinking, because whatever it means, we don't have a whole lot of time to figure it out."

Nick shook his head. "I thought we'd heard the last of Hector's goddamned cult. I guess that was just wishful thinking on my part."

Gabriela was already sitting at her computer. Moments later she let out a gasp.

"Nick, the church around the corner—the address is number nineteen on Rue Saint-Louis on l'Ile."

"It couldn't be that easy," he replied.

"Maybe it isn't, but maybe they want to hit us close to where we live. I think it's worth a call to Alain."

Nick picked up his cell and speed-dialed their old friend and deputy director of the Paris police force.

Alain Moreau was at home, watching his wife set their table for dinner. He glanced at the number on his cell and answered.

"*Bonsoir,* Nicholas. To what do I owe the pleasure of having you disturb my dinner?" The policeman chuckled at his little joke.

"Sorry, Alain, but I've just received a very frightening call, and I need your help."

The deputy director listened intently as Nick described the sinister message he'd just hung up from.

"*Putain de merde*, not that again. I thought we'd closed that case years ago."

"So did I, my friend, but it looks like the snake is back, rearing its ugly head again."

Alain Moreau's meteoric rise through the ranks of France's largest police force was due, in large part, to the man he was now speaking to, and if Nick needed his help, then so be it. He looked at his wife, shrugged, then resumed speaking to the man on the other end of the call. "Sit tight, *mon ami.* I'm on my way."

ψ

Maria Torres, the apostle selected by Philippe Rodriguez to undertake the repugnant task of executing the latest martyr to Quetzalcoatl, had served with the US military in Afghanistan and was dishonorably discharged for sadistically killing a prisoner of war in the bloody conflict. The man was just one of the many unfortunate victims of her perverted psyche. She converted to La Orden de las Serpientes de Cristo while she was visiting her paternal grandfather in Tijuana. José Torres worked in the illicit drug trade and enjoyed a close, albeit subservient, relationship with Philippe Rodriguez. It was her grandfather who showed her the path to her future, a path that led her to an extremist, almost rabid devotion to Philippe Rodriguez and the snake god Quetzalcoatl.

Maria had arrived in Paris at 1:40 p.m. on an Aeroméxico flight and was now sequestered in a seedy nondescript apartment in Place des Fêtes, one of the French capital's most unsavory neighborhoods.

"Have you abducted the woman who's to be glorified by offering her very existence to our great lord Quetzalcoatl?"

Her question, delivered to a ragtag collection of believers, sounded like a threat hissed from between the deadly fangs of the snake god himself.

An earnest-looking man in his early twenties bowed his head in respect to the visiting apostle. "We have, exalted one. She is locked in the cellar of an abandoned warehouse."

The executioner spent the next thirty minutes examining the dossier of Jessica Devlin. The girl was American. She was intelligent and accomplished, and her long dusty-brown hair framed a face highlighted by rosy cheeks and red tulip-shaped lips. She looked like a woman plucked from one of Renoir's famous paintings.

"This one is perfect," said Maria Torres. There was no remorse in her voice, and no tinge of guilt. She sounded like she was selecting a prime cut of meat from a butcher shop counter in the Marché d'Aligre, Paris's famed market in the 12th arrondissement.

She handed the dossier to the young man. "Prepare her for tonight's sacred ritual."

The meeting ended and she picked up her cell phone. Maria Torres had two calls to make that day: one, which she'd already made, to the ex-cop from Chicago who was living in Paris, and the second to El Cardinal on his private line.

ψ

When Alain Moreau arrived at Nick and Gabriela's apartment, he was accompanied by two detectives from the city's Préfecture de Police. He'd asked his wife to keep his dinner warm until he returned home. *Whenever that might be*, he thought to himself.

The five of them sat at the large wooden table in the apartment's neat kitchen and Nick recounted the ominous call he'd received earlier that afternoon.

Gabriela chimed in. "Number nineteen is the mystery." Then she told them about the church, just a few blocks away, at 19 Rue Saint-Louis.

"It aligns with the Rodriguez case that we worked on nineteen years ago. Remember all the murdered girls were discovered on the steps of churches?"

Alain grimaced. "It's not much to go on, but I'll send a surveillance detail there to keep watch." He shook Nick's hand, kissed Gabriela on both cheeks, and went home to his dutiful wife and reheated dinner.

ψ

A small contingent of Paris's finest was sent to the address given to them by their superior. The four officers spent the better part of the evening and the entire night keeping watch on the church, but their vigil turned out to be an exercise in luckless futility. At the first light of dawn, the weary flics called the deputy director and gave him the bad news.

Alain Moreau called Nick. "No one. Nothing. I believe that this is what you Americans call *les recherches futiles,* a wild-goose chase."

ψ

When Jessica Devlin regained consciousness, she found herself gagged and tied to a hard wooden chair in a chamber lit by hundreds of tiny sweet-smelling candles. Her last memory was of being grabbed by two nuns who covered her head with a rough, foul-smelling black cloth. She had fleeting flashbacks of being driven along bumpy cobblestone streets, but that was all.

She blinked, trying desperately to focus, and was finally able to look around the stone-walled room. The flickering candles created terrifying shadows against the ancient walls surrounding her. Empty chairs, placed at even intervals around the dank room, were a sign that she might not be alone for much longer.

Jessica shuddered. *Where am I? Why am I here?* She couldn't move, couldn't cry out for help. An unbearable fear tore at her gut, and her head felt as if it would explode with pain. *Please God, help me. Please help me.* Suddenly, an ancient wooden door creaked open, and a group of robed and hooded men and women filed in and, one by one, took their seats.

Jessica felt the searing agony of pure terror. She wanted to cry out, but her dry mouth, swollen tongue, and gag made any kind of sound impossible. She struggled, but her bindings dug deeply into her wrists, and she felt the sticky trickle of blood oozing down her hands. She began to weep, and then looked around, her eyes pleading for her captors to free her. Tonight, Jessica Devlin was the star performer in a living nightmare from which there was no escape.

Finally, after what seemed like an eternity, one of her captors stood, removed her hood, and walked toward the terrified girl.

"Tonight, you are being glorified to die for the pleasure of Quetzalcoatl, the great and almighty god."

Maria Torres removed the multicolored rope from her robe, placed it roughly around the martyr's neck, and pulled it until Jessica Devlin exhaled the last breath of life from her dry, swollen lips.

The assembled congregation rose and quietly left the chamber. Their mission was to inform the thousands of fanatical devotees that the holy sacrifice, as decreed by the doctrine of their faith, had been fulfilled.

ψ

The murdered girl's body was discovered the following morning on the steps of the Cité des Sciences et de l'Industrie in the city's 19th arrondissement. She was obviously strangled, and her nearly naked body was covered with a coarse black robe. The murder weapon, a multicolored rope, still hung loosely around her neck. There were no witnesses, and the couple who found her, visitors from the Netherlands, were still in a state of shock over their grisly discovery.

The officers who'd responded to the call scoured the area and found no clues. They requested and received CCTV footage from the numerous security cameras at the scene, then left the paramedics to take the woman's body to the morgue. All of this was done before the popular attraction opened its doors to the public at 9:30 a.m.

CHAPTER FIVE

Philippe Rodriguez had returned from the conclave of apostles in Mexico City and was comfortably ensconced, enjoying breakfast, on the upper aft deck of his yacht at the Yacht Club de Monaco, also known as the YCM. His yacht, named *Angelina* after his beloved late sister, was a staggering 320-foot ocean-going super palace complete with every conceivable luxury, including a landing pad for his custom-designed Airbus ACH145 nine-passenger helicopter. It also boasted the most advanced technology for navigation, security, and ultra-secure communications.

A steward, immaculately dressed in a dazzling white uniform bearing the yacht's distinctive logo, removed the remains of Philippe's breakfast and disappeared back into the yacht's sumptuous interior. Philippe scowled at the man's unannounced and unwelcomed intrusion into his morning thoughts. He was about to call the impudent steward back to reprimand him but was interrupted by the ring tone of his cell. He picked it up and checked the caller's name on the screen. "*Buenos días*, Maria. I do hope that you have good news for me." This seemingly innocuous greeting had the undertone of a threat, which didn't go unnoticed by the apostle in Paris.

"Everything has been accomplished as per your instructions, El Cardinal."

"And you made the call to that fucking Palmer guy?"

"Yes, Holiness. Everything was completed exactly as you ordered."

"You will be well rewarded in the afterlife, Sister Torres."

Sadistic bitch. I bet she enjoyed every second of it, he thought as he ended the call.

ψ

Nick and Gabriela sat in stunned silence. The news from Alain was anything but good. First, the stakeout at the church, around the corner from their apartment, had been a complete bust. Then their friend's startling news about the perverted murder of the girl found at the Cité des Sciences et de l'Industrie had brought back memories that they'd just as soon forget.

Nick looked toward his wife. "Well, it looks like the game's the same, but the rules are now very different."

Gabriela was familiar with the area, she had visited the museum many times when the children were younger and knew exactly where the girl's body had been found.

"Cité des Sciences is in the 19th arrondissement. Perhaps that's the number nineteen referenced on the message."

Nick didn't respond. He was deep in thought. *Where the hell is Henri when I need him? Perhaps he'd be able to make sense of what's happening.*

He stood, quietly walked into the bathroom, and looked into the mirror. "Where are you, Henri? Where are you when I need you?"

The reflection of Nick's own gaunt face faded and morphed into the image of a young woman that he didn't know. He stepped backward and steadied himself against a towel rack. It had been almost twenty years since he'd faced the ghostly apparition of a dead girl, and the painful recollections of all the ones he'd seen before flooded into his mind.

"*Buongiorno*, Signor Palmer. My name is Pia Del Forno, and I was murdered one year ago to the day. They discovered my body in the triclinium at the House of the Vettii in Pompeii. I was covered in a black robe, kneeling like I was praying, and the colored rope that I was strangled with was left hanging around my neck like a deadly serpent."

Nick was transfixed. The young woman's gruesome story was all too familiar and brought back nightmarish memories of the horrors perpetrated by the cult headed by Hector Rodriguez.

As the reflection of the beautiful Italian girl faded from the mirror, she uttered one last plaintive plea. "Please help us, Signor Palmer. Please help us and all the others who are ordained to follow."

The girl's face faded and morphed into the weathered countenance of Henri Deneuve. It wasn't the joyful face of the man Nick had loved like a father. Instead, the professor's look was dark and ominous, a grim mask that conveyed the desire for revenge and retribution.

"Nineteen years, and now it is all happening again. Another sacrificial murder to the ungodly deity that we believed had been shattered. It must be stopped. It is our divine destiny Nicholas, yours and mine to destroy Philippe, the son of Hector Rodriguez, and La Orden de las Serpientes de Christo forever."

The reflection of the elderly professor faded and vanished, leaving Nick mystified and uncharacteristically uncertain. *Divine destiny? What the hell does he mean by that? What am I supposed to do now? Where do I even start?*

Loud banging on the bathroom door snapped him out of his trance.

"Nick, are you okay? You've been in there for thirty-five minutes."

He opened the door. "It's all happening again, just like it happened all those years ago."

Gabriela saw the despondent look on her husband's face, raised her eyes to the ceiling, and silently swore to the walls that surrounded them. *Oh god, why us? Why now?*

Their previous case had begun nineteen years earlier in Chicago when a young woman's body was discovered on the steps of a cathedral. The victim's body was covered with a coarse black robe and there were scant clues to her identity or to the identities of her murderers.

In the ensuing weeks, Nick faced the ghostly apparition of Margaux Deneuve, who was similarly murdered in 1942 in Paris. The ghostly likenesses of more martyrs appeared, and their despairing voices helped Nick and Gabriela to successfully conclude the case—or so they believed. Now it seemed that the horrendous nightmare from so many years ago had started once again.

Gabriela turned to Nick. She had a look of determined obstinacy on her face. "Okay, so where do we start? We nailed the bastards once, and there's no goddamn reason that we can't do it again."

CHAPTER SIX

Anna Petersen was dying. The morphine, administered by the team of physicians at the Memorial Sloan Kettering Cancer Center in Manhattan, was just a temporary respite from the agonizing pain she suffered. Her pancreatic cancer had spread, and all hopes for her survival had long since passed.

"Is there anything that I can do for you Mother?"

The young woman was desperately trying to hold back the tears that were welling up in her eyes.

Anna slowly opened her eyes and whispered to her twenty-four-year-old daughter. Sierra leaned in closer so that she could hear what her mother was saying. The words, uttered through the woman's dry, scab-caked lips, were barely discernible.

"Your father was Hector Rodriguez." Anna paused and took a deep breath, which sounded more like a rasp, coming from deep within her sunken chest.

"I was a flight attendant on his private jet." She paused again. "When I told him that I was pregnant with you, he was overjoyed and told me that he would provide for both of us, on the one condition that our affair and your birth must remain a secret forever."

The dying woman's eyes closed again, and when she tried to reach out to touch her daughter's hand, all she could do was feebly lift a finger. Sierra's heart was breaking, and she cursed the cancer that was taking her mother, her only relative, away from her.

Anna started to speak again; her voice was barely audible. "Your father, for all his many faults, kept his word to me. He left me with millions of dollars, and soon all of it will be yours."

The conversation was agonizing, and the tears that Sierra didn't want her mother to see began trickling down her flushed cheeks.

"When I'm gone, call our lawyer." The dying woman took another labored breath. "His card is in the drawer in the bedside table." Her eyes shifted towards the small nightstand next to her hospital bed.

Another heart-wrenching wheeze rattled from between Anna's lips. Sierra took hold of her mother's hand and squeezed tightly.

"You have a half-brother. His name is Philippe Rodriguez. He is your only remaining relative." Anna handed her beloved, well-worn rosary to her bereaved daughter, then closed her once-beautiful eyes and stopped breathing. Sierra Petersen fell across the prone body of her mother and cried. It felt as if everything she'd ever really loved had just been wrenched away from her by the hideous disease.

A nurse tried to gently lift Sierra's still sobbing form from off her dead mother's body, but Sierra's grief made her angry, and she shoved the young woman away. She instantly regretted her actions and turned to the caregiver. "I'm so sorry. I shouldn't have done that." The nurse smiled, silently accepted the apology, and quietly left the room. Sierra pulled the bedsheet over her mother's lifeless face, walked around the bed, and opened the drawer in the nightstand. She removed the lawyer's card and glanced at it.

Jonathan Bloom, LLM, PA. Managing Partner.
Bloom Law Group.

She saw that the lawyer's offices were in the Upper West Side, a short walk from her mother's apartment.

ψ

Sierra Petersen was almost six feet tall. She was strikingly beautiful, with an aura of elegance and poise that belied her youth. Following a short stint studying art history, she switched to economics and earned her master's degree from the Wharton School of Business at the University of Pennsylvania. She earned her diploma in street smarts from her occupation as a world-famous fashion model.

Sierra was an intoxicating mélange of Latina and Scandinavian: a look that was much sought after by photographers, casting directors, fashion editors, and some of the world's top luxury brands. She traveled extensively and turned the heads of both men, and women wherever she went. Sierra was a member of the elite cadre of famous fashion models known only by their first name. A name that, unbeknownst to her, was chosen by her father as homage to the mountain range that runs parallel to the Pacific coast in his native Mexico.

Before that day, Sierra had never known who her father was. She'd asked her mother many times about the man's identity, but every time she'd brought up the matter, her mother managed to subtly steer the conversation to another subject.

Now she knew the answer to her lineage and knew the name of the man who was her father. She went online and searched the name Hector Rodriguez.

The man she read about was a monster. Over many decades, the Mexican cult he'd once headed had carried out literally hundreds of sacrificial murders in the name of an ancient Aztec snake god called Quetzalcoatl.

He was also a world-renowned financier who, as well as fronting his massive legitimate activities, controlled an underworld crime empire with global connections, most of whom had been rounded up by the authorities and were now dead or serving long prison terms.

She discovered that Hector Rodriguez had been murdered by Angelina, his only daughter, who had committed suicide in a Mexican jail cell. Philippe, his only son, was by all accounts a model citizen living in Paris.

Sierra slammed down the screen of her laptop. *Now I know why mother was so evasive. Now I know why she didn't want me to know anything about my father.*

She reached into her pocket and pulled out the lawyer's card.

ψ

Jonathan Bloom's most important client had been the late Hector Rodriguez, but now this exalted position was held by Philippe Rodriguez, the man's son, and to a lesser extent, by Claire, Hector's widow.

The lawyer's primary function for his two most important clients was to deflect any questions regarding the source of their wealth and obscure, as best he could, their unsavory family background. Since the violent demise of Hector Rodriguez nineteen years earlier, and the subsequent loss of public interest in his client's affairs, his job had become significantly easier.

A call he wasn't expecting came on the morning he'd heard about Anna Petersen's passing. He tentatively picked up his private line. "Good morning. Jonathan Bloom speaking."

"Good morning, Mr. Bloom. My name is Sierra Petersen, my mother gave me your card just before she died."

The lawyer sensed the anguish, and a touch of hostility in the young woman's voice. It sounded like she'd been crying.

"My mother suggested that we should meet,"

Bloom offered Sierra his condolences on her mother's passing and spoke fleetingly of his and her mother's excellent relationship. To Sierra, his words sounded vacuous, but before hanging up, she agreed that they would get together at 3:00 p.m. the following day at Bloom's Manhattan office.

ψ

Sierra looked at the back of the lawyer's card, where her mother had scrawled a series of twenty numbers in her shaky handwriting. It was the combination to a safe buried in the wall of her mother's bedroom.

She wandered into the sanctity of the bedroom. Nothing had changed, and nothing had been moved since her mother had been taken to the hospital.

The room exuded her mother's personality. The luxurious decor was sleek and modern and primarily black and white, with color coming only from the art hanging on the walls. It was in stark contrast to Sierra's disorderly 600-square-foot loft in the city's Meatpacking District.

The scent of Chanel No. 5, her mother's favorite fragrance, still lingered in the air, and once again Sierra had to choke back a tear.

The wall safe was hidden behind a painting. Her mother had said that it was a Picasso from the famous artist's Blue Period. Sierra gently touched the surface of the painting. Before becoming a model, she had briefly worked at one of the New York's most preeminent auction houses, and during her tenure there, she'd gained a deeper knowledge than she'd had earlier when studying art at college. Sierra looked closely at the painting. It looked like the real thing, felt like the real thing, but she still wasn't sure if it was a true masterpiece or an excellent forgery. She made a mental note to get it authenticated and appraised later, but now she needed to see the contents of her mother's safe.

Sierra removed the painting, stared for a moment at the safe's shiny black door, then carefully spun the numbers on the dial of the combination lock.

ψ

The following day, at precisely 3:00 p.m., Sierra stepped off the elevator and entered the sumptuously decorated reception area of the Bloom Law Group.

One of the firm's receptionists was obviously anticipating her arrival.

"Good afternoon, Ms. Petersen. Please come this way. Mr. Bloom is expecting you."

She followed the woman through a labyrinth of cubicles occupied by all manner of people busily engaged in the affairs of law until, finally, they arrived at large corner suite.

An impeccably dressed, gray-haired man strode across the room with his right hand extended. Sierra's immediate impression of the man was anything but complementary. *Whew, this guy has slimy lawyer written all over him.*

"Ms. Petersen, so nice to finally meet you. I do, however, wish that the circumstances could have been different." Jonathan Bloom paused and looked directly at Sierra. "Once again, my deepest condolences for your loss." He paused. "Your mother was a truly beautiful person and I'm sure that she'll be missed by all of those who knew her." The lawyer invited Sierra to sit at a round marble-topped table. The view, overlooking Central Park and the city skyline, was breathtaking.

Bloom turned and faced his guest—his tone and demeanor became serious. "I believe that by now you have found out who your father was, and that you know about his reputation?" He paused. "And I am reasonably sure you know that besides your mother, I represented him, and that I now represent his son, Philippe Rodriguez, and Claire Rodriguez, his widow?"

Sierra had been unaware of Bloom's relationship with the various members of the Rodriguez family, but she nodded, implying that she did.

"What you possibly don't know," Bloom continued, "is just how much he cared for you and your mother, but because he was a married man, he kept the secret of your existence from everyone, especially for obvious reasons, his wife, daughter, and son."

Sierra was taciturn. She didn't say a word, but her thoughts were anything but silent. *Sure, he cared for us. That's why we never saw him. Never saw him on my birthdays. Never heard from him at Christmas. Never knew he even existed. Now you want me to have feelings for him. Good luck with that!*

The lawyer continued. "He provided for both you and your mother and left her a considerable fortune."

Sierra's expression remained unchanged, but her thoughts were anything but impassive. *Yeah slimeball, I know all of that.*

"Under the terms of your mother's last will and testament, all of her assets and holdings are to be passed on to you."

Tell me something that I don't already know. I read all about it in the papers my mother kept in her safe.

"I would be delighted to act as your attorney and fulfill all the details of her will."

And I bet you would and get a big fat fee for doing it.

Jonathan Bloom stood and reached out his hand.

"I will be in touch with you very shortly Ms. Petersen so that we can complete all the legal work."

As the lawyer walked her out of his office, he put his arm across her shoulders.

"I look forward to having you as a client of the firm. May I call you Sierra?"

"You can, but I prefer that you wouldn't."

She lifted his arm off her shoulder and smiled at him.

I already have a lawyer, you misogynistic moron, and you'll be hearing from her soon enough.

There was nothing left to say. Her thoughts had said it all.

The lawyer watched the elevator doors close. *Strange*, he thought, *during our whole meeting, she hardly uttered a word.* He shrugged and strolled back toward his office.

CHAPTER SEVEN

Nick, Gabriela, and Alain were comfortably settled into the soft, well-worn leather chairs in the apartment on Île Saint-Louis. Their hushed conversation was centered on Jessica Devlin, the girl whose body had been discovered at Cité des Sciences et de l'Industrie.

Except for the conversation between its present occupants, and the muted chatter of tourists walking along the sidewalk below their open window, the apartment was silent.

"So, where do we start?" asked Gabriela.

Nick replied, "I would suggest that we interview Hector Rodriguez's widow and Philippe, his son. Perhaps they have information that could help us in the investigation."

Alain placed his elbows on his knees and buried his face into his hands. "*Merde*, that would be difficult at best. Their reputations are spotless. They're both good friends of the mayor and, I've heard, even the president himself."

He took off his glasses and rubbed his eyes. "We would be stepping on a lot of very important toes. The repercussions could easily cost me my job and harm both of your reputations. Any other thoughts?"

"But under the circumstances..." Gabriela was abruptly cut off by the Parisian cop.

"Circumstances *être damné*. I'm sure that especially them, or anyone else for that matter, wouldn't want the history of their family raked over the coals."

An uncomfortable silence settled over the room.

Alain got up to leave. "Let's sleep on it. Perhaps by tomorrow the clouds will part."

ψ

When Sierra got back to her late mother's apartment, she stripped down and stepped into the shower. She wanted to wash away the lingering stench of her meeting with Jonathan Bloom.

Her mind was going a mile a minute. *I've met some smooth-talking sleazes in my time, but Bloom is right up there with the best of them.* The steaming hot water streamed over her body and helped relieve the tension that she was feeling in her neck and shoulders. She stayed in the shower for what seemed like an eternity before stepping out. She slipped on one of her mother's plush white terry cloth bathrobes and wandered barefoot into the kitchen.

Sierra looked towards her cell phone. *I'd better call Lucy and tell her what's been happening.*

ψ

Sierra and Lucy Palmer, Nick's daughter, had met at a glamorous studio party during the Cannes Film Festival. Everyone was there—movie stars, directors, celebrity models, big-name film and television producers, editors from fashion and film magazines, and an army of online influencers.

The model and young lawyer hit it off immediately. Both were intelligent, well educated, beautiful, and accomplished. They shared a love of vintage designer fashion, scuba diving, and particular chili cheese dogs bought from a street vendor on the corner of 57th Street and Madison Avenue in Manhattan.

Lucy was in Cannes, sitting in her office when her cell phone rang.

She glanced at the call display and tried to think positively. She hadn't spoken to Sierra since her best friend, and now client, had called and told her the sad news that her mother was dying. *This call's going to be tough*, she thought.

"Hi, Sierra. How's your mom? How are you holding up?"

"She's gone, Luce. Two days ago."

Lucy felt the sadness in her friend's voice and wished that she could be there with her. "I'm so sorry, Sierra. Do you want me to fly over? It's times like these when you really need a friend."

"No, don't worry, Luce. I'll be fine, and we can get together soon when I'm in Paris, but that's not the real reason for my call."

Lucy was intrigued but let her friend keep talking.

"I never knew who my father was. My mother kept his identity secret from me for all these years. She told me his name just before she died." Sierra paused. "Luce, it turns out that he was one of the evilest pricks to ever walk the earth."

Lucy was shocked by her friends unexpected pronouncement.

"How do you know that?"

"I looked him up online. His name was Hector Rodriguez."

Lucy was stunned. This was the very same man that her father and Gabriela had hunted. The same man who'd headed the cult responsible for the murders of literally hundreds of young women. Lucy's normally ordered mind was spinning out of control, and she hardly heard Sierra's account about her meeting with Jonathan Bloom. *Holy shit, should I tell Sierra about my father's connection with Rodriguez? Is this a huge conflict of interest for me, and for my firm? Should I call Dad and tell him? What the hell am I going to do?*

She took a breath. "Look Sierra, let me wrap my head around it for an hour or two and I'll call you back. Don't let Bloom get to you and, once again, my condolences about your mother. I'm really very sorry for your loss."

She hung up, crossed her forearms on the desk in front of her, put her head down, and closed her eyes. *Oh shit, where do I even start?*

Lucy stayed in her office for ten minutes, then stood, brushed off the crumbs from the croissant she'd eaten for breakfast, and went to the ladies' room.

She leaned forward with her hands resting against the sink and looked into the mirror. Her face had a look of foreboding, a result, she thought, of the earlier conversation with her friend. She closed her eyes, but when she opened them again, it wasn't her face that she was seeing in the mirror. It was the kindly face of an elderly man who she remembered from photographs she'd seen many times before, in her father's Paris apartment.

"*Bonjour, ma petite fleur.* It's good to see how beautiful you've become."

Lucy steadied herself against the sink. A slash of crippling panic ripped through her whole body. *This isn't real! This is insane! What the hell's happening to me?* Then she remembered what her father and Gabriela had told her about the apparitions they'd seen in mirrors and how these same "ghosts of angels," as her father called them, had helped them wipe out the cult headed by Hector Rodriguez. She hadn't believed them, but now she faced the truth about all their stories, and it momentarily unnerved her.

"Henri? Professor Henri Deneuve?" she stammered.

"*Oui,* Lucy, it is me. I hope that I didn't frighten you, but because of your recent conversation with the daughter of Hector Rodriguez, I felt it necessary to warn you that there is danger ahead. Heed my warning and step carefully, *ma fleur.* Step very carefully."

Henri Deneuve's image faded and vanished, and Lucy was left staring at herself. She wasn't afraid and wasn't, for some reason, even surprised. *It looks as if I've inherited some of my dad's psychic gifts, and it feels like I'm going to be up to my armpits in trouble. I'd better call Dad and Gabi right away.*

She left the washroom and strode purposefully down the hallway, back towards her office.

CHAPTER EIGHT

Philippe Rodriguez was planning a party and was deeply engrossed in a conversation with the captain of his yacht and his director of public relations.

The guest list contained the names of the most influential and beautiful people in Europe, and the whole world. Besides the usual retinue of politicians, Russian oligarchs, tech billionaires, film stars, and sports celebrities, there was a smattering of internationally renowned rock stars, famous fashion designers, and glamorous fashion models. Sierra's name was near the top of the list of invitees.

"This Sierra girl, do we know her surname?" Philippe's question was aimed at the only female in the yacht's sleek teak-lined salon.

The woman in charge of his public relations and party planning flipped through the list. "Her surname is Petersen, sir. She's from New York, but I understand that she'll be in France for a photo shoot."

"She wasn't at last year's party?"

"No, sir, she wasn't available. Apparently, she was in Africa doing charity work—helping to build a new school for girls in Kenya."

"Great. She's beautiful and a humanitarian to boot. We need more guests like her."

The conversation turned to other aspects of the event: food, libations, staffing, entertainment, decoration, and security.

When the meeting ended, Philippe went back to his cabin, an

opulent retreat where he carried out the business of his various holdings, both legitimate and illicit. *I've got to know this Sierra Petersen better. She'd be the perfect front for my organization—arm candy with an unassailable reputation.* He smiled at the thought.

ψ

Lucy sat in her office, pondering the avalanche of craziness that had occurred during the first few hours of the morning: Sierra's revelations about her father and her meeting with the New York lawyer, followed by the appearance of Henri Deneuve in the mirror of her firm's washroom, and his dire warning for her to be careful. She shook her head. *What the hell is going on?*

She picked up her cell phone and called her father in Paris. "Hi, Daddy, it's me."

Nick was more than delighted to hear from his eldest daughter. The sound of her voice temporarily alleviated his troubled thoughts.

"Hi, Honey. Where are you? How's it going?"

Lucy was reticent to tell her father about everything that had happened earlier in her day, and she wasn't even sure how to start the conversation. However, after a few long seconds, she dove right in, and began telling him about the unexpected, and surreal, events that had interrupted her normally routine morning.

"I saw Henri Deneuve in the washroom mirror at work, and before that I had a disturbing call from my friend Sierra."

The news that his daughter had been visited by his long-dead friend hit Nick right between the eyes. He pushed the middle fingers of his right hand between his eyebrows to elevate the sudden flash of pain. Over the previous twenty or so years, he'd often wondered if his and his mother's "special gift" would be passed from generation to generation, but now he knew for sure.

"Are you sure it was Henri who appeared to you?" he questioned.

"Yes, I'm positive. I remember him from photographs in your apartment."

Nick couldn't hold back. "What did he say?"

"He told me to be careful because there's great danger ahead."

Earlier, Nick had heard much the same from the elderly scholar. Now he was worried about his daughter's safety, and sounded very much like the concerned father that he was.

"I want you to come home to Paris. We've got a lot to talk about."

Then Lucy broke the other piece of news—the revelation about Sierra's father. "Hector Rodriguez was Sierra's father. Her mother confessed this to her just before she died."

Nick, for the second time during their conversation, was stunned. The connection between his daughter's friend's father and himself was unexpected and frighteningly coincidental.

"Then come home right now. I don't want you caught up in something that could be very dangerous."

He pushed the end call button on his cell and turned to face Gabriela, who was hovering behind him. She wanted to hear everything about his call with Lucy.

Gabriela sat in shocked silence as he recounted the conversation that he'd just had with their daughter.

"This is just crazy. Even crazier than the times we saw all the ghosts of girls so many years ago." She plopped down on the closest chair and stared up at Nick. "I wish that I didn't believe you, but goddamnit, I do— what do you think is going to happen next?"

Nick shrugged. He wished he knew the answer to her question.

ψ

Lucy's next call was to Sierra. She'd thought about what she'd say to her close friend. *I'd better lay it right on the line. No use me sugar coating anything, she'll eventually find out the truth anyway.*

Her friend answered on the second ring. "Hi, Sierra. It's me. Are you sitting down?" Lucy began the conversation that could jeopardize their friendship forever.

"My father's name is Nicholas Palmer. He and my stepmom Gabriela used to be Chicago police detectives, and they were the ones responsible for bringing down your father and his whole crooked empire."

There was a long and agonizing silence on the other end of the call. Then Sierra spoke, her voice trembled for a few seconds before it regained the normal self-assured confidence that Lucy had come to know.

"If what you're telling me is true, and I'm not for a second saying that it isn't, then I owe your dad and Gabriela an enormous debt of gratitude."

Lucy felt a surge of relief sweep over her. It was as if a bunch of brightly colored balloons had suddenly been released from their tether and were sailing into a cloudless summer sky. *Whew, that went much better than I expected it would,* she thought. The two friends said their goodbyes' and hung up.

Lucy didn't tell her friend about the apparition of Henri Deneuve. That could wait for another time—or not at all.

ψ

Lucy walked down the hall to the office of her firm's managing partner. She knocked on the door, and upon hearing the woman's invitation to enter, walked in.

The senior lawyer was sitting at her desk behind a large stack of legal papers. She looked up over her thick tortoiseshell eyeglasses.

"*Bonjour,* Lucy. What can I do for you?"

"*Salut,* Denise. Just wanted to let you know that I'm going to take a few days off. My best friend's mother has just passed away and I'm meeting her in Paris. I'll be staying at my parents' apartment if you need me for anything."

The woman looked concerned.

"Oh, *c'est terrible*. Please give your friend my deepest condolences."

"*Merci*, Denise. *Je le ferai.*"

The woman stood and hugged her much-younger associate, then went back to her chair, picked up one of the many files that were cluttering her desk, and got back to work.

Lucy turned her head as she left the room. "*Au revoir*, Denise."

The senior lawyer just waved her away.

Lucy returned to her office, picked up her laptop, and went home to pack for her trip to the French capital.

ψ

Sierra and Lucy had arranged to meet when they were both in Paris, and Gabriela had planned a lunch for them at the apartment on Île Saint-Louis. She hadn't seen Sierra in over a year and was looking forward to seeing both her daughter and her famous friend again.

Nick, on the other hand, was deep in thought. He had an idea, the outline of a strategy that would involve both his daughter and Sierra. It was a long shot, but he hoped that the two young women would agree to participate in his plan.

CHAPTER NINE

Sierra called Jonathan Bloom. "I've decided to retain your firm to represent me regarding my mother's estate." She paused, then continued in a businesslike voice that was devoid of any emotion. "I have to go to Paris on a job. If you prepare the paperwork, I'll sign it when I return home in a week or so."

Then she made her position abundantly clear. "The only stipulation I insist upon is that you reveal nothing of my personal or business dealings to anyone, including Philippe Rodriguez and his mother. I don't want anyone in the world to know that I was conceived by that monster."

Bloom assured her that client-attorney confidentiality was paramount in all his dealings, and she needn't worry about that aspect of their business relationship.

Sierra's thoughts were anything but amiable. *Sure, and if you weren't the lawyer representing my scumbag relatives, I might believe you.* Sierra hung up the phone. *I'll bring Lucy up to speed when I'm in Paris, I'm sure that she'll do a far better job of sorting through the estate than Bloom ever could, and besides that, I'd trust her with my life.*

ψ

After the call with Sierra, Jonathan Bloom went to his wall cabinet, pulled out a bottle of Johnnie Walker Black Label, and poured himself a celebratory drink. *Another fat fee for doing practically nothing,* he thought, then raised the glass to his lips.

ψ

Sierra was looking forward to the photo shoot. The photographer was famous, one of the best in the business, and if everything went well, it could possibly mean a cover on one of the world's most influential fashion magazines. But mostly, she was looking forward to seeing Lucy again. It had been over a year since they last saw each other, and she had a lot to talk about with her friend.

She finished packing, checked her cell phone to make sure that the agency had sent her an airline ticket, took one last look around her mother's lonely apartment, then went downstairs and hailed a cab.

Sierra missed her mother—the hugs and kisses every time she left on a shoot, and the words, "be safe, darling. I love you." Always the last thing she heard as she was leaving.

I'd better get used to it. She's never, ever coming back. Sierra choked back a tear.

ψ

Philippe was anticipating another successful party. In particular, he was excited about meeting Sierra Petersen. The thought of having a ménage à trois with himself, his mother, and the famous model was a fantasy that he hoped would come true in time—as it had with many attractive young women on previous occasions. *Perhaps on the night of the party*, he thought to himself.

His lubricious musings were interrupted by Gisele Martin, the woman in charge of planning his party.

"Sir, we have a minor problem."

Philippe shot the woman a glance indicating his displeasure with her sudden intrusion.

The woman wilted under his gaze and blurted out her concern.

"There's not enough Cristal champagne anywhere in France, sir."

"Then, for fuck's sake Gisele, find some somewhere else. Try calling the office in Singapore, the place is usually floating in the stuff."

The woman scurried from his presence. She knew that her job was on the line, and even though she hated her employer, she realized that duplicating her sizable salary anywhere else would be next to impossible.

ψ

Sierra took a taxi to John F. Kennedy International Airport, checked in at Air France's premier-class departure gate, and was soon comfortably settled into her deluxe on-board suite for the overnight flight to Paris. She was looking forward to the journey, mostly because the service in this exalted realm was nothing less than exceptional. She breathed a deep sigh of relief and closed her eyes. *Whew, I'm glad to be getting out of town for a week or so.*

Her thoughts were scattered. Too much had happened in too short a time. *I hope I did the right thing with that Bloom asshole. I hope the shoot goes well. It'll be great to see Lucy and her parents again. I hope that I'm not putting Lucy on the spot about representing me with the estate. Why didn't mother tell me who my father was earlier?* She accepted a glass of champagne from the courteous flight attendant and leaned back for the seven-hour-and-twenty-minute flight to the French capital. *When mother came to Paris with me for my first big photo shoot, she was so excited, I don't think that we were ever as close as we were on that trip. God, even though we often had our differences, she was still my mother, and at that time, I really did love her.*

Sierra finished her champagne, pulled a blanket up to cover her neck, and fell into a well needed sleep.

ψ

Lucy arrived with great fanfare at Nick and Gabriela's apartment. Her father hugged her, kissed her gently on the forehead, then picked up her bag and took it into the room, overlooking the Seine, which had been hers ever since they'd moved to the French capital many years before. He threw the suitcase onto her bed and left his daughter with Gabriela. *I'm sure they've got plenty of catching up to do.* He smiled at the thought of the two women chatting about every detail of Lucy's life in Cannes.

Ten minutes later, he came back into the room carrying two glasses of wine and interrupted the women's conversation.

"When's Sierra due to arrive?"

"I spoke with her last night, just before she boarded her flight. She was scheduled to arrive in Paris at about six this morning."

Lucy continued, dashing Nick's short-lived anticipation of Sierra coming directly to the apartment. "She's going right to her hotel for a few hours rest before her preproduction meetings with the photographer and fashion editors. I'm meeting her for dinner later this evening."

"So, we're not going to see her until tomorrow?" Nick sounded disappointed.

"Afraid not, daddy. You're just going to have to put up with me for a while." She smiled and shrugged. "So, what is it that you want to know?"

Nick wasted no time getting to the point.

"I want you to tell me everything that Henri told you. Word for word, and don't leave anything out."

ψ

Sierra's flight landed on time at Charles de Gaulle Airport. The flight attendant retrieved Sierra's well-traveled carry-on, and within minutes, she was striding down the jetway toward the unusually quiet arrivals hall. She passed quickly through the formalities of customs and immigration and scanned the group of waiting chauffeurs for Abdullah, her favorite driver, the man she always requested when visiting the French capital.

Abdullah, as always, was immaculately dressed in a black suit, white shirt, and black tie. He stepped forward to take her suitcase, his smile was as wide as Pont Neuf, the Seine's oldest bridge.

Abdullah Mansouri was born in Algeria but had lived in Paris his whole life. He knew the city like the back of his hand and always found the quickest and most under-the-radar route to almost any destination. Because of this talent, and his always amiable demeanor, Abdullah was the favored driver of many of the world's most recognized celebrities. Sierra was one of his favorite clients.

"*Bonjour*, Mademoiselle Sierra. It's wonderful to see you again. Please let me take your bag."

At that early hour, traffic travelling into the city was light and the big black Mercedes-Benz sedan eased through what little congestion there was and reached its destination in record time. The car pulled up in front of a charming little hotel, tucked away on a quiet side street in Saint-Germain-des-Prés. Abdullah rushed around and opened the door for the jet-lagged traveler.

She smiled. "*Merci*, Abdullah. Could you please pick me up again in a couple of hours? I have a meeting to go to in Le Marais."

ψ

Sierra's agency would prefer that she stayed at more high-profile accommodations near Rue Saint-Honoré, one of the city's premier fashion destinations. "It's good for business," they said. But she was happier where she was, away from the gawkers, paparazzi, and social media hounds.

Her first appointment wasn't until eleven, which gave her ample time to crash for an hour or so, shower, and call Lucy.

Sierra's body needed rest, but her mind was spinning like it was on steroids. The reality of even a short nap was next to impossible, so she got up, dropped her clothes onto the floor, and wandered into the bathroom for a long hot shower. She stepped in, closed her eyes, and let the water cascade over her body. *Ahhh, this is perfect—exactly what I need right now*, she thought.

She stepped out from the shower, wiped off the steamed-up mirror with her towel, and looked at her reflection, except the face looking back wasn't hers. It was the face of the young American woman whose body was recently discovered in the 19th arrondissement.

"Hello Miss Petersen. I hope that I didn't frighten you."

Sierra's towel dropped to the floor, and she leaned up against the sink to steady herself. She was shaking violently, not from the cold of her wet body, but from something deeper, more terrifying, and more personal.

She fumbled to find the right words. "Who are you? What are you? What do you want?"

The girl in the mirror looked unfathomably desolate, and a tear of anguish trickled down her ashen cheek.

"My name is Jessica Devlin. I was murdered—sacrificed in the name of an unholy snake god. My body was discovered just days ago on the steps of Cité de Sciences et de l'Industrie. I am just one of many hundreds of women who have died to satiate the inexhaustible appetite of this evil cult." The voice emanating from the ghostly visage hesitated and, when she spoke again, her words carried the weight of unimaginable despair. "You and your friend Miss Palmer have been chosen to bring this depraved sect to its knees, forever!"

The woman's ghostly image faded and slowly vanished, leaving Sierra more frightened than she'd ever remembered being. She stumbled from the bathroom and sat on the edge of her bed. Her thoughts were spinning uncontrollably. *Jesus Christ, this sounds like the stuff my father was into, the crap I read about online when I was checking him out. Oh god, I'm either totally exhausted, or what I just saw was a real message. I've got to talk to Lucy about what just happened. Maybe she can make sense of it.*

There was a gentle knock on her door. She grabbed her robe and went to see who was there.

A young Asian man, dressed in a smart, dark blue valet uniform, handed her a gold-embossed envelope.

"*Pardon, mademoiselle.* This was just delivered to the front desk for you."

CHAPTER TEN

"Have all the invitations been delivered?" It was more of an order than a question.

Gisele Martin, Philippe's party planner, cowered slightly at her boss's gruff tone.

"*Oui,* Monsieur Rodriguez. All have been delivered, just as you requested."

Philippe was lying on his back, stretched out on a massage table in his yacht's pristine spa. The beautiful dark-haired masseuse was naked from the waist up, and her soft hands were gently kneading his neck and shoulders.

"And the one for Mademoiselle Petersen?"

"Delivered to her hotel this very morning, sir."

"Then get the hell out of here. Can't you see that I'm busy?"

The party planner scurried from the room. Seconds later, Philippe's masseuse slipped off her panties, climbed onto the table, and straddled her employer's prone body.

ψ

Sierra arrived at the studio at 10:45 a.m., fifteen minutes prior to the time she was expected. The space was packed with racks of designer clothes and props. Almost everyone involved with the shoot was already there: the photographer, his assistant, the fashion editor and art director from the magazine, a prop person, a stylist, and a social media specialist. The hair and makeup people would be in attendance on the day of the shoot.

"Bonjour, Sierra." The photographer rushed over to greet her, as did the two women from the magazine, both of whom she'd met many times earlier on other photo shoots.

What followed was a frenzied whirl of activity: selecting the appropriate garments, trying them on, sitting, swirling, jumping, doing whatever the photographer, editor, and art director requested of her. It was a full-on dress rehearsal for the real shoot which would occur in two days' time.

It was exhausting but Sierra loved every minute of it, and when they called "It's a wrap." at 5:00 p.m., she changed into a pair of fashionably torn jeans and an oversized white shirt. She draped an electric-green cashmere sweater over her shoulders, waved goodbye to the crew, and stepped out into a pleasantly warm Parisian evening.

Just enough time to get back to my hotel, change, and meet Lucy for an early dinner, she thought as she picked her way through the crowds of happy workers leaving their offices for the day.

ψ

Sierra had arranged to meet Lucy at a restaurant she'd always wanted to try: Les Papilles, a homey wood-paneled restaurant in the Latin Quarter. The room was already busy with chattering Parisians, most of whom took no notice of her arrival. Those who did simply shrugged at seeing the famous model, they'd seen many beautiful women many times over in the French capital.

Upon seeing each other, the two friends rushed into each other's arms and embraced. "Oh my god, it's so good to see you again." The words, from both women, came out in unison, and they laughed at the synchronicity of their feelings.

Lucy and Sierra were shown to their table by a handsome young server who, in a different place and time, would have flirted with them. Uncharacteristically, he was polite, professional, and attentive. Sierra guessed that his deferential demeanor was due, in part, by the presence of the restaurant's owner, who was hovering in the background, near to the table of his famous customer.

Sierra asked the waiter to recommend a wine, and he returned with bottle of a Chablis. He uncorked it with Gallic flair and poured a small taste into Lucy's glass. She sipped it and smiled. "*Merci, c'est très bien.*" She then asked him to return later to take their dinner order.

"I was very sorry to hear about your mother. You said that she was a special person."

Sierra shrugged. "She was, and I'll miss her, but as you know, she carried around a whole lot of secrets."

Lucy was surprised that her friend was jumping into family matters so soon in the evening. She leaned across the table, concerned that their conversation might be overheard by patrons at the next table.

"I never really knew your mother. Tell me what she was really like."

Sierra was conflicted about her and her mother's relationship. She looked down, trying to formulate an answer to the question that she'd never been asked before. She raised her eyes and looked directly at her friend. "Well, she was attractive, intelligent, and had exquisite taste. But ultimately, I guess, she wasn't much more than a high-flying courtesan—a beautiful opportunist who used her charm and classic good looks to get whatever she wanted."

Sierra could see, by the look on Lucy's face, that her scathingly brutal description of her mother had shocked the young attorney.

"But she loved you, didn't she?"

"I guess that she did. She said she did. She paid for my education, encouraged my modeling career, and other than that she pretty much left me alone to deal with life. We never saw much of each other, what with boarding school, university, and her social life, which seldom, if ever, included me."

"But you loved her, didn't you?"

"I'm pretty sure that I did Luce. Toward the end, when I knew that she was dying, I experienced some sort of feelings for her. I guess it was love, it felt like love. I even cried at her deathbed, but sometimes I think that my feelings for her at that moment in time were more a sense of loss than a feeling of love." She paused. "I guess, it's something that I'll have to resolve one day."

Sierra suddenly brightened her tone. "Say, that's enough about me. Let's order, then you can tell me all about what's been happening in your life."

She waved to the waiter and, and when he arrived at their table, they placed their orders, both women chose niçoise salads. "We'll splurge on calories for dessert," laughed Sierra.

Lucy felt that it was the right time to tell her friend about seeing the apparition of Henri Deneuve in the mirror at her office. She recounted her experience in detail, sharing every word of her perplexing confrontation with the apparition of the elderly professor. Strangely, she thought, Sierra didn't seem shocked or surprised.

There was a long and awkward moment of silence when neither of them said anything. *God, I hope she doesn't think I've completely lost my mind,* thought Lucy.

After their salads were delivered to the table and the waiter had left, Sierra broke the silence.

"A similar thing happened to me today in my hotel room. But it wasn't a man, it was the image of a pretty young woman who claimed that she'd been murdered—sacrificed to an ancient Aztec snake god." Sierra paused. "I think it might have had something to do with the cult that my father headed."

Lucy almost choked on her first forkful of food. Sierra continued her story.

"She said that her name was Jessica Devlin, and that her body was discovered here in Paris, in the 19th arrondissement. She was strangled to death."

Lucy reached over and took her friend's hand.

"Apparently, my dad and Gabriela experienced similar apparitions when they were chasing down your father and his cult. My dad called them "ghosts of angels," and the martyred young women he saw in mirrors, helped him, and Gabriela topple La Orden de las Serpientes de Cristo—the Order of the Serpents of Christ."

The two friends stared at each, both seemingly not knowing what to say. Finally, Sierra looked towards Lucy and asked the question that they were both thinking.

"So, what the hell do you think we're supposed to do now?"

"I think our best bet would be to speak to my dad and Gabi when we meet them for lunch."

"But that won't be for a couple of days when my shoot is wrapped."

"It is what it is. Now, how about another glass of wine?"

Lucy's suggestion was a welcome relief from their surreal conversation.

CHAPTER ELEVEN

On the day of the photo shoot, Sierra showed up at 8:00 a.m. The crew was already at the studio preparing for what was going to be a long day.

"*Bonjour, chéri.* Monsieur Moulin is waiting for you in makeup."

The photographer's assistant directed her to a well-lit corner of the room where a portly, bald thirty-something man was talking to the magazine's fashion editor. Marcel Moulin, the makeup artist, was dressed in an outlandishly colored silk caftan that made loud swishing sounds with his every move.

"*Quelque chose d'extrême, je pense.*"

Marcel agreed with the editor's suggestion. "Something extreme, *c'est bon.*"

Sierra smiled warmly at the man, sat in his chair, and prepared herself for the three-hour ordeal. Marcel chatted and gossiped nonstop throughout the whole session about: lovers, friends, parties, films, outrageous fashion gaffes of famous people, and just about anything else that sprung into his creative brain.

When Sierra finally got out of the chair, half of her face resembled a Piet Mondrian painting: rectangles of primary colors, crisscrossed with thin, black lines. The other side looked almost normal, with just a hint of eyeliner and bright yellow lipstick.

The wardrobe, selected by the magazine's staff, reflected the colors of her makeup: bright, billowing sundresses, bikinis, pants, and tops, a graphically stylish interpretation of the season's vibrant color-block collection from one of the world's top designers.

The shoot ended at 8:00 p.m. Marcel removed Sierra's makeup. She slipped into her street clothes and left the studio to applause and a chorus of *merci* from the whole crew.

The photographer was especially appreciative. "*Merveilleux, merveilleux, ma chéri. Merci.*"

Sierra went back to her hotel and collapsed into her bed. She was beyond exhausted.

Across the Seine from where she slept, a different scenario was being played out—a nightmarish conspiracy into which she would inexplicably be drawn.

ψ

The order to assassinate Nicholas and Gabriela Palmer came directly from Claire Rodriguez, Philippe's mother. She believed that their deaths would be a fitting gift for her son on the eve of his big party.

She was lounging in the living room of her luxurious apartment, and the men she was speaking to were two of La Orden de las Serpientes de Cristo's most violent and remorseless disciples.

"I don't care how you do it, just get it done."

The promise of great rewards in the afterlife was more than enough motivation to excite and spur on the two killers.

ψ

Nick was bone-tired. His troubled thoughts had drained every ounce of energy from his body, and all that he wanted was to go to bed in the futile hope of getting a peaceful night's sleep. He slipped into his pajama bottoms, went into the bathroom, and glanced into the mirror.

"*Bonsoir, mon ami.*"

Nick was no longer startled by the apparitions that appeared in mirrors. They seemed, more and more, to be a part of his normal life.

"*Bonsoir*, Henri. Please tell me that you have good news this time." His words seemed to carry the weight of the world.

"I am afraid not, *mon ami*. There are men intent on killing you and the beautiful Gabriela. I do not know how, and I do not know where, so be very vigilant and tread very carefully."

The image of the elderly professor slowly evaporated from the mirror, leaving Nick even more troubled than he was before. It was as if a dark, shadowy shroud had wafted down from the ceiling and settled over his entire body.

Nick slipped quietly into the living room. Gabriela was waiting for him and, like him, was dressed in her usual bedtime attire, a pale blue tank top and blue-striped cotton shorts.

She turned and looked at him. "Ready to call it a day, honey?"

Nick nodded and followed her into their bedroom. "I just saw Henri again. He appeared to me in the bathroom mirror."

Gabriela spun around and faced him. "What did he say?"

"Nothing that I haven't heard before—someone wants to kill us and that we should be vigilant and very careful."

Gabriela punched him playfully on the shoulder. "You weren't going to tell me, were you?"

Nick shrugged. "Didn't want to worry you."

ψ

Sierra dragged herself out of bed, opened the blinds, and was greeted with a dazzling pale-blue sky. The street below her window was alive with a hodgepodge of shopkeepers scurrying around primping and preening their tiny markets and boutiques, making everything perfect for the influx of shoppers and tourists that they knew would soon be arriving in their little corner of the city.

White-aproned waiters were setting up small, round tables and brightly painted wicker chairs on the sidewalks in front of the bistros. There were flower stalls overflowing with buckets of cheerful blooms, delicious-looking pastries being lovingly displayed in the window of a small pâtisserie, and one stooped old man rolling up the dull green louvers that covered the door and windows of his quaint little antique store.

"Good morning, Paris," she said out loud before turning and walking into the suite's elegant bathroom.

Sierra looked at herself in the mirror and noticed that tiny remnants of makeup from the previous day's shoot were still on her face and neck. *Yikes, I'd better get cleaned up before I go to lunch with Lucy's parents.* She slipped her robe off, stepped into the shower, and let the warm spray of water caress her naked body.

She dressed casually: stylishly baggy blue jeans, a white T-shirt emblazoned with a famous designer logo, white sneakers, a black Yankees baseball cap, large dark sunglasses, and a canary yellow silk scarf. She wore no makeup—she didn't need to.

Abdullah, her driver, was standing at the hotel's front entrance, ready to whisk her to lunch at the Île Saint-Louis apartment. Thankfully, there were no paparazzi lying in wait for the famous model.

ψ

Alain Moreau was the first to arrive. Nick had invited his friend from the city's police force for lunch. He wanted the deputy director to hear Sierra's story directly from the horse's mouth, so to speak.

The sound of the doorbell ringing reverberated throughout every room in the apartment. It caused Nick and Alain to interrupt their conversation.

"That must be Sierra," Lucy said as she rushed to open the door.

Hugs, kisses, and noisy chatter engulfed everyone huddled in the entry hall of the apartment. Sierra was happy to be back in the company of her friend's family. "It's so great to see you all again. Let's go in and you can tell me everything that's been happening."

Gabriela took Sierra's hand. "I think that you have a lot more to tell us than we have to tell you." Hinting about the conversation she's had earlier with Lucy about both young women experiencing apparitions in their mirrors. Gabriela smiled knowingly at Sierra and led her into the kitchen. The aroma of boeuf bourguignon, slowly simmering on the stove, was nothing less than intoxicating.

"Ummm, that smells absolutely delicious," said Sierra.

The joyfulness of the moment was shattered by the staccato sound of semiautomatic gunfire, followed by the unmistakable screech of accelerating high-powered Ducati motorbikes.

The small group of friends rushed to the windows and looked down onto the street below them.

Two bodies, a man and a woman, were sprawled out in grossly contorted positions on the sidewalk. Their blood was spreading from beneath them, like a grisly pond of dark red paint.

"Oh my god, it's Louis and Natalie." Gabriela was overwhelmed with dread. She charged out of the apartment, followed quickly by the others.

When they reached the sidewalk, a small crowd of onlookers had already gathered around the bodies, and the distinctive sound of approaching sirens could be heard in the distance.

Gabriela knelt beside the bodies of their close friends, desperately checking for any signs of life. Concurrently the deputy director was using his police credentials to keep the growing intrusion of gawkers away from the horrific scene. The policeman flashed his badge, yelled, and did his best to push back the curious crowd. "*Reculez, reculez.*"

Nick gently lifted his grieving wife off the sidewalk and cradled her head into his shoulder. "I think that this was meant for us," he whispered, as he looked down at their friends' mutilated, blood-soaked bodies. Deep within his gut he knew that somehow Philippe

Rodriguez was the person responsible for the horrific scene laid out in front of him.

Gabriela's whole body was shaking, and tears from the unfathomable anguish she felt began to streak down her cheeks. Nick held her tighter and made a promise to himself that he'd get those responsible if it was the last thing that he ever did.

ψ

Five years earlier, Louis Faucher's mother had passed away from pancreatic cancer, and after settling all the legal hurdles that France is famous for, Louis and his wife Natalie had moved into her apartment, one floor below where Nick and Gabriela lived. The couple were about the same age as Nick and Gabriela, and like them, had children who lived outside of Paris. The two couples shared a mutual love of the French capital, and besides being neighbors, soon became close friends, enjoying many outings and meals together.

The violent murder of their friends hit Nick like a hard punch to his gut. The sensation was a vile combination of anger, anguish, and incomprehensible guilt, all wound up tightly like a huge ball of rubber bands lying deeply in the pit of his stomach. The utter torment he felt was indelibly etched into his face.

"Don't do anything foolish, my friend. I understand how you're feeling, but I would hate to have you arrested for a crime of vengeance."

These somber words, uttered by Alain, didn't resonate with Nick, whose dark thoughts were anything but consolatory.

CHAPTER TWELVE

Even the table looked bereft. The lovingly prepared endive salad, with walnuts and pears, was left untouched, as was the boeuf bourguignon. The thick slices of fresh baguette, usually used to mop up the last delicious morsels of stew, looked pitifully sad in the large woven basket. And the wineglasses sat despondently empty, as if they knew that they wouldn't be filled anytime soon.

Alain was still downstairs at the scene of the crime, collecting what little evidence there was and interviewing potential eyewitnesses. The others huddled quietly in the apartment's living room, alone within their thoughts.

Lucy and Sierra sat staring blankly into space, their distraught faces lined with long-dried streaks running down their cheeks—remnants of the tears they'd recently shed. Gabriela turned toward Nick; her normally confident voice was quavering. The fusion of pleading and utter despair conveyed by her tone would have broken the heart of anyone hearing her. "What are we going to do? What can we do?" She buried her face into her hands then almost immediately lifted her head and scanned the room.

"We're going to get them, get that goddamned Philippe Rodriguez, and make him pay for Louis and Natalie, make him pay for all the murdered girls and shove him and all of his godforsaken religious fanatics into the deepest depths of hell where they belong."

Her words were spoken with such vehemence and decisiveness that she frightened herself and almost all the others in the room. Nick inwardly smiled. *Thanks, honey, my sentiments exactly.*

Gabriela's composure returned, but her resolve for retribution remained locked tightly in her head and heart. She turned to Lucy and Sierra.

"You've both seen apparitions in your mirrors, and both heard their warnings." She paced the room like a caged tiger, then turned back to face the two friends. "Because of what you've witnessed, you're both very much involved in seeing that justice is served."

Nick nodded. "Start thinking people. How do we get to that bastard Philippe Rodriguez, and how do we stop his rampage of depraved killings?"

Sierra looked toward Nick and spoke. Her voice was barely above a whisper. "I've been invited to a party on his yacht in Monaco."

The group stared at her in astonishment.

"Is he a friend of yours?" Lucy sounded perplexed.

"No, I've never met him," she replied.

Nick's mind kicked into overdrive. "This may be the opportunity we've been looking for. Maybe it's our chance to get the evil bastard and put him away for good."

Gabriela glared at her husband. "You can't be serious, Nick. Sierra has no experience dealing with men like Rodriguez, and no knowledge about the level of depravity he's capable of inflicting. It would be like throwing her into a nest full of vipers."

Sierra jumped into the conversation. She sounded confident, even excited. "If there's a plan, you could teach me what you know and tell me what you want me to do—I'm a quick learner."

"And I can be your date to the party," Lucy interjected.

Gabriela wasn't convinced. Sending two inexperienced women to do battle with a man like Rodriguez could easily result in unspeakable consequences—even their deaths.

ψ

"You stupid, fucking morons! You've killed two innocent people, you've got cops crawling all over the place, trying to apprehend the killers, and you've probably warned the fucking Palmer guy that we're out to get him. Get the hell out of my sight, and get the job done properly, or I'll have your balls strung up from the Eiffel Tower." Claire Rodriguez's fists were tightly clenched and her normally perfect complexion had turned a deep foreboding color of scarlet.

The two men scurried from the woman's apartment. They'd heard all about the wrath of El Cardinal's mother and didn't want to be recipients of her venomous rage.

ψ

The mood at Nick and Gabriela's apartment was uncharacteristically somber, and if it wasn't for the relentless *tick-tock, tick-tock* of Henri Deneuve's antique grandfather clock, the silence would have been deafening.

Nick brushed Gabriela's concerns aside and faced the two young women.

"I need to tell you the whole story—a story that began years ago in Chicago when I first stumbled upon La Orden de las Serpientes de Cristo and Hector Rodriguez, Philippe's father."

Sierra interjected. "Hector Rodriguez was my father, too."

Nick acknowledged the woman's remark. "He may have been, but I'm thinking that you have no allegiance, or love, for the man."

"Not one fucking iota," she replied.

"Then let me begin." He stared at the ceiling then returned his gaze to Lucy and Sierra. "When Gabi and I were both detectives on the Chicago police force, a young woman's body was found, kneeling as if she was praying, on the steps of the Holy Name Cathedral on Wabash Avenue . . ."

He continued talking for just over an hour. He described every detail about the case that he, Gabriela, the ghostly apparitions, and police officers on both sides of the Atlantic, had brought to, what they believed, was a successful conclusion—the end of Hector Rodriguez and the cult that he headed.

"Now all of that has changed," he said.

Lucy was stunned. She'd heard snippets of the story when she was growing up, but never the full extent of the horror and challenges her father and Gabriela had lived through. If even half of the things that Nick had said in his horrific story were true, it was a nightmare that needed to end.

Then and there she made up her mind that she'd do everything in her power to finish what her father and Gabriela had started. Put an end to the cult, once and for all. She looked toward Sierra and recognized a similar look of abomination on her friend's face. She was just as horrified and determined as Lucy was.

"Let's get the bastards, Sierra."

ψ

Philippe was focused on his impending party and was totally unaware of the plot being hatched against him in Paris. If he'd had any clue, he would have cancelled his meeting with Gisele Martin, the woman in charge of his party. As it was, their meeting was almost ending anyway, he had just a few last-minute questions for the woman.

"You got the champagne?"

"*Oui, monsieur*. It's on route from the Far East, even as we speak."

"Food? Flowers? Staff? Entertainment?" His questions came fast and furious.

"*Oui, monsieur*. All is well in hand."

"Good. Now get the fuck out of here. I have work to do."

As Gisele closed the door, he picked up his secure cell. "Mother, why don't you come down early? There's business we need to discuss—business relating to the Order."

The thought of her soft, enticing body lying next to him in his yacht's opulent master bedroom aroused his innate carnality.

ψ

Because he was first at the scene of the killing of the Fauchers, and because of his long-standing affinity with the slain couple, Alain Moreau took personal charge of the investigation. He was trying desperately to connect the dots, and no matter how they lined up, he kept coming back to the same sickening conclusion—the couple lying dead on the street in front of him were innocent victims of mistaken identity. The real targets of the vicious attack were his friends Nick and Gabriela.

The murdered couple were roughly the same age, had the same characteristics, and lived in the same apartment building as his two friends. *I'm sure that Nicholas has come to the same conclusion*, he thought.

He left another officer to continue the investigation, then went back into the building. He took the rickety elevator to his friends' apartment and walked in without knocking.

Downstairs on the sidewalk, a young woman from the police force's public relations division was fielding a myriad of questions from reporters gathered at the building's front door.

Alain found his friends and the two young women deep in conversation. They looked toward the cop and immediately stopped talking.

Mon Dieu, I hope that they're not going to go off the deep end and do something foolish. This thought stayed tightly locked up in Alain's head.

CHAPTER THIRTEEN

News of the shooting and subsequent death of the couple on Île Saint-Louis made headlines in all the major news outlets in France: broadcast, print, and online. Similar stories about the double homicide in the French capital appeared, as well, throughout the world.

CCTV footage retrieved from street cameras in front of Nick and Gabriela's apartment building was handed over to the police. It showed the scene exactly as eyewitnesses had described—and more. The killers were obviously amateurs, as they didn't think of obscuring the license plates on their motorbikes.

The plate numbers were run through the database at the city's motor vehicle department, and a positive match of the owners' names quickly appeared on the operator's computer screen. This information was passed on to the police department's homicide division, and a squad of well-armed, well-armored officers was dispatched to an address in one of Paris's roughest districts, an apartment near the Porte de la Chapelle in the northern 18th arrondissement.

Within minutes of their arrival, a squad of GIGN, Paris's National Gendarmerie Intervention Group, entered the building and crept up the stairs towards the suspected killers' apartment.

When the police squad smashed open the door, they were met with a barrage of gunfire. The two killers had bitten off more than they could chew, and within seconds, both men were lying dead on the filthy wooden floor of their living room with an almost unstoppable flow of blood spreading from beneath their bodies. Only one officer of the elite squad of police was wounded. She suffered a flesh wound in her upper left arm, was driven to the nearest hospital, and was discharged two hours later following treatment of her injuries.

In the ensuing search of the apartment, a scrap of paper was discovered. It bore the name, address, and phone number of Claire Rodriguez. There were also six sheets of standard-size white paper that had been downloaded from a computer, printed, and roughly stapled together.

Members of the forensic squad arrived and took over the investigation. They collected two automatic weapons, several clips of ammunition, spent cartridges from both the police officers' and killers' firearms, and other pieces of evidence, which they carefully cataloged, labeled, and bagged.

The accumulation of meticulously processed evidence, along with a detailed report of the takedown, authored by the GIGN officer in charge of the operation, was sent to the man in charge of the murder investigation—Deputy Director Alain Moreau.

The following morning, Alain arrived at his office and was confronted with the box of evidence. He immediately sent the guns, spent cartridges, and ammunition to the forensic lab to determine if the weapons were the same ones used in the murder of Louis and Natalie Faucher. Then he tentatively opened the two clear plastic envelopes, one containing the scrawled note and the second the computer printouts. He reached for his reading glasses and scanned their contents.

The note bearing Madame Rodriguez's contact information was troubling, and the policeman's mind clicked into hyperdrive. *What the hell is Philippe Rodriguez's mother's name doing on a piece of evidence found at the murder suspects' apartment? Did it mean that the woman had something to do with the double homicide in front of his friend's building?* He put the note aside and picked up the computer printouts.

Bon Dieu, what the hell is this? The papers Alain was looking at were indecipherable, a jumble of letters, numbers, and symbols, but one of the carefully drawn icons seemed to jump from the page. It was the image of a snake, curling upward with what looked like a halo hovering above its venomous head. *Oh, merde, this isn't what I wanted to see.*

He picked up the phone to call Nick, then decided against it. *It's better that he didn't get involved right now. He might do something foolish that could jeopardize the whole investigation*, he thought.

Alain leaned back in his chair, removed his glasses, and massaged his temples until they turned an ugly shade of red.

Soon there would be five bodies in the morgue connected to the vile Mexican cult: Jessica Devlin, Louis and Natalie Faucher, and following their autopsies, the two suspected killers.

He knew what he had to do but was disturbed about the consequences that would unfold from his actions.

The phone on his desk rang—the brittle sound snapped the senior policeman from his thoughts.

"*Bonjour, ici L'directeur adjoint Moreau.*"

"*Bonjour, monsieur*. It's Jacques LaPierre down in forensics. We've examined the bodies of the two killers in the Faucher case and found something that you should know about."

The deputy director waited to hear what his colleague had discovered.

"One of the men had a tattoo on the inside of his right arm. It was beautifully executed and read, *Alabado Sea el Sēnor Quetzalcoatl.*"

Alain Moreau was puzzled, but the man on the other end of the call continued. "It's Spanish, and in French it means *Louange à Notre Seigneur Quetzalcoatl.*"

Alain mentally translated the words into English. *Praise be to our Lord Quetzalcoatl.*

He thanked the man from forensics, hung up the phone, and

collapsed into his chair.

Oh, merde, this isn't what I wanted to hear, either.

ψ

The funeral service for the Fauchers was held in the Church of Saint-Louis-en-l'Ile at 19 Rue Saint-Louis, the same church that Gabriela had once suspected to be the site where the murdered victim of Les Serpientes de la Cristo would be found. *Thank God it wasn't*, she thought. The service was a solemn affair attended by the couple's family, friends, and a discrete contingent from the Paris police force headed by Alain Moreau.

The Fauchers' children, Luc and Emilie, had returned to Paris from their studies in Lyon and were ashen faced. Their grief was beyond comprehension, and it showed in their swollen, reddened eyes and in the remnants of tears that marked their cheeks with dried up rivulets. The two of them sat in hushed silence with their distraught relatives, all of them visibly traumatized by the heinous way their beloved family members had been slaughtered.

Nick was asked to give the eulogy. He'd been contemplating what he could say to honor the memory of his deceased friends, all the while thinking. *If not for the grace of God and some downright bullshit luck, it would be me and Gabi lying here in front of the altar, and not our two friends.*

Nick stood at the lectern and slowly began to speak. He didn't use any carefully written or quickly scrawled notes. He didn't need to. The words sprang into his mind as if they'd been indelibly branded into his brain years beforehand. Although he was comfortably fluent in French, Nick felt more confident about expressing his feelings of grief in English. Charles Bernard, one of Natalie's uncles, stood beside him and provided the translation.

"Louis and Natalie were dear friends with whom Gabriela, and I spent many pleasant days and evenings. Their cruel and violent deaths have been an anathema to us and to all of those who knew them. The perpetrators responsible for their murder have been found, and now they too are dead, but their death doesn't make this day any better or brighter. It only reminds us that the men who killed our beloved friends will be unable to perpetrate comparable acts of violence." He paused and looked at the faces before him. "The kind of violence that will result in outpourings of grief, like what each and every one of us here is feeling today." He paused again and looked around the crowded nave at the many mourners, some sitting stoically upright, others silently sobbing, most trying desperately to conceal their grief. "Louis and Natalie will always hold a special place in our hearts. Their contagious laughter and good humor will always be present at our tables, and their hopes and prayers for their children, Emilie and Luc, will be honored by everyone here. Thank you for allowing me to speak. I feel deeply privileged to have been invited to share my feelings of grief about our dear friends."

Nick left the lectern, sat in the chair next to Gabriela, and squeezed her hand. He looked over toward Lucy and Sierra. Much of his hope for retribution lay squarely on their delicate shoulders.

The congregation rose slowly to their feet and watched the pallbearers as they lifted the coffins onto their shoulders. The twelve grim-faced men carried the coffins out into the street. They were followed by a silent procession of grief-stricken mourners.

ψ

Claire Rodriguez was busily packing for her trip to Philippe's yacht in Monaco. She was excited about seeing her son again. It seemed like an eternity since he'd left for his meeting in Mexico City, and they had a lot of catching up to do.

She heard the distinctive sound of the concierge bell and soon thereafter a knock on the front door of her apartment. Almost immediately, Jacqueline, her dutiful maid and confidant, scurried into her mistress's bedroom. "*Madame*, there are gendarmes here to see you."

She handed Claire Alain Moreau's business card as if it was a hot ember, that she needed to quickly rid herself of. Claire took the card and nervously flipped it around in her fingers.

Shit, I need this right now like I need another hole in my head, she thought.

CHAPTER FOURTEEN

Luc and Emilie Faucher were staying in their parents' apartment. They were exhausted. The violent murder of their father and mother and subsequent funeral had taken an immense toll on the young brother and sister. Memories of their *mère et père* and the happy times they'd spent together in the Île Saint-Louis apartment permeated every nook and cranny of the eerily empty rooms. The siblings' overpowering sadness, exacerbated by the countless memories that surrounded them, became unbearable.

"Let's get the hell out of here Em," said Luc. "I know that you're exhausted, I am too, but we need escape the memories of this place for an hour or so."

Emilie knew that what her brother was suggesting would be good for them both. "That's about the best idea you've had since *maternelle*." Luc shot her a look that showed feigned displeasure at her little joke. He pulled a sweater over his head and Emilie grabbed one of her mother's jackets from a hook in the hallway. They left the apartment, ran down the stairs, and bumped into Lucy and Sierra at the building's front door.

Lucy's hand reached out to the young siblings. "Oh my god, I'm so sorry about what happened to your mom and dad. If there's anything you need or anything we can do," Lucy looked towards Sierra, who was hugging Emilie like she was her own little sister, "just let us know."

Sierra released Emilie from her heartwarming embrace. "Say, if you don't have any other plans, why don't you join us for a drink?"

Luc and Emilie answered in almost perfect unison. "*Merci, ça serait sympa,*" Lucy smiled, took Emilie's hand, and the four of them walked to the Pont de Sully bridge and crossed to the left bank and the clamoring activity of the neighborhood's many bars and cafés. They found a small bistro, slightly quieter than most of the others, sat at a sidewalk table, and ordered drinks.

Lucy broke the silence. "So, what have you guys been doing since the funeral?"

"Nothing much," said Luc. "Just messing around on our computers, mostly playing spy games and keeping in touch with our friends at university. But mostly just trying to forget what happened." He paused. "And I guess, there's been a fair amount of crying too." He looked towards his sister and noticed a lonely tear trickling down her ashen face. He reached across the table and gently wiped it away with one of his father's brightly colored handkerchiefs.

Luc's simple act of compassion hit Lucy squarely in the heart. She reached over, took Emilie's hand and gently squeezed it. "Really guys, I meant what I said. If there's anything we can say, or do, to help make things better, just ask."

Luc replied. His voice was raw with emotion.

"I overheard one of the cops at the funeral. She said that the guys who shot my parents were working on somebody else's orders. If you really want to do something, you can help us find out who hired them."

Emilie nodded, her sullen silence reaffirming her brother's sentiment.

"You'll need to speak to my father and Gabriella. I think that they might be able to help."

Lucy's surprising statement struck a chord with the bereaved brother and sister, and Emilie smiled. "*Mère et père* loved your dad and Gabi. Our father told us that they were the police detectives who solved a huge murder case years ago. Is that true?"

Lucy answered Emilie's question. "Yes, and I'm pretty sure they could help find out who the brains were behind your parents' murder." She paused and tried not to look too pessimistic. "But I know they'll tell us that the authorities are doing everything they can to solve the case and they'll only get involved if the police ask them to."

A grim silence engulfed the four friends.

The waiter returned with their drinks, all of which were left untouched on the table.

Sierra recognized that the conversation had petered out and was now at a standstill.

"It's late, and obviously none of us feel like drinking. Why don't we just go home? We'll all get together with Nick and Gabi tomorrow."

ψ

Nick was getting ready for bed. He was in the bathroom splashing water on his face when the apparition of a young woman appeared in his mirror. It was a face he recognized from many years earlier.

"*Bonjour,* Monsieur Palmer. You look exhausted."

He shook his head in disbelief. He was looking directly at the ghost-like image of Margaux Deneuve, Henri's sister, who was the first woman he'd confronted when he was a still a Chicago cop.

"Margaux?"

"I've come to warn you, come to tell you, that the path you are following is deadlier and more dangerous than what you encountered when we first met."

Nick somehow knew that the apparition appearing before him, a woman who was murdered in Paris in 1942, was telling the truth.

Margaux continued to speak. "The evil that is the son far exceeds the evil that was his father."

"But I thought that your soul, and the souls of all of the others, were now at peace."

"*Oui,* Monsieur Palmer. What you say is true, but several of us have returned—returned to help you rid the world of the depraved cult that murdered so many of us. Plan your course carefully Monsieur Palmer, your life and the lives of the people you love depend on it."

As it always had happened, the apparition of the young woman faded and vanished from the mirror's reflective surface.

Nick quickly dried his face and went into the bedroom. "Honey, I think that what's coming down the pike towards us is going to be really ugly." He proceeded to tell Gabriela what Margaux Deneuve had just told him.

Gabriela listened intently, then propped herself up from the pillow she was resting against.

"I think you should call Alain, tell him about your ghosts, and hope to hell he believes you."

ψ

Alain Moreau was sitting across from Claire Rodriguez in her luxurious living room. He had presented her with the evidence implicating her in the brutal murders of Louis and Natalie Faucher and was waiting for her response.

"It is nothing, *monsieur,* just a scrap of paper that could have been picked up from anywhere."

"*Madame*, are you involved, or have any knowledge, of a quasi-religious order called La Orden de las Serpientes de Cristo?"

The deputy director noticed a slight tremor in the woman's marble-cold countenance. "I believe that it was something my late husband was involved in, but now it's gone, apparently wiped out by policemen like you." Her scorn for the officer was palpable, but Alain continued. "We have information that Philippe, your son, has taken over the reins of the organization."

Claire's hackles went up like a dog protecting her brood of puppies.

"Ridiculous. That is pure speculation. Philippe is an outstanding citizen with an impeccable reputation. There's nothing that you, or anyone, could do that would verify his involvement in such an abhorrent organization."

Alain pushed harder. "If that's the case, then I'm sure you won't mind if we escort you to headquarters for further questioning."

"Do you know who I am? Do you know how many friends I have in positions much higher than yours? I can't and I won't come with you." She momentarily stopped her diatribe. "Besides, I'm leaving for the south and won't be returning to Paris for at least a month."

Alain chose his next words very carefully. He knew that any mistake or misunderstanding could very well cost him his job. "*Pardon, madame*, but regrettably, I must insist—and I must also advise you that until our investigation is completed, it would be unwise of you to leave Paris."

He pulled a subpoena from the inside pocket of his jacket, presented the document to Claire, and asked his colleague to take her into custody.

Claire screamed. "I want my lawyer! I have the right to call my lawyer!"

The two officers, and a very frightened Claire Rodriguez, left the apartment and got into the waiting police car.

Jacqueline, Claire's maid, had witnessed the whole encounter. She picked up the phone and called Philippe on his private line.

ψ

Jonathan Bloom was asleep in his Manhattan apartment when the call from Claire Rodriguez came in. His clock radio indicated that it was 4:45 a.m. *Who the fuck is calling me at this ungodly hour*, he thought. *Better be something important, or there'll be hell to pay.*

Claire was livid, screaming into the phone like a woman possessed.

"Calm down, Claire. Tell me everything that's happening."

"I'm in fucking jail in fucking Paris and you've got to get me out of here."

The lawyer was instantly wide awake.

"The bastards think I have something to do with the murders that happened here a few days ago. The killers had a scrap of paper with my name on it." She began to cry.

Oh shit, the stupid bitch probably did have something to do with it, the lawyer thought. "Have they set bail?"

Claire had calmed down and was now quietly sobbing. "No, they haven't officially arrested me. They've only got me here for questioning."

"Then just sit tight and say nothing. I'll contact my colleague in Paris and get him to come and see you right away."

He took down the details of where she was being held, then hung up.

"Fuck, fuck, fuck. When Philippe hears about this, the shit is really going to fly."

He picked up his cell and speed-dialed his associate in Paris.

CHAPTER FIFTEEN

Alain returned to Nick and Gabriela's apartment on Île Saint-Louis. He carried with him photocopies of the scribbled note and the six indecipherable pages of paper they'd found at the killers' address. He dropped the whole package onto the kitchen table without saying a word of greeting.

Nick picked it up and flipped through the papers. "What in God's name is all this?"

Alain shrugged. "I don't know, and he's not saying anything."

He responded to a quizzical look from Gabriela. "We took Claire Rodriguez in for questioning." Alain paused and looked around at their expectant faces.

Nick was too eager for their friend's theatrics. "For God's sake, Alain, get on with it."

Alain smiled. "She was raving. We reached her lawyer in New York, and she spoke to him for about five minutes. Then nothing, her lips were zipped tighter than monkey's . . ." He stopped before completing his thought, and immediately regretted his less than complimentary comparison. "*Pardon, mesdames. Ç'était inapproprié de ma part.*"

Lucy and Sierra were suppressing giggles. Gabriela, on the other hand, was on the verge of outright laughter. "No apologies necessary, Alain. We got the message loud and clear."

The crimson-faced officer glanced sideways toward Nick. "Any ideas, *mon ami*?"

Nick tossed the papers back onto the table. "The note is straightforward, but the pages look like they're in some sort of code. Any idea where they got them from?"

"I'm thinking that the killers scooped them up from somewhere in Madame Rodriguez's apartment, but that's just pure conjecture on my part. There's no conclusive proof for any of it."

Alain's speculation about what happened at Clair's apartment got no response. He was hoping that at least one of them would have a suggestion or suspicion, but no one said anything, it was as if they had all collectively hit the metaphorical, "brick wall."

Sierra jumped up, breaking the uncomfortable silence. "Why don't we get Luc and Emilie to look at the papers? His major at university is computer science, with a focus on artificial intelligence, and she's really computer savvy too." She took a deep breath. "When the four of us were at the café, they mentioned that they liked solving puzzles and playing spy games on their computers. They may be able to untangle the code, and besides that, giving them something useful to do might be just the thing to take their minds off their parents' death."

Alain was unconvinced but agreed to Sierra's suggestion. "Our guys in cybercrime are working on it, but I guess a couple of other sets of eyes wouldn't hurt."

Sierra rushed out of the door, took the stairs two at a time, and barged into the Fauchers' apartment.

"Luc, Emilie, we need you guys to help us solve an unusual problem."

ψ

Luc Faucher looked more like a surfer dude than an academic. He was tall, like his late father, had a mop of unruly blond hair, steel blue eyes, and movie-star good looks. Emilie, his sister, had inherited her mother's fine-boned elegance. Her mother often referred to her as "*Ma petite* Audrey Hepburn" in reference to the girl's uncanny resemblance to the world-famous actor.

The Faucher children shared a grief that was incomprehensible to anyone who hadn't experienced the devastation of losing both parents so violently and took what little consolation they could from being together through sleepless nights and days of gut-wrenching anguish.

Luc and Emilie were both deeply engrossed in their computers when Sierra's unexpectedly noisy interruption surprised them. At the mention of the investigation facing difficulties and that Nick, Gabi, and the police were needing more assistance, Luc jumped up and faced her.

"What problems? What kind of help?"

Sierra explained the enigma contained on the pages of seemingly meaningless gibberish that Alain Moreau had left in the upstairs apartment.

Luc was intrigued. It not only sounded like something that they could help the police with, but it could also be just what he and his sister needed to take their minds away from the recuring nightmares they both were suffering through—at least temporarily.

"What are we waiting for? C'mon Em, let's go upstairs and see what Sierra's talking about."

He took hold of his sister's hand and followed Sierra to the upstairs apartment of Nick and Gabriela.

ψ

The Parisian lawyer that Jonathan Bloom had contacted was almost an exact duplicate of himself. The Frenchman was arrogant, self-assured, and delighted, of course, to have a woman of Claire Rodriguez's social stature as a client. He bordered on fawning over the woman being held in police custody.

"*Bonjour,* Madame Rodriguez. My name is Paul Bonnet, I am an associate of Jonathan Bloom. He requested that I do my utmost to get you out of your present unpleasant predicament."

His smooth French accent and condescending manner did little to soothe Claire's pent-up anger. "I don't give a shit who you are. Just get me the fuck out of here."

"*Oui, madame, oui*, but first tell me, in your own words, what exactly transpired to get you into this very disagreeable situation."

Claire told the attorney what had happened at her apartment earlier in the day. She didn't know about the missing papers, so that small detail was left entirely out of the narrative.

Oh merde, cette chienne est en difficulté jusqu'aux aisselles, he thought.

"Well, *madame*, because there have been no formal charges laid against you, I feel very confident that I can have you out of here within the hour."

"Well, do it. Do it now, you stupid fucking moron."

The lawyer, who seemed impervious to the woman's insulting tone, left the room. *But I'll bet you're going to be in a whole lot of merde de chien before this is all over*, he happily thought.

ψ

Luc and Emilie were pouring over the six pages of indecipherable numbers, letters, and symbols in Nick and Gabriela's apartment. Luc looked up at the apprehensive faces surrounding him.

"*Ouf*, this looks like some kind of code. Would you mind if I scan the pages into my computer?"

"Sure, do whatever you want if you think it'll be of any help."

Nick was less than hopeful that Luc and his sister could untangle the mystifying jumble of characters on the pages, but to his mind, doing anything was better than doing nothing, and besides that, it would help take the kid's minds off the horrific events of the past few days.

Luc laid out the pages and systemically photographed each page with his cell phone, then collected the pages and handed them back to Nick.

"*Merci,* we'll get on it right away." He hurried out of the room, with Emilie following closely behind.

A silence hung in the room after the departure of the Faucher siblings. Nick was the first to speak, he sounded doubtful. "Let's cross our fingers and hope that they'll be able to help us get the answers we need."

ψ

Philippe hadn't heard from his mother since he saw her in Paris. He smiled at the memory but was slightly concerned, it was unlike her not to let him know what her travel plans were.

She's probably hooked up with another handsome gold-digging idiot and doesn't want to be disturbed. He smiled at the thought. *Oh well, practice makes perfect, I guess.*

Phillipe's party was only a few weeks away, and right after the big event, he had a commitment to attend the conclave of apostles he'd decreed to be convened in Mexico.

He'd sent out the encoded agenda by encrypted email several days earlier and hoped each of the attendees would be well prepared to deliver their reports at the clandestine meeting.

Philippe rang for his chief steward. "Marcos, I'll have lunch in my cabin today. Niçoise salad and a diet cola. Make it fast. I'm starving."

He leaned back in his chair and crossed his hands behind his head. It helped him think. *After the party and conclave are over, eliminating that fucking Nicholas Palmer and his family goes right to the top of my to-do list.*

ψ

Luc and Emilie Faucher contacted their respective universities and advised them that they wouldn't be returning to classes for several weeks. The administrators at both schools were sympathetic and offered their personal condolences and further condolences from their entire staff and faculties.

"Okay, Luc, where do we begin?" Emilie's unexpectedly determined look surprised her brother. Luc smiled; his fingers were already flying over the keys on his computer, trying to decipher the seemingly endless arrangement of disparate characters.

At police headquarters, an equally engrossed team of computer specialists had begun going through the same, seemingly futile, exercise.

It was shaping up to be a long stretch of days and nights, with little or no possibility of solving the secrets hidden within the puzzling document.

CHAPTER SIXTEEN

Paul Bonnet arranged to have Claire released from custody. It was a reasonably easy task since no formal charges had been laid against the woman.

Claire stomped out of the police station without acknowledging the lawyer's efforts, or the ill-mannered stares of other detainees and police personnel. She hailed a taxi and returned to her apartment to resume packing for her trip to Monte Carlo.

Jacqueline, her maid, had carefully selected and folded Claire's wardrobe for her, and with a few exceptions added by her employer, her choices were exactly what Claire would have selected for herself.

The final item, destined for inclusion into her luggage, was the printout of the agenda for the conclave in Mexico City.

Claire believed that she'd left it on the antique demilune table in the front hall, but it wasn't there, so she spent the better part of an hour scouring the rooms, trying to find it.

"Jacqueline, have you seen the papers I left on the hall table?"

"*Non, madame.* There was nothing like that when I dusted yesterday."

Claire's breath caught in her throat. *Fuck, Philippe is going to be furious. He specifically ordered me never to print any documents pertaining to the Order.*

She knew that she was in trouble. Her son didn't take lightly to having his orders disobeyed, even if the offender was his mother.

But he knows how lousy I am with computers, she thought. *Perhaps he'll forgive me.*

She knew that her reasoning would fall on deaf ears when Philippe found out about her reckless oversight.

It's got to be here somewhere. No one else has been in the apartment except Jacqueline and me.

Then she remembered the two thugs she'd hired to kill Nick and Gabriela.

Oh fuck, perhaps they picked them up. But why would they? What good would the papers ever be to them?

Her questions to herself remained unanswered.

ψ

Paul Bonnet was on the phone speaking to his counterpart in Manhattan.

"I managed to get Madame Rodriguez released, Jonathan, but I believe that she's going to be in serious trouble when the police dig deeper into the murders on Île Saint-Louis."

Jonathan Bloom could smell trouble, even if it was 3,600 miles away across the Atlantic. He was reluctant to call Philippe but knew that he had no other choice. If he didn't apprise his client in Monaco of exactly what his dilettante mother had gotten herself involved in, she wouldn't be the only one with her with neck in a noose. He shuddered at the thought.

Goddamned stupid bitch. I wouldn't want to be in her shoes when Philippe finds out what she's done.

His attention returned to the lawyer at the other end of the line. "Thanks, Paul. I'll take it from here but stand by. I have a feeling I'll be needing your assistance again very soon."

He hung up and buried his head in his hands. He noticed that his palms were sweating.

ψ

It had been three days since Deputy Director Moreau had handed the six pages of indecipherable numbers and letters to his team in the cybercrime division, and so far, they'd had no luck deciphering the message that the document contained.

He left the crowded computer-filled room and walked slowly back upstairs. *Perhaps the Faucher kids have had better luck*, he thought doubtfully as he entered the equally cramped space that he called his office. He picked up his cell and speed-dialed Nick.

"*Bonjour, mon ami.* Have Luc and Emilie had any breakthroughs in figuring out what the pages say?"

Nick had visited the downstairs apartment earlier in the day. "Not yet, my friend, but Luc said that if they can solve the cryptic precepts of just one word, then the synchronicity of the rest of the message will fall into place—whatever the hell that means."

Alain scratched his head, disturbing what little hair he had left on his almost-bald scalp. "My guys have nothing either. Tell *le jeune homme* to keep working on it. *Le temps presse.*"

"*Oui*, Alain. All of us, know that time is of the essence."

Alain left his office, walked out into the unusually bright morning sunshine in his beloved city, and lit a cigar. He sat down on a nearby bench and drew in a deep breath of the pale blue smoke. *"Ah bon,* this is exactly what I need to clear my head and kick my brain into gear."

A passerby glanced at the policeman and probably wondered why the slightly disheveled man was talking to himself.

ψ

Claire Rodriguez was sitting in the lounge at the Paris-Le Bourget airport, waiting to board Philippe's private jet to Nice Côte d'Azur. The flight would be short, and she knew that Gaston, Philippe's long-time driver, would pick her up for the forty-five-minute drive to her son's yacht. But she was terrified about what Philippe would do to her if he discovered that she'd lost the coded printout containing the agenda for the upcoming conclave of La Orden de las Serpientes de Cristo.

She prayed silently that he would never find out but knew that secrets were his stock in trade, and that sooner or later, he'd come to know about her thoughtless blunder.

One of the airport's courteous concierges gently tapped her shoulder. "*Pardon*, Madame Rodriguez. Your aircraft is ready for you to board."

She left the lounge, boarded the jet, and settled back into one of the cabin's luxurious leather seats. Her thoughts were dark and ominous. It was as if the brilliant sunshine she was heading towards had been obscured by an opaque black cloud.

Claire's imagination was working overtime. *This may very well be my last flight*, she thought.

ψ

"Yahoo! Em, I think I've figured it out. Look at this."

Luc was jubilant and hardly able to contain his excitement. It was like he'd just discovered signs of life on another planet. He passed the coded papers over to his sister. All she saw was the same jumble of numbers, letters, and characters that had always been there.

"So, *garçon génie*, what does it say?"

Emilie's "so what?" reaction didn't exhibit any of her brother's unbridled excitement. Luc ignored her indifference, shrugged, and continued speaking. "It reads: 'AGENDA- LA ORDEN DE LAS SERPIENTES DE CRISTO QUARTERLY CONCLAVE.' And now that I've figured out the code, we should easily be able to translate the whole document."

Emilie was becoming more and more interested in what her brother was saying. "So, smart-ass, how did you figure it out?"

Luc had a smug look on his face and began to explain his hypothesis.

"It's easy once you work out the sequence of numbers and letters—and I have to admit that AI helped a lot."

Emilie looked slightly puzzled. "Go on."

"Well, each sequence of words is broken into sections of ten. In the first section, the number represents the numerical position of the letter of the alphabet minus sequential numbers. A equals one, G equals six, E equals three, and so on."

The girl looked even more confused and rubbed the temple of her forehead with her fingers.

"Would you mind explaining that to me again, please."

"Sure. A equals one. G is the seventh letter in the alphabet, so you subtract one, and the corresponding number for G is six. E is the fifth number of the alphabet, so you subtract two and get the number three."

You could almost hear the wheels in Emilie's mind spinning. "Oh, now I get it—I think."

As Luc continued, his voice got louder and more enthusiastic with each part of his explanation. "In the second sequence of ten, the numbering cycle is reversed. Instead of subtracting numbers, they're adding them. So, S the nineteenth letter of the alphabet, has one added to the number, making S the number twenty, and so on. Then in the third sequence of ten, they revert to adding sequential numbers. It's simple, but very clever."

"So, what's with the letters?" Emilie pointed to the random letters interspersed throughout the document.

Luc looked like the cat who swallowed the canary.

"That one's easy. They're the word breaks. Start with Z, the last letter of the alphabet, then go back three letters to X, then to U, and so on. Then, after they've run out of letters, they've reversed the sequence."

Luc smiled and delivered the final breakthrough. "Then you reverse the whole thing— imagine it's like seeing the words in a mirror."

Emilie looked at him as if he'd lost his mind. "You're kidding— right?"

Luc burst out laughing and hugged his sister. "Just about the mirror thing Em, all the other stuff is true."

He grabbed Emilie by the hand. "C'mon Em, we've got to get upstairs and explain our decryption to Nick and Gabi."

CHAPTER SEVENTEEN

The elegant black Mercedes-Benz Maybach S-Class sedan cruised effortlessly eastward along the Grande Corniche. The spectacular mountaintop highway, which hugged the coastline of France's famous Côte d'Azur, offered breathtaking vistas of the Mediterranean Sea, the towns and villages that hugged its shores, and the spectacular villas clinging precariously to the rugged cliff tops.

The car's lone passenger, Claire Rodriguez, didn't notice or care about the stunning scenery they were driving past. She was consumed with fear, deathly afraid of what her son might do if he discovered she'd misplaced the printout of the coded document that she wasn't supposed to have.

The driver eased the car into a viewing area high above the sea.

"*Pardon, madame.* Just a minute or two for us to enjoy the beautiful view."

Claire quietly nodded her consent and went back to brooding about her uncertain future.

The driver reached into the pocket in the driver's side door, pulled out an air pistol, turned, and fired at the unsuspecting woman.

The dart, laced with venom from the deadly fer-de-lance, a serpent native to Mexico and South America, found its mark in Claire's chest directly above her heart.

The woman's scream fell upon deaf ears.

The driver stepped out of the car, locked it with a remote key, then leaned against the hood and lit a cigarette. *What a spectacular view*, he thought to himself. *Too bad she won't ever be able enjoy it.*

Soon, very soon, Clair Rodriguez's frenzied cries for help stopped, and her prone body lay in a contorted heap on the spacious floor of car's rear seat.

The driver lit another cigarette and waited until a nondescript dark gray van pulled up beside him.

The van's two occupants emerged. They acknowledged the driver, removed the woman's body from the car, and manhandled it into the van. They retrieved her luggage from the Maybach's trunk, and that too was sequestered into the waiting vehicle.

The whole operation took less than a minute and went unnoticed by occupants of other passing cars on the busy highway.

The van pulled out, turned west, and drove toward Marseille, where the body and possessions of Clair Rodriguez were unloaded in a decrepit warehouse on the outskirts of the French city.

Nobody would ever find the body of Philippe Rodriguez's mother or know the circumstances of her disappearance. The whole undertaking was orchestrated by her son and implemented by one of Marseille's most notorious criminal organizations.

ψ

Philippe had several calls that he had to make. The first was to Jacqueline, his mother's long-suffering maid.

"*Bonjour,* Jacqueline. I'm sorry to inform you that my mother won't be returning to Paris or to anywhere else. Thank you for imparting the information about the missing document. I'm sure that with my personal referral you'll be able to find suitable employment elsewhere."

"*Merci,* Monsieur Philippe. I serve at your pleasure."

The maid hung up. She slipped the fat envelope of cash, sent by

Philippe, along with several pieces of expensive jewelry, pilfered from *madame*'s safe, into her suitcase and left the apartment. Her trip to Mexico City, and onward to Puerto Vallarta, was leaving in just three hours and she didn't want to miss her business-class flight.

Philippe's second call was to Jonathan Bloom. When his cell rang, Bloom was sitting in his midtown office high above the maelstrom of people crowding the streets below him.

"*Bonjour,* Jonathan," Philippe said, his voice laced with fake concern. "I'm sorry to inform you that my beloved mother is no longer with us, she passed suddenly yesterday. Please deal with all the necessary details of her estate and close her account with your firm." The matter-of-fact message from Bloom's largest client seemed to carry the hint of a threat.

Philippe's next call was to his beleaguered party planner. "My mother has suffered a serious accident. Take her name off the list of invitees."

Before Gisele Martin could offer her condolences, he'd hung up.

His final call was to Enrique Ortega, head of one of Mexico's most powerful cartels. The man was lounging poolside, surrounded by heavily armed guards, at his multi-million-dollar villa in Punta Mita, the exclusive gated community located just north of the Puerto Vallarta on the country's Pacific coast.

The crime lord saw who was calling, ordered his entourage of men out of listening distance, and answered on the second ring,

"*Hola*, Philippe. To what do I owe the pleasure of your call?"

"There's a woman, Jacqueline Blanchet, arriving on a flight from Mexico City later this afternoon." He momentarily paused. "Please have her picked up and dealt with."

The crime boss knew exactly what his friend in Monaco was asking him to do. "*Mi placer, mi joven amigo*. Consider it done."

Philippe gave the man details of the woman's flight, then added, "And if you could use your considerable influence to have her name removed from the passenger manifest, it would be very much appreciated."

"Again, *amigo*, it would be my great pleasure."

Philippe hung up, and the crime lord at the other end of the call indicated for two of his henchmen to join him.

ψ

Jacqueline Blanchet's flight arrived on schedule at Puerto Vallarta International Airport. The woman deplaned and made her way through the jostling crowd of happy vacationers who were crowding the massive arrivals hall. She picked up her suitcases from the luggage carousel, then passed quickly through security.

A man carrying a sign with her name prominently displayed came over to where she was standing.

"*Buenas tardes, señorita. Estoy aquí para llevarte a tu hotel.*"

The ride to her hotel that the polite young man was offering was, she thought, a much better alternative than trying to find a taxi among the melee of tourists. She gladly accepted, and the man picked up her suitcases and took her outside to a waiting SUV. The vehicle pulled out into the steady stream of traffic and headed south toward the city's hotel zone.

The man who'd met her inside at the airport sat in the rear seat next to her and pointed out the various attractions they were passing. The big black SUV then turned left onto Luis Donaldo Colosio, sped over the highway's numerous speed bumps, and on into the tunnel. It went thought a short section of the city's old town and rejoined Highway 200 heading south.

The winding road hugged the Pacific shoreline. They whisked passed luxurious villas, tall condominium buildings, dusty villages with ramshackle wooden buildings, and street vendors selling fruit and Mexican handicrafts. The traffic became much lighter: just the occasional truck, rusty car, and ancient bus rattling along the road.

Jacqueline became alarmed.

"Where are you taking me?" she asked the man sitting next to her.

"Don't worry, *señorita*, we'll be arriving at your destination in about forty-five minutes."

His calm tone of voice reassured her, so she leaned back against the seat to enjoy the balance of her ride.

They continued driving south, past Puerto Vallarta's world-famous botanical gardens, and onward past the turnoff to the small town of El Tuito. The big vehicle eventually slowed down. They turned left onto a dirt path, drove up into the mountains, and came to a stop at a secluded clearing in the dense jungle.

The young man sitting next to her turned and spoke. This time he didn't seem as friendly.

"We have arrived at your destination, *señorita*."

The terrified woman looked around at the thick jungle surrounding them.

The gangster pulled a multicolored rope from his jacket pocket, wrapped it around her throat, and pulled it until the last breath of life escaped from her mouth.

He and the car's driver pulled Jacqueline Blanchet's prone body from the SUV, stripped off all her clothing and identifying jewelry, and left her body lying in the middle of the clearing.

They waited at the scene, smoking and laughing at the woman's naivety, until they saw several turkey buzzards circling lazily in the sky above them.

"*Salgamos de aquí, mi amigo.*"

The driver nodded his agreement and they drove back down the mountain toward the highway.

The vultures landed then slowly and apprehensively made their way toward the woman's dead body. Within a few days, all that would remain of Claire Rodriguez's trusted maid would be a sun-bleached, partially ravaged skeleton bearing no clues as to her identity.

Several hours later, the newly washed SUV pulled into Enrique

Ortega's opulent compound. The two men presented Ortega with the woman's belongings. *"Gracias mi amigo, ahora perderse."* Ortega pocketed the envelope full of cash, quickly appraised the jewelry, then picked up his cell phone and called the man who was lounging on his yacht in Monaco. He uttered just three words. "It is done."

CHAPTER EIGHTEEN

Luc knocked on the door of the upstairs apartment, then he and Emilie burst in like they were propelled by a hurricane. The young siblings' excitement was palpable, bubbling over like a pot of overly hot potato soup on an ancient kitchen stove.

Their elation was contagious, and both Nick and Gabriela were soon hovering around them to hear what had made the two youngsters so animated.

"We've figured it out! Figured out how to interpret the code." Luc opened his computer, then looked around the room. "Where's Lucy and Sierra?" He wanted everyone to hear about their breakthrough and was slightly disappointed that the two young women weren't there to share their moment of glory.

"They've gone shopping," Gabriela explained. "They've got this cockamamie idea that they're going to attend Philippe Rodriguez's fancy party and need something nice to wear for an evening on the guy's monstrous goddamned yacht." Gabriela's tone of voice implied that she didn't approve of their plan.

"Okay, Luc," Nick sounded impatient. "We're not going to wait for them. Tell us what you guys have worked out."

ψ

It took close to an hour, with several interruptions for numerous questions from Nick and Gabriela, for Luc to explain his hypothesis. Then he went over it again in minute detail until they both somewhat understood the reason for his excitement.

"We can interpret the rest of the document by simply programming the data into a more advanced computer—something like what I have back at the university."

Nick interjected. "Or something like what they might have in the cybercrime division at police headquarters." He looked around at the assembled group. "I think it's time that we called Alain."

ψ

When Nick's call came in, the deputy director was arranging a warrant for the arrest of Madame Claire Rodriguez on the grounds of being an accomplice in the murder of Louis and Natalie Faucher.

When Alain saw who was calling, he picked up his cell. "*Bonjour, Nicholas. How are the bébés doing with their search for the holy grail?*"

"Don't be so dismissive, I believe that they've cracked the code."

The deputy director's tone of voice immediately changed. "*C'est vrai? Tu es sûr?*"

"Yes, my friend. I think that they've really done it."

The policeman needed proof about Nick's claim. "Bring them to the station. I'll summon my people from cybercrime to meet us. When can you get here?"

"Forty-five minutes max. See you soon."

Nick hung up and told the group about the plan. Gabriela left to touch up her makeup and Emilie followed her into the bathroom. She was feeling anxious about meeting the police cybercrime officers. *What if they don't believe our analysis and conclusions? What if they think that we're just a couple of amateurs who think that we're better than them?* She was about to voice her concerns to Gabriela when the ghostly image of Henri Deneuve appeared in the mirror before them.

"*Bonjour, mes belles dames.*"

Gabriela had witnessed these apparitions before, but even she was startled to see her old friend again. It was, however, a totally new experience for Emilie. She screamed, jumped back, and tried to steady herself against the bathroom's rear wall. Hers was a world of facts and science, and what she was seeing was anything but that.

"*Ne t'inquiète pas, ma jolie petite fleur.*" Henri switched to English. "The people you pursue are dangerous and deadly. Be careful and be well prepared. They will soon find out about your discovery and will attempt to stop you in any way they can."

The elderly professor's shadowy countenance slowly faded, then vanished completely.

Gabriela broke the silence that engulfed the small room. "What people? When? Where will it happen?" Gabriela pleaded for the apparition to reappear. "Please Henri, don't go yet. Don't go until you tell me."

Her voice echoed plaintively off the mirror's reflective surface. Emilie was shaking and ashen faced, trying desperately to understand the unexplainable event that she'd just witnessed.

Gabriela took the girl's hand. "Come on, Emilie. Let's get out of here."

Emilie didn't move. She stood, as if she was a stone statue, staring blankly into the mirror. Gabriela tried again to break into the young woman's trance. Her voice was gentle but firm.

"Come on, Emilie. There's no reason to be afraid. I'll explain everything to you later."

Gabriela pulled at Emilie's hand. This time she moved, but still didn't take her eyes from off the mirror.

ψ

Lucy and Sierra were seated on plush blue-and-white-striped cushions at a corner table in the shaded courtyard of a beautiful restaurant on Boulevard Saint-Germain. They had both ordered lunch from the delicious-sounding menu. Lucy was enjoying her chicken Caesar salad, while Sierra had opted for the roasted beet salad and, after one mouthful, declared it to be the best that she'd ever tasted. The pleasant ambiance and hushed conversation of the restaurant's other patrons was shattered by the brittle ringtone of Lucy's cell. She quickly answered it.

"Lucy, where the hell are you?" Her father's excitement was more than apparent. "Get here as quickly as you can. Luc and Emilie have just cracked the message on Claire Rodriguez's notes."

"Sierra and I have just finished lunch. We'll get there as quickly as we can."

"Well for Christ's sake, hurry up. We'll meet you at the police station. Me, Gabi, Luc, and Emilie are meeting with Alain and his computer nerds to go over their findings."

Lucy told Sierra what her father had just told her.

"Well, why are we still sitting here? Let's go."

Lucy waved to their waiter and indicated that she wanted their bill.

The two women were greeted at the front door by a horde of paparazzi, who'd somehow gotten wind of Sierra's presence at the famous designer's restaurant.

One of the store's employees, noticing their plight, quickly ushered them into a taxi. Then they sped away, leaving the melee of pushy photographers and star-porn journalists virtually obliterated in a choking cloud of dark gray exhaust fumes.

ψ

When Lucy and Sierra arrived at Alain's office, the others were already there. Their distinctive dark blue shopping bags were hastily dropped at the deputy director's door, and they elbowed their way through the small group of police officers hovering over Luc's open laptop.

He was just beginning to explain his hypothesis to the dubious group of officers when he noticed that the two young women had entered the room. "Wow, I'm glad you guys could make it. I wouldn't want to go through the whole damned explanation twice."

Luc started his dissertation again, meticulously going through every detail of his process. After an hour or so, when he'd explained the whole thing, he sat up straight and looked around at the assembled group.

"Any questions?"

Bridgette Bélanger, the shy, heavyset woman who headed the police cybercrime unit, spoke.

"*Merci, monsieur.* I think that I speak for the whole group by saying that what you've accomplished is nothing short of brilliant. We'll take it from here and do our best to decipher the entire document."

There were quiet murmurs of congratulations and agreement from everyone. The cybercrime officers left the room, quietly discussing their next steps as they trudged back to their crowded basement offices.

Alain hugged Luc and then Emilie, and planted kisses on both of their cheeks.

"*Merveilleux, mon garçon. Tout simplement merveilleux.*"

Alain left the six friends and followed his police colleagues down to the building's basement.

Nick swung his arms across the shoulders of Luc and Emilie. "Well done you two. I think that we're finally getting somewhere."

CHAPTER NINETEEN

Gabriela and Lucy were busily preparing lunch: a charcuterie board laden with pâté, sliced meats, cheeses, and thick slices of freshly baked baguette picked up from their favorite *boulangerie*.

Emilie walked over to where the women were putting finishing touches on the platter. She looked apprehensively at Lucy, then turned her full attention toward Gabriela and spoke haltingly. Her voice sounded like she might not want to hear the answer to what she was about to ask. "Can you tell me about the elderly man that we saw in the mirror this morning?"

Gabriela stopped what she was doing, took the girl gently by the hand, and led her over to where the others were discussing their morning's adventure at police headquarters. She interrupted Nick as he was in midsentence.

"Nick, honey, Emilie and I saw the reflection of Henri in the bathroom mirror just before we left for Alain's office." She glanced around at the others. "I think that we should tell her and Luc about the ghostly apparitions that sometimes appear to us."

Sierra let out a soft gasp and glanced sideways toward Lucy. "I saw one too, just the other day. I was about to leave for my photo shoot when a woman's face appeared in my hotel room's bathroom mirror. It wasn't a professor; it was a pretty young woman. She said that her name was Jessica Devlin, and that she'd been murdered a few days ago right here in Paris. I checked the internet and saw that everything she told me was true." She paused and looked around.

"What else did she say?" Nick demanded.

"She said that there were literally hundreds of women just like her, and that me and Lucy were chosen to help them rid the earth of the people responsible for their murders."

Luc's head was twisting left, then right, going from one person to another in the small group. "What the hell are you guys talking about?"

Nick felt that he needed to dispel Emilie's and Luc's obvious bewilderment and repeat the story he'd told the others about the apparitions.

"It all began years ago when Gabriela and I were detectives in the Chicago police force . . ." Nick talked, without interruption, for the better part of an hour. Then, when he'd finished, Luc spoke up.

"So, these snake god guys are back to their old tricks, and their victims are appearing to you guys and asking for your help in bringing them down?"

"Yup, in a nutshell, that's exactly what it's all about," Nick replied.

"So, everyone here—except me—has seen them?"

"Seems so." Nick wasn't quite sure where Luc's line of questioning was going.

"Well, why the hell aren't they appearing to me? I'm just as much involved in this shit as you guys are."

Nick didn't know how to answer the boy's question, so he simply shrugged his shoulders and threw his hands in the air.

"Maybe they will and maybe they won't, but I'm guessing that when they believe the time is right, you'll see and hear them too." Luc looked annoyed at being left out.

Lucy remained silent throughout her father's explanation of the paranormal events, then got up from the sofa, looked around, and smiled. "Okay, so I guess that we've been designated to be the good guys in this horror movie. What are we supposed to do now?"

Gabriela clapped her hands, stood, and pointed toward the

still-untouched platter of food. "Now, we should enjoy lunch. We can continue the conversation between mouthfuls."

ψ

Alain had a warrant in his pocket for the arrest of Claire Rodriguez. The deputy director and the three plainclothes detectives accompanying him strode up to the woman's apartment building, rung the bell to her suite, and were granted access by one of building's other residents. The officers took the creaky elevator up to Rodriguez's apartment, and Alain knocked on her door. He knocked again and again until the loud repetitive banging aroused the building's superintendent.

"*Elle n'est pas là, monsieur.*"

"Do you have any idea when *madame* will be returning home?"

The superintendent didn't know if she should say anything to the men standing in front of her, but she quickly changed her mind when Alain waved his police identity badge in front of her face.

"*Non, monsieur*. She left on a trip—her and an enormous stack of suitcases." The superintendent smiled and rolled her eyes. "She was picked up by a limousine and driven away. Jacqueline, *madame*'s maid, left the apartment shortly afterward."

Alain turned to his two colleagues. If looks could kill, both officers would be lying face down on the polished marble floor.

"*Merde*, I specifically ordered the woman not to leave the city."

The deputy director and his colleagues left the bewildered superintendent leaning against her broom.

When they'd reached the foyer, Alain stopped and called his office. The young duty officer who answered the phone immediately recognized his boss's gruff voice.

"Find out where Madame Claire Rodriguez has gone. Check the fucking airlines, check the trains, check fucking everything, and get back to me right away."

The harried young police officer didn't know where to start, or even how to start, so he scurried over to the nearest detective and relayed Alain's message to her.

"*Calme-toi*, Louis," she calmy responded. "It shouldn't be that difficult to locate Madame Rodriguez. God knows everyone in France knows what she looks like."

She picked up her phone and began calling her contacts at the city's airports and train stations.

ψ

Luc was staring into the blank screen of his laptop. His analytical mind was having difficulty processing his friends' claims about seeing ghostly images of dead people in their mirrors.

Why haven't I seen them? I was the one who unscrambled the code, and even the cops couldn't figure that one out. Are they all feeding me a line of bullshit? Goddamn it, I'm just as important to the case as any of them.

He felt as if he'd been kicked off the team by some mysterious beings and was trying desperately to understand the reasons why.

Suddenly, a halo of light began to fill the screen in front of him, and the light morphed into the kindly face of an elderly man.

"*Bonjour,* Monsieur Faucher. My name is Henri Deneuve, and I would like to apologize for not visiting you sooner."

Luc spun around, checking to see if the image was reflecting someone standing behind him. He was alone and slightly afraid. He shook his head and rubbed his eyes. *Shit, I've been staring at the screen for so long I'm beginning to see things.*

The ghostly image of the elderly man on Luc's computer screen smiled at the boy's discomfort. "*Non*, you are not imagining things, and you should not be afraid. I need you to tell my friend Nicholas Palmer that Madame Claire Rodriguez has been murdered, as has her maid, Jacqueline Blanchet. Both in different locations, and both deaths orchestrated by Philippe Rodriguez."

Luc was still staring at the image in disbelief. "Why—why don't you tell him yourself?"

The apparition of Henri Deneuve leaned forward and looked directly into Luc's eyes. "Because you too must believe in our presence. Because you too will play an important role in stopping the evil that is known as La Orden de las Serpientes de Cristo."

Luc's voice quavered. "How can I help? How will I know what to do?"

The words that Henri Deneuve spoke were abundantly clear. "You must tell Nicholas that *madame*'s journey ended in Marseille, and that the body of the woman known as Mademoiselle Blanchet will be found in Mexico, near Puerto Vallarta."

The image of the elderly professor faded, but before it totally vanished, Luc would later swear that Henri smiled and gave him a mischievous wink.

Luc could hardly hold his excitement. He shouted through the bathroom door to his sister, who was soaking in the bathtub, trying to understand the sequence of events that seemed to be engulfing her and her brother's lives—and the lives of their new friends.

"Emilie, I've just spoken to the ghost of Henri Deneuve. I'm going upstairs to tell Nick and Gabi."

He rushed out of the door, took the stairs two at a time, and burst breathlessly into Nick and Gabriela's apartment.

CHAPTER TWENTY

The young Mexican boy was in the mountains, high above El Tuito, searching for a cow that had strayed from his father's herd. He'd seen vultures circling lazily in the air above where he was headed and feared for the worst. If the cow had perished, it would be a great loss to his family, and the last thing he wanted to do was break the news of her death to his father.

He climbed higher and higher up the heavily rutted path until he stumbled into the clearing where the remains of Jacqueline Blanchet's body lay. Three ravenous vultures were picking at the few pieces of flesh left clinging, like glue, to the dead woman's bones.

The boy shrieked and the vultures, frightened by the sudden intrusion, flapped clumsily across the clearing until they reached the speed needed for them to take off. The boy turned and ran back down the incline, tripping and stumbling over the rocks and tree roots that obstructed his path. Finally, he arrived at the dirt yard in front of the shanty his family called home.

His father looked up from his work.

"*Encontraste la vaca?*" the farmer asked his breathless son.

"*No, padre.*" The wide-eyed boy took a deep breath. "Just the bones of a dead person."

The boy's father dropped the shovel that he was using to dig into the hard, sunbaked earth and followed the boy back up the mountain to where the grisly remains of the dead woman were lying.

Two of the vultures had returned to finish their repugnant meal, but once again scattered when the farmer and his son entered the clearing.

The farmer gathered palm fronds to cover the bones, then looked upward to the vultures still circling in the cloudless sky. He waved his fist and yelled at them. *"Malditos buitres!"* Then gave his son urgent instructions. *"Rápido, corre y consigue el agente."*

The boy scrambled back down the mountain. This time, his urgent mission was to summon the police.

The farmer stood over the bones, raised his eyes to the heavens, and made the sign of the cross. Then he walked over to where his errant cow was calmly nibbling on meager strands of grass at the clearing's edge. The man looped a rope over the cow's neck and led the delinquent bovine back down the mountain to rejoin the herd at his farm.

ψ

Several hours after the boy's grisly discovery, a heavily armed contingent from the Policía Federal arrived at the scene. Following a rudimentary inspection of the bones, the scant remains of Jacqueline Blanchet were placed in a makeshift body bag and loaded into the open deck of one of their worse-for-wear khaki-colored half-ton trucks. Photos were taken of tire tracks found at the edge of the clearing, then the officer in charge and his sickened colleagues searched the area for additional clues. Upon finding nothing of consequence, they drove back down the bumpy trail to deposit their grim cargo to their station house.

ψ

Luc rushed into Nick and Gabriela's apartment. His face was flushed, and it took him a few seconds to regain his breath.

"I saw him, I saw him on my computer screen."

Nick tried his best to calm the young man. "Okay, okay, Luc, what did you see?"

"I saw Professor Deneuve, just as you described him. I did. I really did!"

Nick quickly realized that any attempt to quell Luc's excitement was an exercise in futility. "Did he speak to you? What did he say?"

"Yes, he spoke to me. He told me to tell you that both Madame Rodriguez and Jacqueline, her maid, have been murdered. He said that Madame Rodriguez's body was taken to Marseille, and the maid's dead body was in Mexico. He said that Philippe Rodriguez was responsible for both of their deaths."

Nick placed his hand on the young man's shoulder. "Did he say anything else?"

Luc puffed up and a self-important smile flashed momentarily across his face. "Yes, he told me that I'm an integral part of the team, and we should work together to eliminate La Orden de las Serpientes de Cristo—you know, the Mexican cult you told us about."

Luc stood breathless in front of Nick. He had one last question.

"So, Mr. Palmer, what do we do now?"

Nick knew exactly what he had to do. He picked up his cell and dialed Alain Moreau's number.

ψ

Alain was apoplectic. No one in his entire organization had any idea about how, or where, Philippe's mother and her maid had gone. His subordinates and colleagues had exhausted every possible angle, talked to every possible contact, and twisted every possible arm. The two women had simply vanished off the face of the earth, and he didn't know where he should look next.

The cell phone he'd tucked away in his jacket pocket rang; the buzzing sound was muffled by the heavy fabric of his coat. With some difficulty, he dug the offending device from its hiding place and answered Nick's call, just seconds before the incoming message would have switched to voicemail. "*Bonjour, mon ami.* You couldn't have called at a worst time. What can I do for you?"

Nick relayed the information that Luc had just told him to his friend in the police department.

"And how is it that you know all of this?" the disgruntled cop asked.

I guess it's time that I told him about the apparitions too, Nick thought.

"Let's grab a coffee and I'll tell you all about it."

They arranged to meet later in the afternoon at a café close to the deputy director's office.

Nick was thinking ahead. *This is going to be a difficult sell. I'd better bring the others along for backup.*

ψ

Before leaving his office to meet Nick, the deputy director dropped by the department's cybercrime unit to check on what, if any, progress they'd made in deciphering the six-page manuscript. Bridgette Bélanger was smiling.

"*Bonjour*, Alain. We're about halfway through the third page, and the content is mind-blowing. Do you want to look?"

"*Désolé,* Bridgette, I have an appointment in a few minutes. If it's okay with you, I'll stop by again later."

Anxious as he was to see what the cybercrime team had uncovered; Alain knew that he would see it later. His meeting with Nick, however, sounded important, and he didn't want to keep his friend waiting. The deputy director strode out of the building, turned left, and walked to the popular bistro where he'd arranged to meet Nick.

Luc and Sierra had hastily pulled together four tables, and the small group: Nick, Gabriella, Lucy, Emilie, and themselves were discussing the best way to approach the thorny task of telling the pragmatic policeman about the apparitions they'd all seen.

When Alain walked in, their conversation abruptly stopped.

The deputy director smiled. "*Mon Dieu*, have I walked into some kind of ambush?"

He sat down at the only available chair, which Sierra had strategically placed at the center of the group and ordered a double espresso from a pretty dark-haired server.

ψ

The ravaged remains of Jacqueline Blanchet's body were redirected to Puerto Vallarta's police department. Their forensic division was much better equipped to deal with identifying the woman's remains than was the small rural outpost several hours south of the burgeoning tourist city.

The forensic pathologist in charge of examining the remains determined that the bones were that of a woman and that her broken neck had occurred from strangulation. She also ascertained that besides her broken neck, the woman had, many years earlier, suffered numerous gunshot wounds. The woman's right leg also had a metal rod running along the length of her thigh bone—indicating a broken femur, an injury the pathologist determined had also occurred many years prior to her unfortunate demise.

The young pathologist completed her examination, wrote her report, and sent it to her superior. The man reviewed her findings and forwarded the completed report to Mexico City, more specifically to Police Inspector Francisca Ramirez Flores, the officer in charge of the city's homicide division. The report landed on top of a stack of files relating to unsolved murders, which were threatening to overwhelm the police inspector's desk.

Later, the dead woman's remains were also sent to Mexico City for further inspection and DNA testing. As far as the police department in Puerto Vallarta was concerned, their involvement in the case was over.

ψ

For some reason unbeknownst to her, Francisca Ramirez Flores—who usually read the files from the bottom up—picked up the file from Puerto Vallarta and read it. Something about what the report contained struck a chord in her memory bank. She called one of her junior colleagues to join her.

"*Buenos dias*, Alejandro. I seem to remember something that may pertain to this case." She handed her colleague the file. "Will you please check the old files? In particular, find out all that you can about the woman's gunshot wounds and broken femur. *Gracias*."

The man scurried from his superior's office, went back to his desk, and searched the division's cold case files on his computer.

It took him an two hours, going through file after file, but he finally came up with what he believed was a positive identification of the remains of the woman lying in the morgue.

CHAPTER TWENTY-ONE

"Okay, now that you've got me here, what is it you want to tell me that's so damned important?" Alain was a busy man, and the only reason he'd agreed to the meeting was because his long friendship with Nick made it virtually impossible for him to refuse.

Nick was apprehensive, and rightfully so. Explaining the occurrence of apparitions to a man who only saw things in black and white, good or bad, right or wrong, was going to be, as he thought earlier, a tough sell. He began anyway.

"Alain, take your mind back to when we crushed La Orden de las Serpientes de Cristo. At the time I mentioned to you that I had help, help that I couldn't and wouldn't tell you about. Back then I thought that you wouldn't believe me. In fact, I firmly believed that you'd think I'd totally lost my mind."

The deputy director looked puzzled and slightly annoyed. "*Oui*, I remember being, how do you say it in English, really pissed off that you wouldn't confide in me."

"I'm very sorry, *mon ami*, but my mysterious friends have returned and once again are lending their assistance to the case that we're all working on."

"Enough of this childish chatter. Who are these mysterious all-seeing friends that you're talking about?"

Nick took a long sip from his cup. "They're more than friends, *mon ami*. They're angels—ghosts of angels."

The dubious cop shook his head in disbelief and stood to leave.

"Please sit down, Alain, and hear me out. You at least owe me that much."

Nick told the story once again, beginning with the appearance of Margaux Deneuve, the young woman who was murdered in Paris in 1942.

"I hate to say it Nicholas, but all of this sounds like pure unadulterated *merde*. I don't have the time or the patience for this nonsense. *Pardon*, but I must get back to the station." The policeman stood, pushed his chair back, and began walking toward the café's door.

Luc Faucher jumped up and wildly gestured to the departing officer.

"*Non*, Monsieur Moreau, I saw them too. I saw Henri Deneuve on my computer screen, and he told me that a woman's body, found in Mexico, would be relevant to the case we're all involved in."

The deputy director turned towards the young man and shook his head in disbelief.

Cries of "I saw them too" emanated from all the others.

Waiters and other customers in the café looked toward the group with puzzled glances.

Alain returned to the table. He looked first at Nick then at all the others. "So, tell me my friends, what did these 'ghosts of angels' say about the mess that we're now faced with?"

His question was met with silence, none of them knew how to convince the dubious policeman that what they had experienced was not figments of their collective imaginations. Alain took a moment to scan their faces then gave an exasperated shrug, stood, and left the café.

Emilie was the first to speak. "Okay, you guys, so what do we do now?"

ψ

"*Hola, Señorita Flores, ¿tiene un momento?*"

Alejandro was quickly ushered into Francisca's cluttered office. She took a moment to finish reading one of the many reports on her desk before looking up at him.

"*Buenas tardes*, Alejandro. What did you find out?"

He handed Francisca a printout from his computer.

"A female passenger, fitting the description of the dead woman, deplaned an Aeroméxico flight from Paris to Mexico City several days ago. She boarded a connecting flight to Puerto Vallarta, and that was the last time that anyone saw her. Strangely though, all records of her being on the aircraft have vanished."

The young police officer continued. "Witnesses said that she carried a French passport made out in the name of Jacqueline Blanchet, but the DNA report I received from the guy's downstairs identified her remains as being that of Sophia Perez, a felon who escaped custody over twenty years ago." The young officer paused. "The woman was believed to be connected to a cult called La Orden de las Serpientes de Cristo." Alejandro looked at his superior and delivered the last startling piece of information. "You were the arresting officer in the case."

An overwhelming flood of bad memories surged into the police inspector's mind, but her facial expression showed none of the emotion attached to what she was thinking. "*Gracias*, Alejandro. That will be all."

Francisca got up from her desk and took the elevator to the basement, where the department's overwhelmed pathologists carried out their grisly work. *I've got to see what's left of this woman for myself and check to make sure that their report is all that they say it is.*

The attending pathologist met Francisca at the morgue and showed her the remains. Francisca studied the report, and after accepting the accuracy of the physician's findings, she returned to her office, picked up her cell, and called the only person she knew in the PPD.

A sleepy Alain Moreau picked up his cell. He had long deleted the telephone number of the Mexican police inspector, so he was surprised when he heard her voice—even though he immediately recognized her lyrical Mexican accent. He sat up in bed, careful not to arouse his sleeping wife, and whispered. "*Bonjour*, Francisca. To what do I owe the pleasure of your call at this ungodly hour?"

Francisca laughed at her colleague's greeting. "*Buenos dias*, Alain. It's been a long time. Too long if you ask me, but I have some information that you may find very interesting."

Alain simply grunted.

"There are remains of a woman's body in our morgue. We've identified her as one Sophia Perez, but you may know her as Jacqueline Blanchet."

When Alain heard the name of Claire Rodriguez's maid, he leaped from his bed. His wife turned, opened one eye, sighed, then went back to sleep, she'd lived through this scenario many times before and would live through it many more times to come.

"*Merde,* Francisca. Tell me everything that you know."

Francisca recounted every detail of their investigation to her friend in the Paris force. "I'll send you our pathologist's report the minute we hang up," she concluded.

Alain Moreau felt that he should share the meager results of his investigation in France and proceeded to tell his Mexican colleague about the case that he and Nicholas Palmer were working on, which related directly to the grisly remains of the woman now lying on a slab in Mexico City.

Francisca listened intently, then exhaled. "Whew, Alain, it looks like the snake cult has raised its venomous head again. Let me know if there's anything that I can do to help."

"*Merci*, Francisca. With this case, I believe that I'll need all the help I can get."

Francisca understood how he felt. She'd been in similar situations many times in her career.

"*Adios*, Alain. Now go back to sleep."

The two officers, both on different continents, knew that sleep for the Parisian cop would be next to impossible.

ψ

Alain Moreau's apartment was in Paris's Marais district. It wasn't as large, or as luxurious, as Nick and Gabriela's residence on Île Saint-Louis, but it was where he and his wife, Marie, had raised their two sons, and where he usually found solace away from the gritty underbelly of heinous crime that constituted most of his waking hours.

He meandered through the rooms in his pajamas, retrieved a cigar from a half-empty humidor, and opened a window overlooking the street below. Marie didn't approve of his smoking and definitely didn't like the smell of cigar smoke permeating the rooms of their apartment.

He leaned over the railing of their tiny balcony and lit the offending tube of tobacco. Morning was beginning to stalk the streets of the French city, and the rising sun was casting subtle streaks of pink light across the neighborhood's centuries-old buildings.

Alain was thinking about his conversation with Francisca and his earlier meeting with Nicholas and his friends at the café. In particular, he was thinking about the revelation from Luc Faucher that the ghost of Henri Deneuve had told him that a woman's body would be found in Mexico.

Perhaps what they were telling me about the mirror ghosts is true. Perhaps I should have believed what they said. Who the hell knows what's true, and what's not true, in this crazy goddamned world.

He flipped the ash from his cigar onto the empty street below, hid the leftover butt in one of the many flowerpots crowding the small balcony, then went into the kitchen and made coffee.

I guess it's worth listening to them. Who knows where all this nonsense will lead.

He wandered into the bathroom, leaned his hands against the rim of the sink, and looked at his worried countenance in the mirror. Suddenly his face morphed into that of someone else.

"*Bonjour*, Deputy Director Moreau. Do you remember me from so many years ago?"

The harried police officer couldn't believe his eyes. The manifestation of Henri Deneuve, the late professor, was a contradiction of everything he ever believed in, but somehow the ghostly image of the kindly old man he'd once known felt very real.

Alain rubbed at his eyes to make sure that he was still awake, then tentatively reached out to touch the face in the mirror. His fingers hesitated then touched the reflected image. His hand immediately recoiled; instead of feeling the soft wrinkled face of an old friend, all he felt was the smooth surface of reflective glass.

Henri Deneuve smiled.

"Would that we could, my old friend. Would that we could touch and embrace like we used to, but I'm here to impart information that you may not know about the recently departed Jacqueline Blanchet—the woman whose birth name was Sophia Perez."

To say that the deputy director was startled would be a vast understatement. He stared at the apparition with a look of total disbelief on his face.

The elderly professor continued to speak.

"Sophia Perez was a high-ranking member of La Orden de las Serpientes de Cristo. She was one of the cult's most ruthless *discipulas*, and countless murders and atrocities were committed by this woman whose soul now resides in hellfire."

Henri's demeanor displayed a look of both horror and unimaginable grief.

"Mademoiselle Perez's one and only encounter with the police resulted in her being seriously wounded. She suffered several life-threatening gunshot wounds to her chest and a bullet from an officer's weapon shattered the femur in her left leg. She was picked up and, under guard, taken to a hospital in Mexico City, where she was successfully operated on. Following her surgery, she spent eleven months recuperating in a heavily guarded facility in the hospital's basement."

Henri continued, his voice becoming more and more agitated. "She was guarded around the clock, but after so many months of boredom, an errant junior constable left his post to get coffee from the hospital's café. During the officer's unfortunate lapse of care, other members of the Order absconded with Perez and took her to a secret hideaway in the Polanco district of Mexico City."

Alain Moreau was so engrossed with what the professor was telling him that he barely heard his wife knocking and calling from outside the bathroom door.

"Alain! Alain, what are you doing in there? I need to use the toilet."

Henri stifled a chuckle.

Alain turned to answer. "*Bon Dieu, madame.* I'll be out in a minute." He quickly looked back towards the mirror, and Henri continued speaking.

"Hector Rodriguez, the cult's leader, met her there. He praised the woman for her many years of faithful service to La Orden de la Serpientes de Cristo and then told her what she already knew. Because of her injuries, she'd no longer be required to carry out her normal duties as a *discipula*."

The deputy director wanted the story to end but was apprehensive about asking the elderly scholar to speed things up.

"Rodriguez then offered the woman an alternative. Live in Paris, under an assumed name, as his wife's maid, and act as his spy. He wanted to know exactly what his wife Claire, his son Philippe, and daughter Angelina were plotting when he wasn't present. His psychotic distrust of everyone, including his family, was what led to his eventual downfall."

"*Alain, dépêche-toi là-dedans. Je dois y aller.*"

Alain shrugged at his wife's evident discomfort.

"The rest, as they say, is history. She boarded Rodriguez's

private jet, was flown to Paris, and assumed her duties as Madame Rodriguez's maid and confidant."

The professor's image began to fade.

"I hope, *mon ami*, that this answers some of the questions you've been searching for. Now, I believe that you should offer your ever-patient wife the relief she so desperately needs."

Henri's face vanished from off the mirror, and the deputy director opened the door for his long-suffering wife to enter.

What Henri Deneuve had said corroborated the information that Francisca had told him about the woman's remains: the ravaged bones that the boy in Mexico had found in the hills high above his father's farm. Mostly, though, it allayed all his skepticism about what his friends had told him. Now he knew, beyond a shadow of a doubt, that the apparitions they claimed to be seeing were not just figments of their combined imaginations but were, in fact, mystifying truths.

CHAPTER TWENTY-TWO

Philippe Rodriguez was thinking about his mother. He missed her. Missed the lazy afternoons in her Paris apartment's sumptuous king-size bed. Missed her soft caresses, her gentle lovemaking. What he didn't miss about the woman was her reckless carelessness and her frivolous indiscretions. Claire was privy to every aspect of his far-flung business enterprises and therefore a threat to everything he'd worked for. Over the years, he'd cautioned her many times about her thoughtless habits and warned her about the dire consequences of her irresponsible actions. Printing the coded agenda for the upcoming enclave and allowing it to be stolen was the last straw, and although he felt a fleeting tinge of remorse, the foolish woman got exactly what she deserved.

Claire's position on the Order's council of apostles was honorary. She had no power, no vote, and no veto prerogatives. She was there only because Philippe had decreed it. He had no moral imperative to replace her and no desire to do so. He also had no obligation to explain her absence to other members of the council.

As for Jacqueline, his mother's maid, it was simply a matter of housekeeping. The hapless woman was too close to his mother and may or may not have had sensitive information about the Order and all his other businesses. Philippe couldn't take the chance that she knew more than he wanted the world to know about.

With those unfortunate pieces of business taken care of, it was time to address yet another pressing problem. He picked up his cell and dialed a number in Marseille belonging to his most trusted *discipulus,* the name given to a select group of assassins who were responsible for delivering the final coup de grâce to young women selected as sacrificial tributes to Quetzalcoatl.

The man answered on the third ring. "*Bonjour*, Master. Is it time?"

"Not yet, my dear friend. The assignment that I have for you today is slightly different."

The assassin listened intently.

"The Russian oligarch Nikola Volkov is attempting to assume control of the Order's pharmaceutical distribution interests in Eastern Europe. I believe that the time has arrived for us to make an example of him—so that others with similar ambitions will think twice about embarking upon the same foolish path."

The assassin understood his mission.

"*Oui,* Master, consider the matter resolved."

Philippe ended the call. His twisted smile revealed his thoughts. *Fucking Russian should know better than to try and muscle in on my drug distribution business.*

ψ

Volkov's mega yacht was moored in the Old Port of Marseille. The floating 340-foot behemoth was crewed by an army of heavily armed mercenaries and a large contingent of highly experienced men and women who were charged with the vessel's ongoing operations.

Security personnel, sailors, personal staff, and stunningly beautiful Russian courtesans validated the yacht's reputation as being one of the world's most notorious on-water pleasure palaces. The constant presence of all these people would make the *discipulus*'s assignment next to impossible.

The assassin took several days to consider his options. He had an arsenal of potential choices at his disposal which, one by one, he discarded.

He placed a call to Philippe Rodriguez. "*Pardon*, El Cardinal, but in order to complete my assignment, I must request a favor from you—approval for what I must do."

Philippe considered the assassin's plan. "What you are asking is regrettable but necessary to me and to our faith. For this you have my blessing, and my deepest respect and admiration."

ψ

A large black Rolls-Royce Phantom pulled up next to the boarding ramp of Volkov's yacht, and the emissary from Philippe Rodriguez stepped out from the car's luxurious rear passenger compartment. The man was immaculately dressed in a dark blue Italian suit, suede loafers, white silk shirt, and a thin multicolored necktie. He was thoroughly searched by the yacht's security detail before being allowed to board.

The Russian wasn't happy about this uninvited intrusion into his private realm, but the call from Philippe Rodriguez requesting the meeting was an ultimatum that he couldn't ignore.

I wonder how much the prick Rodriguez knows about my plans? he thought as he waited for Philippe's emissary.

There was a gentle knock on the door of his private stateroom, and the man from the Rolls-Royce, accompanied by two of the Russian's security detail, walked in.

The visitor turned toward the two guards.

"Please excuse us. This is a private meeting."

The Russian nodded to his guards, and they left the room to take up duty outside the door.

The *discipulus* and the Russian sat side by side on one of the room's buttery-soft white leather sofas. The Russian, who was casually dressed in a striped T-shirt and white linen pants, had a

GLOCK 19 handgun hidden within easy reach behind one of the seat's plush cushions.

"Tell me, my friend, what the fuck does Philippe want?"

The emissary loosened his necktie, as if to be more comfortable. "In a nutshell, sir, he wants you to keep your fat Russian fingers out of his business interests here in Europe."

"Well, in a nutshell, you can tell him to go and fuck himself—competition is good for business."

Volkov reached for his gun, but his visitor was faster. The emissary knocked the weapon from the Russian's grip, removed his necktie in a lightning-fast swish, wrapped it around the Russian's fat neck, and twisted. He heard the unmistakable sound of his host's neck snapping. Nikola Volkov was dead in seconds.

The visitor heard the oligarch's guards pushing open the stateroom door. He grabbed the Russian's weapon, put the muzzle into his mouth, and pulled the trigger.

The man's blood, flesh, scull fragments, and brain residue spattered indiscriminately over the sofa's pristine cushions and all over the disbelieving faces of the Russian's guards.

ψ

The following morning, news of the murder and apparent suicide on a private yacht in Marseille was the lead story in all online, broadcast, and print media. The stolen Rolls-Royce was discovered by officers of the Commissariat de Police de Marseille behind an abandoned warehouse in the city's huge port area. Forensic experts from the Commissariat found no fingerprints or identifying evidence in the vehicle, and following a second thorough examination by Interpol officials, the car was eventually returned to its owner.

Officials in Marseille had no clue as to the killer's identity, except that the man was Asian, possibly from the Philippines. They also had no idea that Claire Rodriguez, the allegedly missing woman they'd been ordered to locate, and the recent murder-suicide on the Russian's mega yacht were in any way connected.

Philippe Rodríguez and La Orden de las Serpientes de Cristo had made their point. There'd be no more poaching or encroaching on their territory: not for a while, anyway.

Philippe sat silently in his stateroom. His head was bowed in respect for the fallen *discipulus*. He whispered softly, "Thank you, my dear friend. You will be handsomely rewarded in the afterlife."

ψ

Dmitriy Egorov, a high-ranking official in the FSB, Russia's Federal Security Service (the notorious successor of the infamous KGB) was in his office when he received news about the murder-suicide in France. The corpulent bureaucrat slammed his fat hairy fist down on the ornate mahogany desk and swore revenge.

No one, not even fucking Philippe Rodriguez, is going to get away with killing my partner. I'm going to lose a fortune in American dollars—my share of the real money I need to get away from this stinking hellhole and the maniac who's running things from the fucking Kremlin.

He didn't express his thoughts into words because he knew, that even with his exalted position, the walls had ears, and his opulent office was very probably bugged.

CHAPTER TWENTY-THREE

Alain Moreau was uncharacteristically conflicted. He believed that what he saw in his bathroom mirror was real, but it went against all that he thought to be true.

There were two things that he did know for sure. First, he owed Nick and his friends an apology for his misgivings; and second, he needed to bring Nick up to date about his conversations with both Francisca and Henri. He picked up his cell phone and dialed Nick's number.

"Bonjour, *mon ami*. We need to talk. Are you available later today?"

The two friends agreed on a time: 3:00 p.m. at Nick and Gabriela's apartment.

ψ

Bridgette Bélanger, the officer in charge of the PPD's cybercrimes division, knocked on Alain's office door. A large sheaf of papers and her laptop were precariously cradled her arms, and because she had rushed up several flights of stairs carrying the results of her colleague's findings, she was breathless with exhaustion. She was also still, however, bubbling with excitement.

"*Bonjour, directeur adjoint* Moreau."

Bridgette stopped, took a deep breath, and waved the batch of papers toward the deputy director. "We've managed to interpret the entire document, *monsieur*." Her facial expression looked exactly like the cat that swallowed the canary. "Once we programmed in the code that young Monsieur Faucher and his sister provided us, it all fell into place—they are to be commended for their brilliant work."

Alain was anxious to see what the woman had brought and reached out his hand for her to give him the evidence that was making her so animated.

He flipped through the document, his practiced eye picking out all the relevant details outlined in the papers. He looked up and saw that Bridgette was still standing in front of him.

"*Pardonne moi*, Bridgette, please take a seat." He motioned toward a chair opposite him. She sat on the edge of her chair and watched as the deputy director continued scouring through the report. After a short while, he looked up and faced her.

"This document details the agenda of an upcoming meeting of disciples of La Orden de las Serpientes de Cristo. Reports to be delivered by the heads of human trafficking, narcotics, prostitution, gambling, robbery, collusion, and much more. What it doesn't tell us is where and when this meeting will take place. Any thoughts on those details, Bridgette?"

Bridgette was clearly distressed. She lowered her eyes and stammered her response.

"*Non, monsieur,* nothing concrete, but we did find a clue indicating that the meeting may take place in Mexico sometime this month."

A flashback about the secret chamber, hidden behind the crypt in the Mexican cathedral that Nick had told him about, sent an involuntary shudder up Alain's spine. "*Merci,* Bridgette. Excellent work. Please thank your colleagues in cybercrimes on their brilliant efforts."

Alain watched Bridgette stand, give him an almost imperceptible bow, and respectfully back out of his office.

This is something else I'll have to discuss with Nicholas, he thought as he looked at the stack of transcripts on his desk.

ψ

At precisely 2:55 that same afternoon, Alain Moreau arrived at the apartment on Île Saint-Louis. He knocked on the door and was greeted by Gabriela. She hugged her friend and invited him in. Nick, Emilie, and Luc were sitting at the kitchen table waiting for the police officer to arrive, their impatience to hear what the deputy director wanted to meet about was beyond obvious.

Alain sat facing them. He had a conflicted expression on his face: it conveyed a feeling of both satisfaction and remorse, as if he didn't know where to begin. He planted his elbows firmly on the table in front of him and placed his hands together, as if he were about to pray.

"First, *mes amis*, I would like to apologize for doubting you about these ghosts of angels you all spoke of."

His words were received with looks of shock and surprise. Alain smiled then continued. "In fact, I have recently experienced a similar occurrence in my bathroom mirror at home."

Nick, Gabriela, and the others looked as if they were all suddenly hit with the same strange malady—their eyes and mouths suddenly opened wide in disbelief. Several long seconds passed before Nick spoke. His voice conveyed a sense of incredulity. "What? Who appeared? What did they say?"

Alain had already placed both hands flat on the table and was laughing out loud at their looks of utter astonishment. Then, after the final sputter of laughter had emanated from his mouth and he'd wiped the tears from his eyes, he told them, literally word for word, the conversation he'd had with Henri, then he recounted his conversation with Francisca Ramirez Flores in Mexico City.

Gabriela smiled. She had a soft spot for the Mexican police officer who had possibly saved her life so many years ago. "Please, Alain, tell me how Francisca is doing. I keep meaning to write her—"

Alain cut her off in midsentence. His eyes flashed back and forth between Nick and Gabriela.

"She's well. In fact, she passed on her best wishes to both of you. And now, what I must show you next may result in you seeing the beautiful Francisca soon, very soon indeed."

He pulled the decoded transcript of the cult's agenda out of his briefcase and laid it on the table.

"My colleagues have unraveled the entire contents of the stolen documents."

Nick and Gabriela each grabbed for the papers. Gabriela won the tug-of-war and immediately began reading the incriminating document. As she completed each page, she passed it on to Nick and the others. It took them about twenty-five minutes to read and digest the entire contents.

Nick spoke for all of them. "Wow, this is heavy stuff, but not the kind of hard evidence we'll need to arrest Philippe Rodriguez. There are no names, no dates, no times, and no location about where this secret meeting is going to take place."

"Not quite, *mon ami*. The officers in cybercrimes believe that the meeting will take place sometime this month in Mexico." Alain smiled and continued. "Within the original pages, they discovered a reversed numerical code outlining travel arrangements to Mexico City and information saying that further details of the conclave's date, place, and time would follow."

Gabriela's analytical mind went into overdrive.

"The only person that we know who will be attending the conclave is Rodriguez. We have no idea who any of the other disciples are or where they're coming from. If we can somehow track his movements . . ." She stopped speaking and her eyes widened. "His private jet needs an authorized flight plan before it can travel anywhere, right? All we need to do is ask the authorities to notify us when they submit the flight plan."

Nick shook his head. "Great idea, Gabi, but this guy is very well connected and extremely devious. He has enough bribe money and influence to do just about anything he wants." His train of thought was speeding along the track. "That said, if I were him, I'd have several alternative plans up my sleeve."

The deputy director agreed with Nick.

"The best idea, *mon ami*, if we can pull it off, is to have him followed."

Suddenly, the front door burst open, and Lucy and Sierra tumbled into the apartment. The young women's faces were flushed from their recent workout. They dropped their gear onto the hallway floor and stared at the solemn group.

"So, what's happening guys?"

They said the four-word question in almost perfect unison.

CHAPTER TWENTY-FOUR

"When Lucy and I go to his party, I'll charm him into telling me anything you want to know. I'm pretty good at getting what I want, when I need it." Sierra smiled seductively at Nick, then laughed.

Nick ignored Sierra's flippant come-on as if it didn't even happen. "That's great of you to offer, Sierra, but it would be far too dangerous, and as for Lucy going with you, I'm not sure that's such a great idea either."

Lucy began to debate the point but was quickly cut off by her father. "He will recognize your surname, put two and two together, and rightfully conclude that you're my daughter, I know that's what I would do." Nick was adamant. "I'm positive that sneaking into the party, which I'm sure will be under super-heavy security, will be almost as impossible as getting into Fort Knox. So, my answer is no. No, Lucy, I don't want you to go." Then he grudgingly acquiesced. "But you're a grown woman, very capable of making your own decisions, so do what you have to do, but please be very careful."

Lucy looked over toward Alain.

"Can you get me some false identification or something?" she asked hopefully.

Alain shook his head. "*Désolée*, Lucy. This time I must agree with your father. It would be far too dangerous."

Sierra jumped right into the conversation. "But I can still go, and if you teach me what to do, it'll be easy. Like I told you guys before, I'm a very fast learner."

Sierra was adamant, and Alain, Nick, and Gabriela knew that trying to talk her out of going to Philippe's party would be an exercise in futility.

"Well then, young lady," Gabriela said, "your training starts right now." She took Sierra by the hand and led her into the library.

ψ

Luc and Emilie had been quietly listening to the whole conversation. Finally, Luc spoke for him and his sister. "We can do something too. I'm sure that Rodriguez has an online presence that we could hack into—and, with any luck, maybe steal information that could help us."

Nick winked at Alain. "I'm sure that what you're suggesting is very illegal, but if Alain agrees to turn a blind eye to your suggestion, it would be greatly appreciated by all of us."

"Did you say something? *Merde*, my hearing just isn't what it used to be."

Emilie smiled at the policeman's obtuse approval of the plan.

"Perhaps I can also get my cybercrime people to dig into Rodriguez's online activities," Alain continued. "I'm sure his computer's activity is heavily protected with who knows how many passwords and codes, but any little lead could help."

Alain struggled out of his chair, picked up his jacket, and left the apartment with a wave of his hand. "*Mon Dieu*, we must all be crazy."

His departing words were met with a foreboding silence.

ψ

Dmitriy Egorov was seething. The FSB bureaucrat was planning to use any asset at his vast disposal to rid the world of Philippe

Rodriguez. The how, when, and where were the only questions he had yet to determine.

He pulled a bottle of Imperial Collection Super Premium Russian vodka from a hidden compartment in his desk, poured himself an absurdly large drink, and downed the crystal-clear liquid in a single gulp. The alcohol seemed to clear his racing mind.

Some of our decadent fucking oligarchs will be attending the party on Rodriguez's fucking yacht. Perhaps I can convince one of the rich pricks that a small dose of poison would be good for their future health—and wealth. And if one of them gets the job done and offs Rodriguez, who gives a shit if they get caught? I don't owe any of those rich, ostentatious pricks anything anyway.

Another thought entered his mind. *The firm has a pretty good track record for quietly eliminating enemies of the state—all that I must do is make a call.*

Egorov poured another glass of the costly vodka, downed it, and pulled an encrypted cell phone from his jacket pocket.

ψ

Lucy was reluctant to leave Paris, but the managing partner of her law firm had called several times to inquire when she'd be coming back to the office. *Best not to annoy the boss any more than necessary,* she thought. She packed, said a tearful goodbye to Nick, Gabriela, and Sierra, and took a taxi to the Gare de Lyon railway station and the high-speed TGV to Cannes.

Sierra checked out of her hotel suite and relocated herself into Lucy's room on Île Saint-Louis. Nick and Gabriela felt it was the right move. With her staying at the apartment, they could more effectively keep track of her training. As Alain had suggested earlier, "Better Sierra stay with you so that her coaching won't be interrupted by the comings and goings of a busy hotel."

To accelerate her clandestine education, Moreau assigned two

GIGN tactical forces and one of his cybercrime officers to assist his two friends in the arduous, fast-tracked instruction program. Sierra, as she had told them earlier, was a quick learner, and was soon adequately skilled in self-defence and spy craft. She even became proficient in the ins and outs of high-tech surveillance, which delighted her instructor from cybercrime.

Two weeks later, when they had completed Sierra's rudimentary training, the officers from GIGN felt reasonably confident that their student could handle almost anything that Rodriguez could throw her way. As the three officers were leaving the apartment for the last time, they turned to say goodbye. "*Au revoir et bonne chance*"—goodbye and good luck.

Now all that anyone could do was wait for the evening of Rodriguez's sumptuous party in the principality bordering the French Riviera.

ψ

Jonathan Bloom's gold-edged invitation had been hand-delivered several weeks earlier to his Park Avenue penthouse on Manhattan's exclusive East Side. He felt that it was more of a command than a polite request to attend his client's annual soiree, so he kept it a secret from his socially ambitious wife. He knew full well the frenzy it would cause once she found out.

Tonight, he'd break the news and tell her that it would be impossible for him to take time away from the office to fly halfway around the world for a goddamned party. He hoped she'd agree that they shouldn't attend.

Yvonne, Bloom's wife, felt differently. For her, it was an exciting opportunity to mingle with some of the world's richest, most famous, and most notorious citizens.

"Oh my god, Jonathan, this is so fabulous! I can't believe that you don't want us to go. Will we be staying on Philippe's yacht? What do you think I should wear?" Her stream of questions seemed, to him, to go on forever.

Sometime, at about halfway through his wife's animated onslaught, he tuned her out. *Shit, this is going to be awkward. Should I ask him if he's invited Sierra Petersen? She's famous and beautiful enough to be included on the guest list. I wonder if Philippe has found out that she's, his half-sister? Should I tell him?*

When he snapped out of his trance-like thoughts, his wife was still chattering. He placed his arm around the woman's shoulders, surrendering to the fact that this was a battle he was never going to win.

"Okay, I'll RSVP saying that we'll be attending. However, I'm sure that we won't be invited to stay on the yacht." Bloom tried to alleviate his wife's obvious disappointment. "But let's plan on taking a few extra days on the Med—just you and me." Then, handing her purse to her, he added, "Go and buy yourself something fabulous, sweetheart. You deserve it."

Yvonne kissed and hugged her wary husband. "Thank you, darling. Oh, thank you." The lawyer shrugged, released himself from his wife's grip, wandered into his library, and poured himself a tall glass of scotch. He heard his wife talking excitedly to one of her friends. She was still chattering when the door to their apartment opened and closed. He smiled. *I guess that it's never too early to start shopping.*

ψ

Levi Heifetz, Philippe Rodriguez's head of security, was an alumnus of Mossad, Israel's infamous intelligence force. He stood five feet ten inches tall, was wire-thin and cobra-tough. For this meeting with his employer, he wore casual white slacks and a brightly patterned short-sleeved shirt. His taut, heavily muscled right arm bore an unusual series of tattoos: three lines each of ten tiny silhouettes of men lined up one after another, much like the kill markings on the nose cone of wartime combat aircraft. Those familiar with the man knew that his unusual tattoos represented the number of individual kills Levi Heifetz had made during his illustrious clandestine career.

He knocked on the door of Philippe's onboard office, entered the inner sanctum, and sat opposite the man who paid his exorbitant salary.

Philippe looked up. "Good morning, Levi. Have you finalized security protocols for the party yet?"

Philippe had both loathing and respect for the man sitting in front of him, and Levi knew it. He also knew that, if push came to shove, he could use his power of intimidation and seldom-mentioned expertise for remorseless brutality against his employer.

"Is this a good time to review the arrangements?"

The security chief didn't wait for an answer. "Pre-event security begins at entry to the dock. Each guest will be required to show their invitation and identification—nothing less than a valid passport will be accepted."

Philippe placed his palms together, rested them against his chin, and looked directly into Heifetz's eyes. This ineffectual attempt at unnerving the hardened soldier failed miserably.

Levi continued. "Every passport will be verified with the world's latest scanning technology: the exact same, top-secret system and programming used in high-level security by international intelligence and diplomatic services. Think of it as airport security protocols on steroids."

Levi rightfully believed that the specifics of the security technology would not be understood by the man he was facing and getting into them would be unnecessary, at best.

"Guests will be required to check any electronics, including cell phones. Pens, liquids, weapons, or anything else that could be used as a weapon will also be securely locked until they can be picked up at the end of the evening when guests disembark."

Philippe was about to say something but was cut off before he could voice his concern.

"At the boarding ramp, guests will be subjected to a full-body X-ray scan and patted down. Any questions, sir?"

"It sounds like it would be easier for a thief to break into Fort Knox."

Levi grimaced. *You got that right,* he thought.

"One other thing," Levi continued. "We've completed extensive background checks on all your guests and have discovered something that you should probably know about." He paused, more for effect than anything else. "The model, Sierra Petersen, is the daughter of Anna Petersen, one of the flight attendants who worked on your father's private jet."

Then Levi stood, turned, and left the room before his employer had a chance respond.

He smiled. *I bet that was a surprise for the ostentatious prick.*

CHAPTER TWENTY-FIVE

Maxim Morozov was a wealthy man, a billionaire many times over, thanks to his close personal relationship with the president of the Russian Federation. He didn't like being told what to do or where to go, but when summoned to dinner by one of the highest-ranking officers of the FSB, he had no choice. To refuse the man's invitation could cause serious damage to both his wealth and well-being.

The restaurant in the magnificent Hotel Metropol in the heart of Moscow was a favorite of high-ranking government officials, not only because of its proximity to Red Square and the Kremlin, but also because the cuisine was reputed to be the finest in all of Russia. Dmitriy Egorov entered the restaurant and was ushered to the oligarch's VIP table by the establishment's formally dressed maître de. The corpulent bureaucrat reached out his hand.

"Maxim, apologies for my lateness. Business first, you know."

Morozov reluctantly shook the man's fat, hairy hand and accepted the apology. "It's good to see you again, Dmitriy. It's been far too long. How are Olga and the children? Well, I hope." Morozov's thoughts were anything but sincere pleasantries. *I wonder what kind of favor the fat prick wants this time.*

"They're all well, my friend. Unfortunately, I don't get to see them very much. Too busy these days. You know how it is."

Morozov shrugged. *Too busy sucking back vodka, fucking whores, putting your fat nose into other people's business, and plotting against decent Russian citizens.*

A waiter cautiously approached the table to take their order. She knew both men by reputation and didn't want to elicit displeasure from either of them. The two powerful Russians scanned the menu and ordered. Egorov gently touched the girl's arm.

"Bring us a bottle of your finest vodka. I haven't seen my friend here for many months and I want to toast to his continued good health."

The girl scurried away to place their orders and get the bottle of vodka.

"Now, my friend," Morozov said, "I feel that you want more from me than a shared dinner and idle conversation."

Egorov smiled. His nicotine-stained teeth reminded Morozov of a day, many years earlier, when he'd witnessed the intelligence chief torture a woman accused of treason, although the accusations against her were unfounded and never proven. The flashback brought back memories of just how evil his host was and how evil and perverse the man had always been.

Egorov glanced around the room, making sure that they were out of earshot from other diners. "I understand that you've been invited to attend a party aboard the yacht owned by Philippe Rodriguez, the decadent western criminal. I also understand that security surrounding the event will be as tight as a donkey's arse."

"You've always had a way with words, Dmitriy. What's your point?"

Egorov once again scanned the room, his tiny, squinty eyes touching every table within a hundred yards of where they were sitting. "Well, my friend, it seems that this Rodriguez prick has been interfering with the well-being of some very important people in our government. He needs to be dealt with, and dealt with permanently, if you understand me."

Morozov understood the man explicitly and knew that the *very important people* Egorov was referencing was himself. What he didn't know was exactly what role he was going to be asked to play in Rodriguez's murder.

Goddamn, this fat prick has me in a corner. If I don't do what he wants, he'll figure out a way to totally fuck me over and kill me. If I do what he wants, I'll probably end up on the wrong side of the grass anyway. Fuck. Fuck. Fuck.

"So, tell me, Dmitriy, how can I be of assistance?" Morozov's words were spoken through tightly clenched teeth.

The server rolled a trolley over to their table, placed their first courses in front of them, then carefully set the bottle of vodka between them. Egorov poured two glasses of the potent, clear liquid and raised his glass in a toast.

"Here's to good friends and to a successful conclusion of our business together."

The bureaucrat removed his heavy, round tortoiseshell eyeglasses, raised his glass, and downed its contents in one large swallow. His guest's glass remained untouched on the table in front of him.

ψ

Philippe's already-immaculate yacht was, at his orders, getting a bow-to-stern cleaning. The disgruntled crew was scrubbing the decks and hull, polishing brightwork, and washing and buffing every item of stainless steel, silver and gold. This monumental task was being overseen by Gisele Martin, Philippe's party planner, who closely followed the crew around the huge ship armed with a clipboard, white gloves, and a take-no-prisoners attitude. Philippe strode up to the fastidious woman as she was berating a crew member for folding the dazzling white napkins incorrectly.

He smiled at his party planner, his look was more threatening than it was cordial. "The party is in three days Gisele, I hope, for your sake, that everything is under control."

"Yes, sir. Everything is proceeding perfectly. We'll be adding the decorations and most of the finishing touches tomorrow."

Philippe acknowledged her work with a dismissive wave of his hand. He was too preoccupied with what his security chief had told him about Sierra Petersen to chastise, praise, or comment on her efforts.

On his way back to his quarters, Philippe dialed Jonathan Bloom on the man's private line. His call was answered on the third ring.

"Jonathan, Philippe here. Do you know, or know anything about, Sierra Petersen?"

The lawyer hesitated for about four seconds before answering. "Isn't she the famous fashion model?"

"Yeah, that's the one. Levi informed me that her mother once worked for my father, apparently as a flight attendant on his jet. I've invited her to my party, so I want you to do some digging for me and find out everything you can about her. Where she lives, what she likes, what she doesn't like. All the background stuff you can find out about her."

Jonathan Bloom was faced with a quandary. He'd taken an oath to honor client-attorney confidentiality and knew that whatever decision he'd make could land him in a cauldron of scalding hot water.

"I'll see what I can find out, Philippe. Get back to you soon. Oh, by the way, Yvonne says hello and that we're really looking forward to your party."

Bloom hung up and buried his head in his hands.

Fuck. Damned if I do, damned if I don't.

ψ

At ten o'clock on the morning following their dinner, Maxim Morozov strode into Dmitriy Egorov's opulent office in the imposing Lubyanka Building at 2 Bolshaya Lubyanka Street, a prime location on the edge of Moscow's downtown Meshchansky District.

Construction on the neo-baroque Stalinist edifice began in 1919 and for many years it housed the headquarters of the now-defunct KGB. It was now headquarters of the FSB, the successor agency of its more famous predecessor, and contained the offices of numerous senior intelligence officials, among them the man Morozov was scheduled to meet.

"Come in, my friend. Come in and make yourself comfortable."

Egorov waved his guest toward a well-worn dark-brown leather sofa then sat down next to him. He opened a bottle of vodka and filled two crystal goblets with the liquor. He raised his glass and toasted his hapless guest. "To Mother Russia."

Dmitriy Egorov didn't waste any time in getting down to business. "Many years ago, some of our country's most esteemed scientists developed a chemical called Novichok. It's a powerful nerve agent that our operatives have successfully utilized to rid ourselves of enemies of our great state."

Although Morozov normally didn't drink, he raised his glass and took deep swallow of the powerful, clear liquid.

Egorov continued. "Most recently, our dear comrade, Alexei Navalny, was miraculously saved after accidentally encountering the toxin. As you undoubtedly heard, the unfortunate man died naturally in prison, where he was paying penance for his disgraceful remarks about our government."

The corpulent bureaucrat poured another shot of vodka. "You also may have heard about other dissidents who succumbed because of their careless handling of Novichok, but nonetheless what's done is done and history, as you know, cannot be reversed."

Egorov stood and walked over to his desk. He opened the top right-hand drawer and pulled out a letter-size sheet of paper.

"What I am about to tell you is top secret, and fully endorsed by the president himself."

He passed the sheet of paper over to the man sitting on the sofa. It was a direct order, on official presidential letterhead, and signed with the president's distinctive signature.

Morozov removed his eyeglasses from the inside pocket of his jacket and read the letter. When he handed it back to Egorov, his hand was visibly shaking. Morozov knew that he had no other choice but to comply. What he didn't know was whether he'd still be alive after completing the undertaking.

CHAPTER TWENTY-SIX

Philippe's Gulfstream G650ER was parked at Nice Côte d'Azur Airport, a thirty-minute drive from his yacht in Monaco. Although their flight plan had yet to be filed, the luxurious jet's crew knew that their next trip would probably take them across the Atlantic to Mexico City. The innocuous online chatter between the aircraft's pilot and her lover in Paris was being monitored by Luc Faucher, who applied the skills he learned at the National Institute of Applied Sciences in Lyon, the fabled French city in the country's Auvergne-Rhône-Alpes region.

He was using a pirated version of Pegasus, an online spyware technology developed in Israel. The program allowed him to penetrate encrypted messaging platforms on computers and cell phones, giving him access to texts, photographs, and real-time surveillance via microphones and cameras.

Identifying the aircraft's crew, then hacking into their private data and online activities using Pegasus wasn't a huge problem for Luc, and getting prior information on the big jet's flight schedule could give Nick and Gabriela a head start on Rodriguez's travel plans.

Hacking into the online activities of the yacht's crew, however, had proven to be more difficult because the high level of security, ordered by Levi Heifetz, was near to being bulletproof. Luc did, however, gain access to the guest list for Rodriguez's upcoming party and was running around-the-clock monitoring programs on their online conversations and activities.

After the second harrowing day of scrolling through calls, emails, and text messages, he picked up his cell phone and called Nick in Paris. His call was answered on the third ring.

"*Bonjour,* Nick. It's Luc. The only thing that's slightly out of the ordinary to report is that there's been a substitution on the guest list. Some fucking Russian bigwig couldn't make it, so he's sending a guy called Maxim Morozov in his place. I looked him up and he's an oligarch, not as rich as some of the other guys, but still worth a couple of billion."

Nick was silently wondering whether this tidbit of information had anything remotely connected their investigation. Luc continued, and by the elevated tone of his voice, he obviously believed he was on to something important.

"He recently had a meeting with a guy named Dmitriy Egorov at the FSB building in Moscow. He apparently didn't like the way it went, and after leaving the building, called his wife."

Nick didn't ask the young scholar how he'd managed to infiltrate the Russian's devices, but the explanation came anyway. "I hacked into his cell, turned on an instant-translate program, and listened to their whole conversation. It seems that neither of them is excited about attending the big blowout in Monte Carlo. He also said that he's been ordered by the president and FSB to do something that could be disastrous for them both. He didn't say what it would be."

Nick was both intrigued and alarmed by what Luc had told him. He immediately thought of Sierra. *Jesus Christ, the FSB doesn't fuck around, and whatever they're planning to do could be dangerous to everyone at the party, including Sierra.* A wave of nauseating panic rippled through his body. It was as if his equilibrium had been replaced with dread and foreboding. He heard a distant voice emanating from his cell phone.

"Nick, are you still there? Are you okay?"

"Yeah, Luc, I'm good. Let me know if you get any more intel. And thanks, you're doing a great job."

Nick flopped down on one of the room's big leather chairs and buried his head in his hands. *Goddamn it, how am I going to tell Sierra that she shouldn't attend the party—and will she even listen to me?*

ψ

Philippe was alone in his onboard suite. He'd shut down all his devices—except for his ever-present cell phone—and the only disturbance that affected his thoughts came from the gentle rocking of the big yacht caused by the wake of smaller boats as they passed by his mooring. He was thinking about what Heifetz had told him, and he was intrigued by the thought that Sierra Petersen could be his half-sister.

Fuck, what if we're related? I wouldn't put it past old Hector to screw his flight attendant halfway across the Atlantic. He smiled at the thought of his father pumping up and down on the beautiful woman. *Shit, I've done the same thing many times myself.* He continued smiling. *Fuck, old Hector and I are both charter members of the Mile High Club.* Philippe shook his head at the thought, picked up his cell, and called his head of security. The call was answered immediately.

"Levi, I want you to get something that we can use to test Sierra Petersen's DNA. I need to find out if she's somehow related to me."

"No problem, boss, but it will probably have to wait until after the party." Levi Heifetz knew that this wasn't what Rodriguez wanted to hear.

"I want it before the party. Do whatever you need to do to get the test done."

Philippe clicked off and screamed through the door for his steward. "Where the hell is my lunch?"

ψ

Levi got lucky. He went online, found Sierra Petersen's agent, then called her, pretending to be the creative director of a large Israeli advertising agency.

"We're interested in hiring Sierra for a cosmetic commercial," he explained into his phone. "Is she in Europe or in the States?"

"I believe that she's still in Paris, sir. Sierra has just completed a fashion spread and is taking a few days off to visit friends there."

Levi feigned relief.

"Wow, that's great. Who's the photographer who did the shoot with her?

The agent sensed the possibility of a lucrative deal for her client and gave Levi the name of the photographer.

"You wouldn't mind if I called him directly, would you?"

"Not a problem, Mr. Heifetz, but I'm not sure that he shoots film. If you like, I can recommend a commercial director who we also represent."

Levi covered his ass with yet another lie.

"No, *madame*, that won't be necessary. We've already contracted a film company to shoot the commercial, but we may want to use your photographer for the print campaign that we're planning to run in conjunction with the promotion."

Satisfied, the agent gave Levi the name and phone number of the photographer.

"Is the campaign imminent?" she asked.

"I'll call you the instant we finalize our plans. Thank you for all your help."

Levi called the photographer and repeated, almost verbatim, the story he'd told to the man's agent.

"We'd like to shoot the campaign in Paris, if that's convenient for you?"

"*Oh, oui*, Monsieur Heifetz. My studio is in Le Marais. it would be very convenient."

Levi smiled at the man's naivete. *Hook, line, and sinker*, he thought.

"Because it's for a cosmetics company, we'll obviously have to use the client's makeup artist, but if you could give me the name and contact information for the stylist you used on the recent shoot you did with Sierra, it would be very helpful."

The photographer gave Levi the woman's contact details and hung up.

Levi wasted no time calling the stylist. He couldn't believe that things were falling into place so quickly and easily, and as he dialed the woman's number, he couldn't help but hum a little tune he'd learned from his *bubbe* when he was growing up in Jerusalem.

When the woman answered, Levi retold his story for the third time.

"One more thing, *mademoiselle*. My youngest daughter is a huge fan of Mademoiselle Petersen. You don't, by chance, have a clip of her hair that my daughter can put into a locket?"

The stylist thought for a moment. *Locket? Jesus Christ, the kid is right out of the dark ages.*

"*Oui, monsieur,* I believe that I do. I've been out of town visiting a friend in the country and didn't finish cleaning my combs and hairbrushes from the shoot. Should I send what I have to you?"

"*Non, mademoiselle,* I don't wish to trouble you any further. I will have my colleague in Paris pick it up from your apartment. Once again, *merci*. You're going to make a little girl very happy."

The security chief hung up. He had a smug look on his thin, deeply lined face. *Looks like Rodriguez will have the DNA results, as requested, before his goddamned party.*

CHAPTER TWENTY-SEVEN

As the day of Rodriguez's party grew nearer, the mood at the apartment on Île Saint-Louis got darker. Nick was still trying to convince Sierra that going to Rodriguez's party would be foolhardy, but as he'd somehow known, she couldn't be talked out of attending the glitzy event.

"Look, Nick, I know that you're concerned about my safety, but you and Alain's men have trained me well and, quite frankly, just sitting around here doing nothing goes against everything we've planned. Besides, I bought this amazing dress, and it shouldn't be wasted."

She flipped her hair, smiled mischievously, and strode out of the room.

Was that a natural mannerism or something she'd picked up from being around Gabi? Nick shook his head.

ψ

Sierra's temporary room on Île Saint-Louis was cluttered with clothing and designer shoes picked up during her shopping sprees with Lucy. Pride of place, lying atop her bed, was the dress she planned to wear to Rodriguez's fancy shindig. She picked it up, held it in front of her, and looked into the full-length mirror that was mounted on the inside door of the room's antique armoire.

Suddenly Henri Deneuve's luminous face was staring out from in the mirror in front of her. The apparition's surprise intrusion startled her. She jumped back, dropped the dress to the floor, and swore at her clumsiness. Henri laughed out loud at the girl's unladylike reaction.

"*Oh, mon Dieu, ma jolie princesse.* Such awful words coming from such a beautiful mouth."

Sierra smiled and shrugged her shoulders. In truth, she was delighted to see the kindly face of the old professor again. "*Bonjour,* Professor Deneuve. It's wonderful to see you again."

Henri's demeanor suddenly became serious, as if the anguish on his face was reflecting the deep darkness in his heart. A black ominous cloud seemed to envelop the room. Sierra shivered and wrapped her arms around her bare shoulders.

"I fear that you are stepping into something far more dangerous than you could ever imagine. The evil that you will encounter will tear you apart piece by piece and leave you a hollow shell. Be careful. Be very careful that the unholy person you'll meet doesn't drag you down into his web of depravity."

Sierra was transfixed and more frightened than she'd ever remembered being, but as the ghostly image of the professor began to fade, he uttered words that gave her the tiniest glimmer of hope.

"Your strength and unwavering commitment to the inherent goodness of men and women can lead you safely through the tunnel of darkness."

The dark clouds dissipated, and the room got warmer, yet Sierra still felt tremors of fear and trepidation. She sat on the floor in front of the armoire and looked at her reflection in the mirror. She started to shake uncontrollably. It was as if her whole being was at the epicenter of a tiny earthquake. Then the tears came.

ψ

Gabriela heard the sound Sierra's sobbing coming from behind the bedroom's closed door and gently knocked.

"Sierra, are you okay? Is everything okay in there?"

A muffled voice answered, and when Gabriela entered the room, she saw Sierra sitting on the floor with tears streaming down her puffy, reddened cheeks.

"Henri appeared again, right here, right here in the mirror." She pointed toward the huge armoire.

Nick had silently entered the room and was standing next to his wife. "I hope he told you that you shouldn't go to Rodriguez's party."

Sierra looked up and glared at him. Her tear-stained face was defiant, and Nick knew that his words of concern had gone unheeded, blown away like so many leaves in an autumn windstorm.

"He did, and he didn't. He told me to be very aware and to be careful that I don't get sucked into Rodriguez's web of evil."

Her words did little to alleviate Nick and Gabriela's concerns.

"He also told me that I'm strong enough to deal with any difficult situations—whatever they may be."

She paused, took a deep breath and looked up at her two friends.

"I am going to the party, and that's final."

ψ

Levi Heifetz knocked loudly on the door of Rodriguez's private suite and, without waiting to be invited, strode into his boss's inner sanctum. Rodriguez looked up from his desk, ready to berate the insolent person who had the audacity to enter without permission. When he saw who it was, he managed to hold back the barrage of vitriol he'd intended to release on his unsuspecting victim.

Levi remained standing as he spoke. "I've managed to acquire a hair sample from Mademoiselle Petersen. What I need from you is a sample of saliva so that I can determine whether you and the girl are related."

Rodriguez leaned back and laughed.

"Do you want me to spit at you, or would you like me to dribble saliva into a jar or something?"

Levi pretended to look amused. "Either would work, but why don't you just spit on a piece of paper for me."

Rodriguez hawked onto a clean sheet of paper, folded it, and handed it over to his chief of security. "Don't go selling my secret identity to anyone—if you know what's good for you." Then he laughed again.

Levi took the folded sheet, placed it into an envelope, and left the room. Sometimes he wondered whether the crap that he endured from the man he worked for was worth the aggravation, or even worth the exorbitant amount of money that he was paid.

ψ

The thirty-something blonde attendant at the laboratory in Nice took the two envelopes that Levi handed her and promised that she'd have the results of the DNA tests back to him within two or three days. She peeked into the envelope containing the few strands of Sierra's hair, nodded, and then opened the one containing Rodriguez's saliva. She unfolded the paper and grimaced at the sticky yellow glob at its center.

"*Mon Dieu.* I hope this didn't come from out of your mouth."

Levi shook his head and smiled at the woman. "Non, *madame*, it came from the mouth of a snake, so be very careful, it might be venomous."

The lab attendant quickly folded the piece of paper and put it back into the envelope.

After receiving assurance that the woman would call him immediately when the result of the test became available, Levi left the laboratory, got into his car, and drove to the Promenade des Anglais, the seven-mile stretch of road running parallel to the Mediterranean coast in the southern French city.

He parked, strolled to an unassuming little café overlooking the harbor, then sat at a sidewalk table to enjoy a quiet meal: away from Philippe Rodriguez, away from the yacht, and away from the million and one things on his to-do list.

Levi ordered a glass of inexpensive red wine and steak frites from the young server, then sat back to enjoy the parade of high-priced cars streaking past him on the busy thoroughfare. Three middle-aged men, obviously Russian by their accents, were deep in conversation at a table just ten feet away from where he was sitting. The men didn't notice the black Mercedes-Benz S-Class sedan until it was too late. Levi jumped from his chair and screamed.

"Get down! Get down now!"

The startled men looked up, but it was too late. A devastating hail of bullets spewed out from the barrel of a semiautomatic gun protruding from the big car's right rear window. The weapon was held by an elderly woman, perhaps in her late sixties, the car's driver was indistinguishable.

Levi quickly ascertained that the short black weapon was a Heckler & Koch MP5SD6 silenced submachine gun, set to fire three-round bursts—he'd used the same weapon many times before in his previous occupation. The staccato blast of gunfire wreaked havoc on them and the surrounding area. Seconds later, the car and its deadly passenger sped away along the busy thoroughfare, leaving a scene of horror and devastation in its wake.

Levi, other patrons of the café, and innocent bystanders had dived for cover, trying desperately to find shelter from the scene of mayhem and carnage surrounding them.

Levi pushed himself up from the ground and rushed over to where the Russians were seated. What he saw sickened even him. The head of one man was virtually severed from his body by the fusillade of bullets and was hanging by a few strands of glutinous flesh. Mutilated torsos of the man's two companions lay in sickly, contorted positions around the terrace. Blood, severed limbs, bone particles, and shards of wood and glass from what was left of their table and chairs were fused together in a viscous concoction of death.

Suddenly, Levi froze, fell to the ground, and curled into a fetal position. He had absolutely no control of his body and was shaking uncontrollably. Sweat spewed from every pore in his being, and past images of death and destruction swirled around inside his head. He saw the grossly mutilated bodies of people he'd assassinated—enemies of the state, his superiors had told him—but mostly he relived a scene at a café in Palestine, where he and two Mossad colleagues had suffered an attack similar to the one, he'd just witnessed.

During the attack in Israel, Levi's two friends were killed instantly, but he had miraculously survived. His broken, blood-stained body was airlifted to the Sourasky Medical Center in Tel Aviv where, following a harrowing fifteen-hour operation to repair a shattered right leg, numerous bullet wounds to his upper torso, and shards of glass and wood piercing his entire body, he was wheeled into the intensive care ward, which was to be his home for the next nine weeks.

The next step in his recuperation was the Loewenstein Rehabilitation Hospital, where he underwent nine months of intense physical and occupational therapy. When he was finally discharged, his body was healed, but the mental pain and anguish bought on by the incident, he knew, would last a lifetime. Even today, the deeply slashed wounds in his mind remained open and sore.

Levi suffered from severe post-traumatic stress disorder, which the psychiatrists, assigned to him by Mossad, were unable to cure. It was after the psychiatrists' final diagnosis and report that Levi was asked to retire from Mossad, an organization to which he'd devoted most of his adult life.

ψ

The *he-haw* sound of French police sirens echoed off the walls of surrounding buildings, and within minutes, nine of the force's distinctive white cars, emblazoned with blue-and-red stripes, pulled up in front of the café.

One of the officers, a man in his mid-thirties dressed in combat fatigues, knelt next to the stricken man and gently rested his hand on Levi Heifetz's still-shaking body.

"*Êtes-vous blessé?*"

Levi struggled to his feet and assured the concerned officer that he was okay. "I'm just a little shaken up, thank you. It will pass."

In his heart of hearts, Levi knew that his nightmares would never pass. The horrors he'd experienced would remain in his conscious mind forever.

The policeman had a notebook in his hand, ready to take down Levi's name, contact information, and his statement about what he'd just witnessed.

Levi put up his hand. "I saw nothing."

He stumbled away from café. All he needed was to be alone: alone with his thoughts, alone to reassess his priorities, alone to determine, once and for all, whether he wanted to be on the side of good or evil.

He quickly reached a decision.

Why the fuck am I working for an asshole like Rodriguez? He and his whole fucking organization need to be eliminated.

ψ

As Rodriguez's head of security, Levi was privy to many of the man's numerous dealings. Killing him wouldn't be an issue, but eliminating the quasi-religious order and crippling the hidden illicit businesses that the man headed was a problem that Levi would need help to accomplish.

CHAPTER TWENTY-EIGHT

When Sierra's cell phone rang, she was in the process of dressing for dinner. Lucy, Luc, and Emilie had just returned to Paris and were joining her for what promised to be an exceptional meal at a recently discovered restaurant recommended by one of her Parisian friends.

Sierra picked up the phone and saw the words *caller unknown* prominently displayed on the device's screen. Normally, she wouldn't have answered, but a voice in her head, sounding very much like Henri Deneuve, told her that she should. Sierra shook her head, picked up her cell, and answered. "Hello," her voice sounded tentative.

"Am I speaking to Mademoiselle Sierra Petersen?"

The man on the other end of the call had a guttural accent that Sierra immediately recognized as belonging to someone from Israel.

"Yes."

"Then it's very important that we meet. My name is Levi Heifetz. I am head of Philippe Rodriguez's security force."

Sierra was so shaken that she almost dropped the phone. *This can't be real. How did he get my number? Why does he want to meet me?* A thousand and one unanswered questions raced through her mind, none of which made any sense.

The man continued speaking. It sounded like he was pleading with her.

"Your name is on the guest list for Philippe Rodriguez's party, and I have conclusive evidence that you're his half-sister and his only remaining relative."

Sierra couldn't believe what she was hearing. It was a secret that only she, her close friends, and her smarmy New York lawyer knew about.

She feigned her response. "What are you talking about? I don't believe a word that you're saying, and I don't want to meet you, not for anything. Got it?"

Sierra pressed the end call button on her cell and fell back onto the bed. It was as if every secret, every fear, every doubt she'd ever felt was colliding like a million tiny atoms ready to explode. She was frightened and her whole body began to shake. She felt that, more than anything, she wanted to throw up.

There was an urgent knock on her door. It was Luc.

"Hey Sierra, are you almost ready to go? Our reservation is in half an hour."

She took a deep breath, stood, smoothed her dress, and walked over to the mirror in the armoire. Suddenly, the familiar countenance of Henri Deneuve appeared. His gaze looked foreboding, and he had a worried look on his ashen face.

"*Bonjour,* Mademoiselle Petersen. You must meet this Heifetz man and hear him out. He is the one who can help solve the adversity that we all face. He is the one who offers the solution we need to rid ourselves, and the world, of Rodriguez and La Orden de las Serpientes de Cristo."

Henri's face slowly faded, and Sierra was once again faced with a reflection of herself wearing a blue-and-white floral dress. She continued staring into the mirror. *This dress is way too pretty for my mood. I should be wearing black.*

The knocking on her door sounded even more insistent.

"Say, Sierra, are you coming or not?" This time, it was Lucy who spoke.

"Yeah, hold onto your britches. I'm coming."

She opened her door and faced her three friends.

ψ

Dmitriy Egorov was seething. The FSB bureaucrat paced around his office like a caged lion. If his thoughts could be heard, more than half the population of Europe would be raped, murdered, and burned. He had no doubt that the shooting in Nice, which instantly killed three of his most trusted lieutenants, was the work of one man—Philippe Rodriguez.

He slammed his fist down on the ornate desk that occupied a place of prominence in the gloomy room, then picked up his phone and screamed to his assistant.

"Get me fucking Morozov on the phone!"

Then he flopped down into his plush leather desk chair, opened a drawer, and pulled out an unopened bottle of vodka. He didn't bother with a glass. Instead, he opened it, raised the bottle to his lips, and downed a full quarter of the crystal-clear liquid in several long gulps. He choked and spewed his last mouthful in a spray of spittle and booze all over the top of his desk.

"Fuck, fuck, fuck."

He flung the bottle across the room, releasing its contents in an aerial waterfall worthy of the famous Orekhovskiy Vodopad cascade in his country's Sochi National Park. Then his whole body collapsed into a fit of shaking, sweating, and unextinguishable rage.

Egorov's phone rang. It was his assistant—the man sounded terrified about what he was about to tell the irrational FSB boss.

"Apologies, Minister. Comrade Morozov is unavailable. He's airborne—on a flight to France."

Egorov slammed down the phone. His mood was darkening. It was as if an inky black cloud was quickly approaching, ready to unleash a torrential storm across the entire Russian landscape.

ψ

Sierra and her three friends were comfortably seated at an unobtrusive table, artfully sandwiched between two large pale-green planters in the opulent window-blanketed restaurant in one of Paris's most famous hotels. The courteous maître d' wanted to ask his famous guest for a selfie of them standing together, but discretion prevailed, and he remained silent. Their waiter had no such misgivings. He quietly asked if Sierra would mind if one of her friends took a photo of them together. She agreed to the man's request, and Luc snapped a photo of the grateful server and the beautiful model side-by-side.

"I would really appreciate it if you don't post it on social media until after I return to New York next month."

The man smiled, nodded, and scurried away to get their predinner drinks. Even in his excitement, he knew that his job could be jeopardized if he didn't agree to Sierra's request for privacy.

When they were alone, Sierra told the others about her brief conversation with Levi Heifetz, the subsequent visit from Henri Deneuve, and his suggestion that she should meet with this mysterious man.

The barrage of questions she was expecting were put on hold by the server, who delivered their drinks and took their dinner orders.

Lucy was the first to ask the question on everyone's mind. "Are you going to go through with it? Are you really going to meet this Heifetz character?"

Sierra looked at the expectant faces of the people facing her. "At first I wasn't going to, but after Henri spoke to me, I think that I should."

Luc was on the verge of being angry and locked his hands on top of his head in exasperation. "It's craziness, I tell you. Not only are you going to the prick's party, but now you're seriously thinking about meeting the guy's head of security? Don't do it Sierra. Don't get sucked into this. He can't be trusted and it's way too dangerous."

Sierra reached over and gently touched her friend's shoulder.

"Thanks for caring, Luc, but if what Henri said is true, then meeting the guy just might give us the opportunity to destroy all that Rodriguez represents."

"But if what Heifetz said is true, then you're related to him. He's your only living relative and you are his only living relative. How do you feel about destroying your brother?"

These words, spoken by Lucy, resulted in an overwhelming silence.

The server arrived with their dinner orders. He noticed the pall of uneasiness hanging over the heads of his patrons but carried on with his duties as if nothing had happened.

"*S'il vous plaît, profiter de vos dîners.*"

The group acknowledged the man's polite invitation to enjoy their dinners, but none of them were hungry. The implicit knowledge about the many dangers and challenges that were facing Sierra had robbed them of their appetites.

CHAPTER TWENTY-NINE

Philippe Rodriguez was in an uncharacteristically good mood. He'd just learned, from one of his most faithful followers, that three of Dmitriy Egorov's Russian henchmen had been executed, gangland style, at a café in Nice. He knew that his order to kill the men would start a turf war between him and the FSB bigwig, but the stakes were astronomically high, and he knew that in this game he held the winning hand. The only thing worrying him was the absence of his head of security. He hadn't heard from Levi in several days, which was unusual. He wondered where the man was and what he was up to.

He screamed for one of his assistants. "Denise, find Heifetz and get him here. I need to speak to him— NOW!"

The beleaguered woman rushed off to try to obey her employer's virtually impossible order.

ψ

Sierra and Levi arranged to meet at the base of Marie de' Médici's statue in Paris's famous Jardin du Luxembourg. He'd taken the TGV high speed train from Nice earlier that morning expressly for their meeting and was anxiously waiting for the famous model to appear.

The popular attraction was packed with tourists and Parisians alike enjoying the gardens, the fountains, and park-like ambience that straddled the boundary between Saint-Germaine-des-Prés and the Latin Quarter. The crowds and frenetic activity made it an ideal location for their clandestine rendezvous.

Sierra had disguised herself, as best she could, in a wide-brimmed hat, large, framed sunglasses, an oversize sweater, and fashionable wide-legged jeans. Levi recognized her immediately and indicated his identity with the prearranged signal—cleaning his sunglasses with a bright red handkerchief.

The oddly mismatched couple strolled to the large octagonal pond fronting the Luxembourg Palace, found two chairs, then sat and watched as children, and their ever-protective parents, played with model sailboats. To those who may have noticed them, they were just another couple enjoying the sights and sounds of this charming city oasis.

Levi broke the silence. "For many, many years I've fought for what I've believed in. For millennia, my people have been subjugated to evil men and their zombie-like acolytes. Men like Hitler, Stalin, and others before and after them, have persecuted and killed Jews and other innocent peoples who don't fit within their twisted view of the world, or who don't blindly follow their doctrine of hate."

"Then why are you working for a monster like Philippe Rodriguez?" Sierra asked.

"After I resigned from Mossad, I vowed to exact revenge on all those individuals who personify evil and who think only about the power and personal gains they can achieve by whatever means they can think of." Levi rested his elbows on his knees and buried his head in his hands. "I've killed many men who fit this description and have suffered no regrets for my actions."

Sierra leaned down and touched the man's shoulder.

"So, you're some kind of vigilante? A one-man god who decides who should live and who should die?"

Levi straightened up and looked directly into the model's eyes. He suddenly became defensive.

"I did what I did, and do what I do with no shame and little regret."

Sierra pushed her line of questioning. "You still haven't answered me. Why are you working for prick like Rodriguez?"

"Because I needed to get close to him, needed to find out the true extent of his empire of evil, needed to have him trust me implicitly."

"You could easily kill him yourself. Why did you want to meet with me?"

"You're right, I could easily kill him myself, but I can't kill his whole organization. For that task, I need your help."

Sierra was confused and conflicted. Levi continued speaking.

"Philippe Rodriguez is your half-brother. You are his only living relative, and the only person who can, upon his death, assume rightful leadership of La Orden de las Serpientes de Cristo, the ancient cult that is the base of his power."

Sierra couldn't believe what she was hearing. She was being asked, by a man she didn't know, to be an accomplice to the murder of a brother she hadn't met.

"When you assume leadership of the cult, you will have the power to dismantle and destroy it by simply turning all of their records over to the authorities."

"How will the followers know that I'm his half-sister? What happens if they don't believe me? What happens if they reject my claim?"

An errant soccer ball, kicked by a pretty little girl in a brightly colored striped dress, landed at Sierra's feet. Sierra smiled and kicked the ball back to the giggling child.

"They'll believe you because I have the DNA proof that you'll need to convince them, and they'll accept you because succession of bloodline is strictly ingrained into their doctrine."

Levi stood and began to walk away. After two steps he turned back.

"Think about it, and remember that I'll always be there, covering your back."

Sierra sat for another fifteen minutes before she too stood and walked back to the apartment on Île Saint-Louis.

Her mind was as jumbled as an unsolved jigsaw puzzle, a puzzle that she was desperately trying to piece together. She could only hope there were no missing pieces.

ψ

Nick and Gabriela listened. In these new circumstances, it was all they could do. It now seemed that the permanent eradication of Philippe Rodriguez and the Serpents of Christ cult had been passed on to the next generation. Nevertheless, Gabriela jumped into the conversation, she was like a mother eagle, hell-bent on protecting her hapless fledglings from the danger that she knew was coming.

"I don't like it. I don't like it one little bit. We don't know this Heifetz character, don't know if we can trust him, and if it wasn't for the message from Henri, I'd forbid you all from getting involved. It's far too dangerous."

She plopped down next to Nick, folded her arms in front of her chest, and scowled.

Nick rubbed his eyes until he felt the beginnings of tears.

"Henri can only warn and advise you. He can't protect you."

A hush settled over the room. It was as if the ghosts of angels had drawn a collective breath, sucking all the air from out of the apartment. Sierra's tentative voice shattered the silence.

"I think I can trust him. This thing with Rodriguez must end, and it seems like I'm the only one who has a chance to do it."

Her shoulders dropped with the daunting realization of what she'd said.

ψ

Levi entered his employer's sumptuous onboard office. Rodriguez quickly shuffled a large stack of papers and deposited them into a desk drawer. He obviously didn't want his head of security to see their contents.

"Where the fuck have you been?"

The words were hissed out between clenched teeth. Heifetz could almost imagine the tongue of a viper flicking out from between the man's thin lips.

"I've managed to get conclusive DNA proof that Mademoiselle Sierra Petersen is your half-sister."

Levi went on to tell Rodriguez about how he had obtained samples of the young model's hair and about his visit to the laboratory in Nice where the tests were conducted. He didn't mention his quick trip to Paris or his close call at the café on Promenade des Anglais. He rightfully suspected that the man he was facing was somehow implicated in the brutal attack on the Russians.

"Does she know?"

Levi smiled. The bait had been placed in the trap.

"I'm not sure, but I'm confident that she has her suspicions."

Rodriguez stood, walked around his desk, and placed his hand on Levi's shoulder.

"You've done well my friend, very well indeed. Please make sure that housekeeping prepares the VIP cabin for my sister. I want everything to be perfect for her."

Levi stood, swiped his boss's hand from his shoulder, and left the room.

This, my evil fucking friend, is the beginning of your downfall.

Levi shoved his hands deep into his pants pockets and secretly crossed his fingers.

CHAPTER THIRTY

Maxim Morozov and the president of the Russian Federation had been friends for many years. They'd grown up together in Leningrad, now known as Saint Petersburg, and shared a common affection for the northern city. Their school years took a parallel course, and they remained close until the now-president entered service in the KGB and Morozov became a junior executive in the country's burgeoning oil industry. When Mikhail Gorbachev initiated perestroika and glasnost programs to decentralize many of the state-controlled industries, their paths crossed once again. In the turbulence following their country's transition towards a more capitalistic state, Morozov became extremely wealthy, and with the power of his contacts and riches, helped his childhood friend ascend to the position of power that he now occupied and enjoyed.

The two friends were comfortably seated opposite each other in the president's ostentatious home office. His pillared, yellow-painted summer mansion, Novo-Ogaryovo, located in an exclusive suburban neighborhood just west of Moscow, was equipped with state-of-the-art security surveillance and a large presence of heavily armed guards.

Neither of the men liked alcohol, not even vodka, the preferred beverage of their colleagues. Instead, a sterling silver tea service with fine porcelain China sat on the ornate white-and-gold-trimmed table between them. Morozov spoke first; his tone of voice was respectful but also confrontational.

"I'll get right to the point. That fucking asshole Dmitriy Egorov wants me to poison Philippe Rodriguez when I attend his party in Monaco. I'm not an assassin, and I know that far too many things could go wrong if I screw it up." He stared angrily at the man he was facing. "And I can't believe that you, one of my oldest friends, would sign a fucking letter giving him the authority to do whatever he wants with me."

The president's stoic face was like a blank canvas, devoid of any real or perceived emotion. "I am aware of Comrade Egorov's extracurricular activities, even though he believes otherwise. He's greedy, and believes that because of his high-ranking position, he has total impunity. His one failing however, besides his goddamned bombastic temper, is that he doesn't like sharing his ill-gotten gains."

The president-for-life placed his palms together in a prayer-like position, and for a split second an almost imperceptible smile appeared on his smooth, parchment-like white face. He turned his cold, ice-blue eyes toward his guest.

"I am also very aware of what our friend Philippe Rodriguez is involved in, both above and below the precepts of Western law, and it is my opinion that you should proceed with whatever Egorov wants of you."

Morozov was about to protest, but the president raised his hand and stopped him.

"Maxim, my dear friend, you take care of Rodriguez, and I will take care of Egorov. With them both gone, the opportunities for us will be immense."

Their conversation was interrupted when the telephone on the president's desk rang, and he stood to answer it. He held his right hand over the receiver and indicated to his friend that their meeting was over.

Maxim Morozov was in more trouble than he ever thought possible. Using his power and prestige to quell the request from Egorov would be easy, compared to ignoring a direct order from the president of the Russian Federation. To do the latter would result in certain death for him and his whole family. The implications sent an ice-cold shiver up his spine and throughout his entire body.

ψ

Rodriguez's guests had already begun descending on the tiny, jewel-like principality on the northern shores of the Mediterranean Sea. All the most luxurious hotel suites in Monaco had been booked months in advance, and the owners of sumptuous homes and mega yachts, moored at the yacht club, were busily preparing accommodation for their rich and famous friends. Staff and crew members of these high-rise and floating palaces were given explicit instructions as to the likes, dislikes, foibles, and eccentricities of their employer's party-going visitors.

Sierra was packing for her trip to France's sunny south. The casually elegant Armani outfit she'd selected to wear to the party was carefully folded, wrapped in tissue, and placed on top of her other clothes in the vintage Louis Vuitton suitcase that had accompanied her on all her travels.

She would stay at Lucy's apartment in Cannes, which was a picturesque one-hour drive from Rodriguez's yacht in Monaco and change into her party clothes at the apartment of a photographer friend in Monte Carlo. She was totally unaware that the host of the elegant shindig had other plans for her accommodation.

ψ

Jana, Maxim Morozov's wife, was excited to be attending Philippe Rodriguez's quayside party and didn't understand her husband's reticence.

"Everyone will be there, darling. It's going to be one of the most glamorous events of the year."

She kissed her husband gently on the cheek, grabbed her purse and went shopping. The troubled man was left alone to consider his fate and, very possibly, the fate of his beautiful wife and three young children.

Morozov fiddled with the small vial of Novichok that Dmitriy Egorov had given him. He thought about the implicit orders given to him by the president and became even more despondent.

If I succeed, I'm a dead man, killed by Rodriguez's henchmen. If I don't succeed, me and my whole family will be assassinated by Egorov's FSB thugs.

He opened the vial, put a small amount of the deadly nerve agent on his tongue, and waited for the poison to end his anguish.

When Jana Morozov returned to their yacht to show her husband the curve-hugging, pale pink dress she'd purchased for the party, she found him lying on the floor of their cabin. All his bodily functions had shut down, and in the final stages of his tortuous death, he'd succumbed to heart failure.

The opened vial of Novichok lay next to his body. Thankfully for her, she didn't reach down to pick it up.

ψ

News of the oligarch's death spread like wildfire. The president of the Russian Federation took a nanosecond to mourn the passing of his friend, then immediately returned to the business at hand, which consisted of being massaged by one of the country's leading female gymnasts.

Dmitriy Egorov had no such distraction. He paced around his office swearing obscenities and punching out at everything that came within reach of his fat fist.

Philippe Rodriguez called his security chief.

"That fucking poison was meant for me!"

He was screaming into his cell phone at Levi Heifetz, who was listening, and thinking.

Too bad the fucking Russian failed. It would have made my life a whole lot easier.

"Well, the good news, Monsieur Rodriguez, is that he didn't kill you, and the better news is that we'd have caught him before he even got the chance to kill you."

Levi's words of consolation did little to alleviate Rodriguez's wrath.

"Hire more security people. I don't want anything or anyone fucking up my party."

Levi shrugged his shoulders and answered in his calmest possible voice.

"No problem, sir. I'll get on it right away."

At this late date, all I'll be able to get are the dredges of inexperienced idiots who think they're Schwarzenegger.

He hung up and smiled.

Perhaps that wouldn't be such a bad thing after all.

CHAPTER THIRTY-ONE

Jana Morozov and her three small children were reported missing. Unbeknownst to authorities responsible for the security of high-ranking government officials, and other important individuals in the Russian Federation, even their most stringent efforts to find Maxim Morozov's family would be fruitless.

The order for their immediate removal had come directly from the sumptuous office in Novo-Ogaryovo. The Russian president, in a rare moment of empathy, ordered that his friend's family be moved to a secret location, where they could live safely for the rest of their lives. The whereabouts of the four missing persons were never disclosed, and after a frenzy of speculative gossip and news, the mystery of their disappearance quickly evaporated.

Following several days of intense diplomatic maneuvering, Morozov's yacht was deemed to be property of the Russian Federation and it immediately set sail for Novorossiysk, the huge Russian military port in the Black Sea. Orders for the yacht's expeditious voyage also came directly from the office of the Russian president.

None of this news interested residents of the apartment on Île Saint-Louis, who were seated around the kitchen table discussing what, if anything, they could do to ensure the safety of their friend.

Sierra, who up until that moment, had remained silent, let the others know exactly what her feelings were about attending

Rodriguez's party.

"I'm going, and there's nothing that any of you guys can say that's going to stop me."

Nick was about to respond to Sierra's adamant statement when the ethereal voice of Henri Deneuve filled the room and stopped him dead in his tracks.

"Sierra must attend the party."

Gabriela's head spun around looking for the source of the voice. "Henri, you can't be serious. It's dangerous, far too dangerous. It would be like sending a lamb to its slaughter."

The spectral voice of Henri Deneuve continued speaking. "There is no other choice Gabriela, no other way to rid the world of the evil dynasty controlled by Philippe Rodriguez."

An uneasy silence settled over the room, and all eyes turned toward Sierra.

"Well, that settles it then. I guess I'm going to meet my half-brother."

She stood, kissed her friend's goodbye, then she and Lucy left the apartment for the Gare de Lyon railway station and the five-hour train ride to Cannes—and her uncertain future.

The mood in the apartment was as dark as the clouds of an incoming thunderstorm.

Nick was the first to speak.

"Get your stuff together, we're going to Monte Carlo. There's no way in hell that I'm letting those two girls do this thing alone."

ψ

Dmitriy Egorov was still seething about the apparent suicide of his would-be assassin when the call came in. His secretary barged into his office and breathlessly announced that the Russian president was on the line for him. He almost dropped the glass of vodka that he was holding.

Fuck, what does he want with me? I've never met him, never even spoken to him. Fuck, I don't even know how I should address him.

He tentatively picked up the receiver, placed it against his ear, and prayed that the man on the other end of the call wouldn't be able to detect his fear and trepidation.

"Good morning, Excellency. Dmitriy Egorov here."

He immediately recognized the voice that he'd heard many times over in speeches and on broadcasts. "Good morning, Comrade Egorov. I hear that your little plan to rid us of Philippe Rodriguez has gone sideways."

Fuck, how does he know about that?

The eerily calm voice of his ultimate boss continued. "I do hope, for your sake, that you have a suitable backup plan."

"Yes, Excellency. I'm working on it as we speak."

"Good, keep me informed."

The line went dead, as dead as he knew he'd be if he didn't come up with something fast.

Egorov buried his head in his hands. His mind was spinning like a Catherine wheel—the circular firework that spins, spitting sparks and fire, until it dies unceremoniously into a small pile of dead ashes.

Shit. Think man, think. If I don't come up with something fast, I'll be as dead as poor Morozov.

Egorov's secretary couldn't ever remember the time that her boss had been so quiet and dispirited.

ψ

The compartment that Lucy and Sierra occupied on the train to Cannes was uncommonly quiet. Most of the train's other passengers were either deeply engrossed in reading or silently dozing. Even the usual droll wordplay, smart banter, and impromptu laughter that made up much of the friends' everyday conversations were notably absent. Both their thoughts were about the party and Sierra's role in bringing down Rodriguez and La Orden de la Serpientes de Cristo.

"What are you thinking about?"

The seemingly innocuous question, uttered by Lucy, seemed to startle her friend.

"Oh, I don't know, just thinking about the cult that Rodriguez heads, thinking about all the innocent women they've murdered, wondering how it's all going to end, and if I'll even be around to see the final scene."

Lucy gently placed her hand on her friend's knee.

"Don't worry. You've always been amazing at figuring things out, and you have friends who'll have your back whatever happens."

Lucy raised her eyes and scanned the train's compartment.

"You'll even have help from those in the heavens."

Sierra was humbled by the thought of Henri Deneuve and the hundreds of martyred girls, who seemed to be guiding and warning them of impending danger.

"Yes, that's reassuring, but I only wish they could hold and use guns."

The two women hugged each other tightly, and Lucy whispered into her friend's ear.

"Don't worry. Everything is going to be fine. The good and the gods are on our side."

ψ

Luc and Emilie were on the same train as Sierra and Lucy, albeit several coaches behind. Because of the dangerous circumstances of the trip, Nick and Gabriela thought that the four young friends shouldn't be seen traveling together.

Luc was busily pounding the keys of his laptop, stopping only occasionally to ponder what he'd been working on. Emilie, on the other hand, was engrossed in a book about ancient Mesoamerican religions. She slammed the book shut and turned to face her brother.

"There's nothing, Luc. Not a word or whisper about La Orden de la Serpientes de Cristo in this stupid book. Only a lot of details about hundreds of other ancient beliefs and religions."

Luc looked over at his sister.

"That's because, in the narrative of theology, it's a relatively new faith. Here, let me see if I can find anything online."

He clicked onto a search engine and within seconds his screen was filled with accounts of how Nick and Gabriela had wiped out the sect of evil that was formed many years earlier in Mexico. It was a story like the one he'd often heard from his parents.

As they were looking at the screen, the face of Henri Deneuve morphed onto the flat, reflective surface. "*Bonjour,* Mademoiselle Emilie. *Bonjour,* Monsieur Luc."

This was the second time that Emilie had witnessed the ghostly apparition of the elderly professor. She fell back against her seat; her eyes were as wide as the small white plates used for serving croissants or macarons.

Henri smiled and a soft glow of relief spread throughout Emilie's entire body. It was as if her soul had been wrapped in a warm blanket.

"*Bonjour,* Professor Deneuve," she said. "It is a great pleasure to see you once again."

Henri continued smiling. "The sentiment, *mademoiselle*, is mutual."

Then his countenance turned serious, and his words became foreboding. "You and your companions are fast approaching an unspeakable danger that I, and others like me, cannot stop or assist you with. You must tread carefully and put your trust in the man from Israel. Only he can guide you, only he can lead you to the righteous conclusion of your journey." With those words, the professor's face faded from the screen. Emilie was at first silent, then she turned toward her brother.

The girl broke down, tears streamed down her cheeks as she remembered the horror of her parents' violent deaths. She missed them more than she ever imagined she could: missed their laughter, missed their hugs and goodnight kisses, missed the joy of family holidays, missed the quiet moments, and the crazy antics that her father had often amused them with. She felt empty and more alone than she'd ever felt in her life. She reached over, hugged her brother, buried her face in his slim shoulder, and continued sobbing.

"You won't leave me? You're all I have in the world. Please promise me you won't ever leave me."

Luc held her lovingly in his arms. "I promise, Em. I promise."

No words were spoken but they both knew, deep within their hearts, that what she was asking might be next to impossible.

CHAPTER THIRTY-TWO

The horrific report about the eviscerated, partially decomposed remains of a woman found in dumpsters in and around Marseille's port district and in shallow graves scattered throughout several of the city's upscale neighborhoods was covered by most of the world's press and online news sites.

"It was the stench of rotting flesh and the rats," said one disgruntled, oft-quoted, expat resident. "Neither of which is very pleasant."

The Englishman's blunt assessment of the murder was translated into French, Italian, German, and Spanish. Murder has always been bad for business, and soon the hotels, tour guides, restaurants, and other Riviera attractions were experiencing cancellations from visitors and locals alike.

Town mayors and municipal officials in the stricken area began pressuring their harried police forces to quickly solve the grisly murder. "Our economies cannot withstand this kind of publicity" became the oft-repeated protestation from officialdom.

Body parts of the unfortunate victim were assembled at the morgue in Marseille. DNA tests were undertaken to ascertain the dead woman's identity. Results of these tests, along with meager physical descriptions of the victim were sent to police jurisdictions throughout France.

ψ

The police report from Marseille popped up on Alain Moreau's computer screen, and after a quick glance at the content, he knew beyond a shadow of a doubt that the dead woman it referenced was Claire Rodriguez. He went online, scrolled through the department's confidential directory of French police services, then picked up his phone and dialed the officer in charge of the murder investigation in the southern city.

"*Bonjour, Détective Charlotte Allard à la parole.*"

The police officer in Marseille sounded young, like Lucy, his friend's daughter.

"*Bonjour,* Mademoiselle Allard. This is Director Adjoint Alain Moreau of the PPD. I believe that I can help identity the murdered woman described in the report you circulated."

"*Pardon, monsieur*, it's Madame Allard now. I recently got married—but please call me Charlotte."

"My apologies, *madame*. I should not have made that assumption."

Alain's tone of voice became more serious. "We believe that the woman you're attempting to identify is Madame Claire Rodriguez. She is wanted in connection with a double homicide here in Paris." He let out an exasperated sigh. "We went to her apartment with an arrest warrant and discovered that she'd skipped town." Alain leaned in to look at the message on his computer's screen. "Up until I received your communiqué, we had no idea as to her whereabouts."

"Is this the same Claire Rodriguez who is the big-deal socialite? The same Claire Rodriguez who is Philippe Rodriguez's mother?" Charlotte sounded slightly apprehensive.

"*Oui, madame*, the very same woman." Alain still hadn't worked himself around to calling her Charlotte. "And if you have no objections, I would like to share your findings with some colleagues here in Paris who have a particular interest in the case."

The young detective was trying to digest the information she'd just been told. *Merde, when this gets out, all hell's going to break loose. I'd better alert the chief. It's way too big for me to handle alone.*

She quickly regained her composure. "*Merci,* Monsieur Moreau, I will relay the content of our conversation to my superior officer and get back you."

Alain Moreau hung up and sank back into his chair. His thoughts were anything but cheerful.

If Rodriguez had anything to do with his own mother's murder, then my young friends on their way to Cannes are in even greater danger than any of us imagined.

ψ

Charlotte Allard raced upstairs to her superior's office. She had to tell her boss about the conversation she'd just had with the senior police officer in Paris.

The stern woman stood, paced around the small room, then finally stopped and spoke to Charlotte. "Call the deputy director back and ask him if he would be able to come and assist us with the investigation. If the victim is wanted for a double murder inquiry in Paris, then this is as much his case as it is ours." The next thought she kept to herself. *God help us, when news of this gets out, we're going to need all the assistance we can get.*

She ushered Charlotte out of her office and plonked down in her chair.

Bon Dieu, it looks like I'll have to postpone my vacation again.

ψ

As Charlotte and her superior had rightly predicted, the news that the victim of the grisly murder in the southern city was the famous socialite Claire Rodriguez made the front pages of news outlets throughout France—and the world. Within hours, reporters from all the city's print, broadcast, and online news outlets were crowded around the imposing front door of le Commissariat de police on La Canebière in Marseille's 1st arrondissement.

Uniformed gendarmes were stationed outside the headquarters with the futile task of appeasing the pushy group of journalists. Inside, the department's public relations team was huddled in a small back room, composing a press release and attempting to author a strategic plan to deal with the fallout that they knew would soon be coming.

ψ

Philippe's personal assistant barged into his plush stateroom aboard the *Angelina*. Philippe looked up from where he was working and was about to scream an obscenity at the woman. She cut him off before any words could escape his lips.

"*Monsieur*, your mother has been murdered. Her body was discovered in Marseille."

The woman was apoplectic, wide eyed, and out of breath. Her face was dark red, like the color of a squishy over ripe peach.

"Calm down, Marie," Philippe said, his voice steady. "Calm down and tell me what you've heard." He indicated that she should sit in the chair opposite him.

"It's all over the news, Monsieur Philippe. Her body was cut into little pieces and spread all over Marseille." She took a deep breath. "There are reporters crowded around the yacht club's front gates wanting to speak with you."

He turned and switched on the television mounted on the room's opposite wall. An official police spokesperson was addressing reporters gathered in front of the headquarters building.

"Forensics and DNA testing have confirmed that the victim of this horrific murder and dismemberment has been identified as Madame Claire Rodriguez, mother of Monsieur Philippe Rodriguez, the well-respected businessman and philanthropist. Our sincere condolences go out to him and to the family's many friends, with assurances that the police will apprehend the perpetrators in a timely fashion." The spokesperson stepped away from the microphone, ignoring questions being hurled at him by the mob he faced.

Philippe clicked off the television and turned to his distraught assistant.

"Thank you, Marie. You may leave me now."

Marie stood and scurried from the room, muttering as she left, "*Je suis tellement désolé, tellement désolé pour ta perte.*"

When the door closed behind her, Philippe clenched his fists so hard it felt as if his fingernails would penetrate the skin of his palms.

His thoughts were anything but being overwhelmed with grief. *Dumb fucking bastards, I ordered them to dispose of her body where it would never be found. Now I've got to act like a bereaved fucking son to all the sons of bitches who know me—and her.*

He stood and began pacing the room. *Everyone will expect me to cancel the party. Fuck them, fuck them all. I'll tell them that she wouldn't have wanted me to do that.*

There was a knock on his door and Marie, her cheeks still stained with tears, entered the room to announce that the police were here to see him. Detective Charlotte Allard and her superior officer, Inspector Claudette Girard, stood motionless in the doorway.

"*Bonjour, Monsieur Rodriguez. Veuillez accepter nos condoléances et nos excuses pour vous avoir imposé et cette période de deuil.*"

Philippe graciously accepted the inspector's condolences and apologies and invited his visitors to be seated. "My assistant informed me about my mother's death this morning—just before you arrived." He wiped a crocodile tear from his eye and continued. "I need you to find the person, or persons, who committed this heinous crime and bring them to justice. I promise that you will have my full support, wherever and whenever you need it." He stood and opened the door. "Now, if you'll please excuse me, I have arrangements to make."

The two police officers stepped out into the dazzling Mediterranean sunshine.

Claudette Girard crossed her arms. "*Je pense que quelque chose sent le poisson.*"

Charlotte looked toward the water, and then toward her boss. "*Oui*, something does smell fishy, and it's not the harbor."

CHAPTER THIRTY-THREE

Alain Moreau, Nick, and Gabriela were on the ultra-fast TGV train on route to Marseille. The 480-mile trip from Paris's Gare de Lyon to the Gare de Marseille-Saint-Charles in the southern city had them rocketing through some of France's most picturesque countryside vistas, little of which any of them took the time to enjoy.

Gabriela looked first to Alain and then to her husband. "I'm glad that we're going. We may not be much help in solving the murder of Madame Rodriguez, but being closer to the kids, if they need us, eases my mind."

Both men nodded their agreement, and then, lulled by the gentle rhythm of the train and murmuring chatter from the train's other passengers, the three friends settled into their own ominous thoughts of what might lie ahead.

ψ

Lucy and Sierra arrived at Lucy's apartment. The air in the small rooms was Sahara-hot and overbearingly musty from being locked up during Lucy's trip to Paris. Sierra threw open the windows, shoved a small bunch of cheerful flowers into a vase, and placed the modest bouquet on the kitchen counter.

Lucy loved growing up in her parent's apartment on Île Saint-Louis, but the well-worn leather, precious paintings, and beautiful Persian carpets had no place in the sunny south. Instead, she'd decorated her apartment in bright blues and whites more appropriate to the Mediterranean climate. Sierra took a moment to survey the rooms in her friend's home. "Wow, this place is gorgeous. Now I know where all your outrageous fees go." She laughed and hugged her friend.

ψ

Luc and Emilie were also in the process of unpacking and getting settled. The Airbnb that they'd booked was not as charming as Lucy's apartment, but it was comfortable, convenient, and ideally suited their purpose.

Luc placed his laptop on the tiny desk that occupied a corner of the apartment's living room. He flipped open the computer and scanned the screen for any updates on his unsanctioned probes into Philippe Rodriguez's comings and goings.

"Y'know Em, I'm not sure how we fit into the plan, but I've got a gut feeling that this is exactly where we're supposed to be."

His sister was staring out of the room's only window. "The listing said that we'd have a view of the Mediterranean, but all I see is a sliver of blue between the buildings." She sounded disappointed.

"We're not here for the view, Em. We're here to help in any way we can." Luc heard the blip of an incoming message. The email from Sierra grabbed his attention: "Hi, guys. I'm going to meet with the guy from Israel. Do you want to get together for dinner later?"

"*Putain de merde*. Em, look at this."

Emilie looked over her brother's shoulder. She let out an audible gasp.

"What guy from Israel? Could this be the man that the professor said could help us?"

Luc had already sent his reply. "Dinner sounds great. Let us know where and at what time?"

He turned around and faced his sister. "We can ask her what the Israeli thing is all about later, when we have dinner together."

Emilie was silent. A lone tear escaped from her eye and trickled slowly down her flushed cheek. "Y'know, Luc, I think that I could kill Rodriguez myself."

Luc stood and wrapped his arms around his stricken sister. She buried her head into his chest.

"I could too, Em. No mercy, no hesitation, no remorse—the bastard deserves nothing less for what he did to *mère et père.*

He released his grip and held his sister at arm's length. "But I don't know how we'd ever get close enough to do it."

Luc dropped his arms to his sides and turned back to his laptop. He didn't want Emilie to see that he too had tears in his eyes.

ψ

When Sierra arrived at the café on Rue Hoche, she was waved over to a small outdoor table by a wiry, deeply tanned man who she instantly recognized as Levi Heifetz. The man stood and offered his outstretched hand to the beautiful model.

"*Bonjour,* Mademoiselle Petersen. It is a pleasure to see you again."

Sierra looked around the virtually empty café—she needed to assure herself that their conversation would go unnoticed and unheard. Sierra removed her wide-brimmed straw hat and oversize sunglasses and focused her gaze directly on the man facing her.

"*Bonjour,* Monsieur Heifetz. Now, what is it that I can do for you?"

Levi's response was interrupted by the waiter, who quickly took their orders and scurried back through the café's front door to retrieve their coffees.

After the waiter's departure, Levi continued. "As you well know, your half-brother, Philippe Rodriguez, is perhaps the most morally depraved person in the world. Never in my long career of dealing with such vile animals have I ever encountered such a malevolent individual." Levi stared, unblinking, into Sierra's eyes. "He and the organization that he heads are perpetrating an infinite list of illegal and reprehensible crimes that are well beyond repugnant."

He stopped speaking, took a deep breath, and continued. Levi's voice was barely above a whisper. "As I told you at our earlier meeting, I took the job as his head of security in order to assassinate him, but soon realized that me killing the man would not end the infestation of rats and snakes that he, by right of birth, controls."

Levi's ice-cold eyes seared into Sierra's brain. "To accomplish the outright destruction of Philippe Rodriguez and his entire organization, I need your help."

The waiter returned to the table carrying their drinks; double espresso for him and a less-potent caffe latte for her.

"And what exactly is it that you think I can do?"

Levi looked furtively around the café. Sierra did the same, then she leaned in to hear exactly what the man's plan entailed.

ψ

Aleksei Sidorov was bored. He'd been sitting around the tiny Ukrainian village for more days than he cared to remember, waiting for the country's president to arrive.

Aleksei was a highly regarded spetsnaz officer, and one of his country's most efficient snipers. At that moment, his thoughts were anything but complimentary about the seemingly false information provided him by the FSB regarding his target's movements.

He fiddled with his weapon. *Shit, we don't have a hope in hell of winning this fucking war if we must depend on Egorov and his band of so-called intelligence officers. Stupid pricks probably couldn't predict the date of New Year's Eve.* He silently laughed at his own little joke, then sat on a pile of broken bricks to continue his seemingly fruitless vigil.

The elite sniper felt the vibration of his cell phone from deep within his combat jacket. He fumbled through the garment's many layers and put the device to his ear.

He said just one word. "Sidorov."

The voice on the other end of the call was his friend and commanding officer. "Looks like they need your talents somewhere else, Aleksei. Report to headquarters in Moscow and they'll give you a full briefing." The man paused, then added, "You lucky bastard."

ψ

Dmitriy Egorov was smiling. His backup plan for the elimination of Philippe Rodriguez was straightforwardly simple: a single sniper's bullet right into the prick's head.

Too bad I can't be there to see Rodriguez's blood and brains splatter all over his shiny fucking boat. Oh well, you can't have everything you want in life.

Egorov scooped his jacket from the back of his chair and left his office.

"I've a meeting at spetsnaz headquarters and won't be returning until the morning."

His dutiful assistant looked up, nodded, and continued working.

ψ

Luc, Emilie, Lucy and Sierra were gathered around the small kitchen table in Lucy's apartment. They were all intently listening to Sierra as she outlined the plan that was given her by Levi.

"The only hiccup is that we'll have no backup. Nobody, if needed, to cause a distraction. Nobody in the crowd to be our eyes and ears." Sierra lowered her eyes. "I know I shouldn't have agreed to it without speaking to you first, but I volunteered all three of you to be there in case we need help."

Lucy spoke first. "That's easy for you to say, but how do we get in? None of us have been invited."

All eyes turned toward Sierra.

"Levi screens all the security and serving staff employed for the Rodriguez party. He assures me that getting you in will not be a problem."

Luc jumped up from the table. "Count me in."

Lucy and Emilie were slightly more apprehensive, but within minutes, they too agreed to participate in Sierra and Levi's risky plan.

CHAPTER THIRTY-FOUR

A private jet carrying Aleksei Sidorov landed at Marseille Provence airport at 8:45 a.m. He deplaned, passed easily through French customs and immigration, and was picked up by a driver from the Russian consulate offices on Av. Ambroise Paré in the southern city. No words were exchanged between Sidorov and the driver.

The car drove through the consulate's gates and pulled up to the front entrance of the imposing château-style building. Aleksei was sitting in the car's rear seat. He grabbed his small carry-on, stepped out of the big SUV, and strode up to the building's front entrance. He was greeted by an efficacious-looking woman and escorted to a private office on the consulate's second floor. Then he was left alone.

The sniper dropped his bag and opened the black rectangular-shaped plastic box that was sitting on the room's only table. He opened the case, lifted the American-made Remington M24 Sniper Weapon System from its custom-molded case, and examined the weapon through the eyes of an expert. He slipped the Mark 4LR/M1 fixed power scope to the rifle, raised the gun to his shoulder, and peered through the scope.

Satisfied with his superior's choice of weaponry, he took the box of 51mm hollow-point cartridges from the case and thought about the devastation that he would soon unleash on his unsuspecting target.

Aleksei smiled, this is what he was trained for, and he loved his job.

ψ

Sir David Fitzgerald, before he retired, was a successful money market manager at one of London's most prominent investment firms. To avoid the UK's often-inclement weather, but mostly to evade the country's onerous tax bite, he and his wife, Lady Margaret Fitzgerald, moved to a sumptuous three-bedroom condominium in Monte Carlo.

Their apartment, on the twenty-third floor of a relatively new building, had spectacular vistas of the Mediterranean and unimpeded views of the magnificent yachts moored in the principality's famed harbor. The location, elevation, and lush foliage on their home's spacious terrace provided an ideal cover and line-of-sight position for the Russian marksman to successfully fulfill his mission.

ψ

At exactly 4:00 p.m. on the day prior to Philippe Rodriguez's party, the intercom in the Fitzgerald's apartment rang, and the concierge informed the elderly residents that a man from the building's landscape consulting company was coming up to inspect the foliage on their terrace.

Mrs. Fitzgerald gave her approval to send him up and opened the door to a man dressed in green coveralls and carrying a bag of gardening tools. She led the man onto the terrace and left him alone to complete his duties.

Aleksei Sidorov fumbled among the various plants, pretending to know what he was doing. Then, midway through his charade, he selected the ideal vantage point from which to complete his assignment. He stood, went back through the elegant French doors and faced the lady of the house.

"*Pardon, madame,* but I've discovered blight on some of your plants. I don't have the correct chemicals with me today, so would it be convenient if I stopped by again tomorrow to give them the necessary treatment?"

The elderly woman smiled, thanked him, and gave her approval for a second visit. Aleksei bowed his head slightly toward the woman and left the apartment.

Margaret Fitzgerald found her husband in his study. "My oh my, David. What a polite young man the landscape company sent," she gushed.

ψ

On the same day, Levi was huddled with the four friends in Lucy's apartment. He was briefing Luc and Emilie on what their duties would be as servers at Rodriguez's party and telling Lucy what she'd be expected to do in her role as one of the yacht's security staff. Then, for emphasis, he reiterated, word-for-word, what he'd told them earlier.

"Remember, your primary function is to keep your eyes and ears open for anything strange or unusual and to create a distraction if, or when, needed."

Levi paused. He wasn't sure how his next words would be construed by the small group of amateur conspirators. "I will kill him. I'll spare you the details about how I'll do it, but rest assured, Philippe Rodriguez will die on the night of his party."

He turned his attention to Sierra. "All of the incriminating records, intelligence, and details of his legal and illegal businesses, as well as his murderous involvement as leader of La Orden de las Serpientes de Cristo, are either on his laptop or in documents locked in his safe."

As he spoke, the resolve in his tone and manner became more and more apparent. "Rodriguez is occasionally careless, and over the months that I've been employed by him, I've learned the combination to his safe." Lucy, Luc, and Emilie were hanging onto the security chief's every word. "I will remove his computer and all the incriminating papers from the safe and somehow get them to Mademoiselle Sierra." He turned and stared directly at Sierra, "Then it will up to you to pass them to the authorities."

A deathly stillness engulfed the room until Luc finally broke it. "What about you, Levi? What happens to you after it's all done?"

Levi smiled, not a happy-to-see-you kind of smile, but a goodbye-it's-been-nice-knowing-you kind of smile. "If I'm not dead by the end of the evening, we'll all meet up for a grand celebration."

He stood, and on his way out the door, stopped and turned. "Goodnight and get lots of rest tonight—we'll all need it."

ψ

"Madame Fitzgerald, the gardener is here. Should I send him up?"

The call from the building's concierge was readily agreed to. Margaret Fitzgerald glanced into the mirror, patted her pale cheeks to add a little flush, and answered the door.

Aleksei Sidorov entered the apartment. He was wearing the same green coveralls he'd worn on the previous day, but this time he carried a different case—it was long and made from heavy black plastic.

He placed the case gently on the kitchen table, reached inside his coveralls, and pulled out a Soviet made Makarov PB handgun equipped with an integral suppressor. The formidable weapon, favored by Russian FSB agents, is capable of firing 30 rounds of lead cartridges per minute, specifics that Sidorov was going to mention, but had second thoughts about. *This old woman doesn't give a shit about the capabilities of this remarkable weapon.*

The sniper pointed the pistol toward the frightened woman and asked her to call her husband. The undeniable panic in her voice elicited an immediate response from Sir David. He rushed into the room and, upon seeing the gun, stopped dead in his tracks. "Good lord, what the hell is going on here?"

The Russian sniper smiled at the man's upper-class British

pomposity and used the gun to gesture toward their bedroom. "Please, if you do as you're told, I won't be forced to harm either of you."

The elderly couple were ushered into the master suite's sumptuous bathroom. Sidorov patted them down, took both their cell phones, and ripped the intercom phone from off the wall. "Now, if you know what's good for you, you'll be quiet—very, very quiet." He left the bathroom and pushed a heavy cabinet in front of the outside door, effectively locking the couple inside.

The two elderly expats sat facing each other, Lady Margaret on the toilet and her husband on the edge of the bathtub.

"Well, Maggie," Sir David began, "what do you think we should do now?"

"He didn't take this, darling." The woman reached into her blouse and pulled out the medical alert device hanging, like a necklace, between her breasts.

"Well damn it, woman, press the button! Press the damn button!"

ψ

An alarm sounded at the security company's office in Nice, and paramedics were immediately dispatched to the Fitzgerald's condominium building in Monaco. Because of the elderly couple's distinguished stature in the principality, the Sûreté Publique de Monaco, Monte Carlo's police force, was informed of the potential emergency.

The police officer taking the call notified his superior who, in turn, requested a patrol vehicle be sent to the Fitzgerald residence "*pour offrir de l'aide, si nécessaire.*"

An ambulance carrying two young paramedics, a man and a woman, and a police vehicle with two officers arrived at the building's front entrance within seconds of each other. The four first responders rushed into the building's elegant lobby, enlisted the concierge, and rode the elevator up to the twenty-third floor. The concierge used her pass key to open the door to the Fitzgerald's apartment, and the paramedics and police officers rushed into the rooms looking for the elderly couple who had set their sudden intrusion into motion.

The Russian sniper heard them, spun around, raised his handgun, and fired at the first person he saw. The unfortunate woman fell to the floor, blood spreading across the front of her pale blue uniform shirt. Before Sidorov could squeeze off a second shot, he was hit by a hail of bullets fired by the police. Dmitriy Egorov's assassin was dead before his body hit the floor.

Alarms were sounded and, within seconds, nosy residents from within the building began crowding around the Fitzgerald's front door. They were quickly ordered back to their homes by one of the officers who had first entered the Fitzgerald's apartment. Then, less than ten minutes after the crowd of grumbling residents had dispersed, a cadre of additional police and emergency vehicles pulled up in front of the building.

The Fitzgerald's were released from their marble-clad prison and were being interviewed by the police. Sir David's first bumptious words, as he looked around at the devastation, were "What the hell took you chaps so long?"

ψ

Dmitriy Egorov received two calls on the afternoon of Philippe Rodriguez's party. The first, from an FSB agent in Monaco, informed him about the circumstance of Aleksei Sidorov's death. The second, more ominous call, came from an assistant to the president of the Russian Federation. "Good afternoon, Comrade Egorov. The president wishes to see you immediately. A car will be at your office's front door within five minutes." The phone went dead before Egorov had the chance to speak.

Twenty minutes later, two dour-faced men sat in the front seat of the car carrying Egorov to his meeting with the president. The man in the passenger seat turned around and handed the FSB deputy director a crystal goblet. "Perhaps, Comrade Egorov, you'd welcome a drink before you meet with the president." He half-filled the glass from a bottle of the country's finest vodka.

Egorov raised the glass to his lips. "*Na Zdorov'ye*, comrade," he said, then downed the drink. Thirty seconds later, his lifeless form collapsed onto the floor of the car's rear compartment.

The car sped west on the A106 past Novo-Ogaryovo towards its destination: a secret graveyard with no headstones and no markers, reserved exclusively for traitors of the Russian Federation—and enemies of the president.

CHAPTER THIRTY-FIVE

The *Angelina*, Philippe Rodriguez's massive yacht, was a beehive of activity. The floating, black-hulled behemoth was crawling with close to one hundred people polishing, primping, and preparing for the evening's lavish soiree.

Philippe was nervously pacing around his cabin. He'd heard earlier about the police takedown of a Russian sniper and was wondering whether the marksman's intended target was him or one of the evening's many prominent guests.

He opened his cabin door and screamed to his assistant. "Get me fucking Heifetz! I need to see him right now!" He could have used his cell to summon his chief of security, but earlier in his life, he realized that he got a perverse pleasure from bullying his subordinates.

Marie scrambled to her feet and ran out to find Levi.

Philippe closed the door and turned back into his cabin. The custom-tailored blue linen blazer and white slacks that he was planning to wear for the evening's festivities had been carefully laid out on his bed.

He was admiring the garments when Levi knocked and quietly entered the room. "*Bonjour*, boss. You called?"

ψ

Lucy, Luc, and Emilie arrived at the main gate to the Yacht Club de Monaco three hours prior to the start of the evening's festivities. They were huddled among a small group of temporary staff hired for the Rodriguez party. Levi was on hand to meet them and take them through the rigorous, predetermined security ritual.

Levi isolated five of the group, which included Luc and Emilie, and pointed them toward to the ship's galley. "Go to the galley and report to the head steward. She'll provide you with uniforms and give you details of your duties at tonight's party." He ordered the four men he'd recruited from a local security firm to take up strategic positions along the big ship's gunnels, then took Lucy by the elbow and led her in the opposite direction, toward his onboard office. "I want you stationed at the foot of the gangplank. Your job is to check and confirm that all guests are included on the manifest, examine their passports to confirm their identity, and pass them through to the person manning the X-ray scanners."

He chuckled. "Don't get starstruck, Lucy. There'll be a lot of famous people coming tonight, including some very handsome movie stars." Then the man's demeanor returned to being deadly serious. "When all the guests have boarded, come and see me on the upper aft deck—that's action central for tonight's party."

He handed her a laminated identification card: it included a fictitious name and a photograph of her taken by one of the security chief's permanent staff. She checked the card and hung it around her neck. Tonight, she'd be Camille D'Chantel.

ψ

Hordes of paparazzi, fans, and curious onlookers had already begun crowding the boulevard surrounding the harbor—each of them jostling for prime positions in the hope of glimpsing of their favorite celebrity as they boarded Philippe's yacht. Harried police officers from the Sûreté Publique de Monaco were doing their utmost to control the growing mayhem, but as the crowds grew larger, all hopes of the police retaining control evaporated. The best they were able to achieve was to form a cordon surrounding the red carpet that led from the arrival drop-off point to the yacht's security installation and gangplank.

Levi escorted Lucy to a small table at the receiving end of the carpet. "This is your station. It's going to be crazy around here—so be aware and be very careful."

ψ

Philippe Rodriguez stepped out of his shower, pulled on a plush white terry cloth robe bearing the yacht's distinctive logo, and peeked through a window at the horde of people crowded around the stern of his yacht. He selected a dazzling white Armani T-shirt from his wardrobe, put on his slacks and blazer, and checked himself out in the floor-to-ceiling three-way mirror in his dressing room. He folded a canary yellow silk handkerchief and carefully positioned it in his blazer's breast pocket. Finally, he slipped on a pair of dark-blue designer boat shoes and walked out into the paling glare of the setting Mediterranean sun.

"I trust that everything is in order." His remark, directed to his harried party planner, sounded more like an ominous threat, than a casual inquiry.

ψ

Stretch limousines and exotic cars began pulling up and discharging their passengers. It was a who's who of the glamorous, famous, and influential, all dressed in their best casual finery.

Lucy was busy checking the passports of each and every famous guest against the manifest given to her by Levi. Only one marginally famous actor gave her any trouble. "Why do I need identification?

Everyone knows who the hell I am," he blustered indignantly. He finally produced his British passport and was allowed entry through to the next level of security.

Rodriguez stood at the top of the gangplank, personally greeting each guest. He assumed the persona of a true gentleman. Charm oozed from every pore of his being as he shook hands, kissed cheeks, and offered kind words of welcome. When Sierra arrived to where he was standing, he became particularly attentive. "Welcome aboard, Mademoiselle Petersen. I believe that you and I have a lot in common—perhaps later, when the party's over and all my guests have disembarked, we can have a quiet drink together?"

Sierra smiled, thanked him for inviting her to his party, and quietly responded to his offer. "It would be my pleasure, Monsieur Rodriguez."

He turned and watched her stroll provocatively into the noisy crowd of partygoers.

ψ

The heady scent of expensive perfume, flashes of diamonds, mountains of chilled Beluga caviar, and seemingly bottomless well of champagne fueled the loud conversations and animated laughter of partygoers. Emilie dodged her way through the crowd carrying a tray of champagne flutes. The nearly full glasses of crystal stemware were quickly scooped up by Rodriguez's guests, and she often found herself rushing back to the bar for refills. Luc, on the other hand, was running in and out of the cacophony of madness they called the galley with tray after tray of sumptuous hors d'oeuvres.

ψ

Sierra noticed Jonathan Bloom leaning against the bulkhead in a far corner of the main salon. His wife was working the crowd, chatting up celebrities and collecting bits and pieces of gossip that she would later relate, with great delight, to her coterie of wealthy Manhattan friends.

Bloom was quick to speak as Sierra approached. "I didn't say a word about your relationship with Philippe."

There was no, "How wonderful to see you again, Sierra." No, "You're looking beautiful this evening, Sierra." No, "I do hope that you're enjoying the party." Bloom was on the defensive, and every muscle in his face betrayed his discomfort. He was a man determined to protect the fees that both Sierra and Philippe represented.

"I know, thank you." Sierra turned and sauntered into the melee of glamorous guests, many of whom she knew from previous parties and galas.

The band had just begun playing their rendition of "The Girl from Ipanema" when Rodriguez stepped up beside her. "May I please have this dance, Mademoiselle Petersen?"

She felt her whole body tighten but smiled anyway and graciously accepted his invitation. He led her to the dance floor, and they were soon gently swaying to the intoxicating samba beat. "So, *mademoiselle*, how are you enjoying my party so far?" His words were courteous, charming, and gentlemanly, and for a moment Sierra forgot all about the unspeakable evil that her handsome dance partner was capable of inflicting.

Luc came into the salon and saw them dancing. An unquenchable rage rose in his gut and engulfed his whole body, it was as if a volcano had erupted in belly. He raced back to the galley, slipped by the busy kitchen staff and scooped an eight-inch chef's knife from the galley's stainless-steel counter. He hid the knife beneath a tray of hors d'oeuvres, returned to the party, and wove his way through the crowd until he came close to where Sierra and Rodriguez were dancing. He threw the tray to the ground, took hold of the knife, and lunged at Rodriguez. "*Bâtard, tu as tué ma mère mon père!*"

Before he could reach the startled couple, Luc was tackled and pinned to the floor by Levi. The crash of the falling tray and Luc's violent proclamation accusing Philippe of murdering his mother and father brought festivities to an abrupt standstill.

"Get him out of here!" Rodriguez shouted.

Levi lifted Luc's limp body from the floor, handcuffed him, and handed him over to Lucy who, with the aid of a second security guard, escorted the overwrought young man off the yacht.

Lucy turned toward the other guard. "You go back. I'm sure that they'll need you at the party. I'll call the police and wait here for them to arrive." She watched the guard leave then called the only person that she knew could help them. Her call was answered on the first ring. "Daddy, we've got a huge problem, and I need your help."

CHAPTER THIRTY-SIX

Sierra was visibly shaken by Luc's brazen attack. She stood on the dance floor, not moving a muscle; it was as if she was frozen in place. As one of Rodriguez's other guests later remarked, "The woman who was dancing with Philippe reminded me of a beautiful marble statue that I recently saw in a gallery in Firenze. Can't for the life of me remember who the artist was, though."

Sierra heard the muffled voice of Rodriguez resonate through the fog that clouded her brain. "Sierra, are you okay? Are you okay?" She simply nodded and watched as Rodriguez stepped in front of the band and grabbed a microphone from one of the musicians.

"My dear friends, my sincere apologies. I'm extremely sorry about the recent incident and hope that it does nothing to spoil the rest of your evening. The young man who attacked me and my guest is obviously disturbed and delusional. He is now safely in custody and will be dealt with accordingly." Rodriguez paused and scanned the faces of his guests. "I will not be pressing any charges but will recommend to the authorities that he be taken to a hospital where his mental condition and state of mind can be closely monitored and perhaps taken care of."

Rodriguez paused again and lowered his eyes. Everyone aboard the yacht saw that their host's demeanor had turned even more solemn. "Mental illness is a serious global issue and because of it, a major portion of the money you've so generously donated at this fundraising event will be given to institutions involved in the research of and potential cures for these debilitating diseases." He smiled widely and spread his arms. "Now let's get on with the party!"

The band began playing again, there was enthusiastic applause and cheering from most of the guests, but Sierra was still in a state of shock. Meanwhile, Levi was wondering when the axe would slam down onto his thin, well-tanned neck.

ψ

"Where's Luc now?"

"He's in my car. We're driving toward Cannes. He's in terrible shape, Daddy." Nick heard the sobs of the distraught young man through the cell's speaker. "I was supposed to call the police."

"Well, in a way, you have. I'm here with Alain and Gabi. Find a spot where you can safely stay out of sight until we get there—and don't go to your apartment!"

ψ

The party aboard the *Angelina* was in full swing. Bottle after bottle of champagne were emptied faster than they could reappear. Truckloads of caviar, tray-loads of exquisite truffled hors d'oeuvres, and other mouth-watering delicacies were quickly being vacuumed into the mouths of rapturous guests. The attempted killing of their host was virtually forgotten by nearly everyone. It was, however, clouding every thought of the gregarious, ever-smiling host as he made his rounds through the throng of well-heeled merrymakers. He caught up to Sierra who was standing alone next to the bar.

"My darling sister, I've had my staff prepare a guest cabin for you. You'll stay here onboard with me tonight."

"I'm sorry, brother but I can't. I've already made other plans for tonight—arrangements that are impossible to cancel." Sierra lowered her eyes. "But perhaps some other time soon."

Her acknowledgment of their relationship took Rodriguez by surprise. "I didn't know that you knew."

She smiled, kissed him on both cheeks, and said goodnight. "*Bonne soirée, frère. Merci pour cette soirée inoubliable.*" Rodriguez watched in awe as she drifted effortlessly through the crowd of merrymakers toward the stern of the yacht and her waiting limousine.

ψ

When Sierra arrived at Lucy's apartment, her friend was nowhere to be seen. She picked up her cell and called her. "Lucy, where the hell are you? I saw you and some other security guys take Luc away in handcuffs. What the hell's going on?"

"I'm sorry, Sierra. Luc and I are in my car waiting for my dad, Gabriela, and Alain. They told me to stay put until they arrive."

"Is Luc, okay? What in God's name got into him, attacking Rodriguez like that?"

Luc was listening in on Lucy's speakerphone. "I'm sorry, Sierra. I saw that slimeball and just saw red. *Oh mon Dieu, j'ai tout foiré.*" He buried his head in his hands and began quietly sobbing.

"Jesus Christ, Luc, you may have fucked up the whole operation, and there's a good chance that you already have. Pull yourself together, and we'll try to salvage whatever's left of the plan."

Sierra hung up, leaving Lucy and Luc fully aware that their beautiful friend had taken full charge of their conspiracy to destroy Philippe Rodriguez.

ψ

Nick was racing along the A8 from Marseilles to Cannes. At the speed he was driving, he believed that he could easily clip thirty minutes off the normally two-hour trip. His two white-knuckled passengers, Alain Moreau and Gabriela, were grilling him on the brief conversation he'd had with his daughter.

"Is everyone okay? What the hell was Luc thinking?" Gabriela's somber tone of voice expressed the concern that each of them felt.

"*Merde*, as much as I hate to say it, we'll have to turn the boy over to the authorities,"

Nick turned and glanced at Alain, who sat in the seat beside him. "There's no fucking way we're going to do that, Alain. We're likely going to need his talents again before this shit show is over."

A brief but ominous silence fell over the three friends as they sped toward Cannes.

Gabriela looked at Nick. "Where are Lucy and Luc now?"

"They're at the Square Méro, not far from the harbor. We're going to meet them there." The car sped past the exit to Vidauban, just over the halfway point to Cannes. At this hour of night, traffic was light, so Nick pressed harder on the accelerator.

"Watch your speed, Nicholas. This road is well patrolled," Alain's warning came a few seconds too late.

As if on cue, flashing blue lights and the distinctive siren of a police car interrupted their conversation.

"*Tu vois, je l'avais dit.*" Alain's recriminating warning did little to alleviate Nick's mounting annoyance. He pulled the car off to the side of the road and waited for the officer to approach.

The highway patrolman stuck his head in the driver's side window. "*Savez-vous à quelle vitesse vous allez?*"

Alain pulled his police identity card from an inside pocket of his jacket and showed it to the cop. "*Il s'agit d'une urgence policière. Nous devons nous rendre à Cannes au plus vite.*"

The patrol officer, realizing that they were on urgent police business, quickly demurred and asked if they needed an escort.

Alain shook his head. "*Merci, mais non, nous ne voulons pas annoncer notre arrivée.*"

The officer waved them off, saying that he would radio ahead to his colleagues to let them pass but warned them to drive carefully. *"Conduisez prudemment. Je vais appeler mes collègues par radio pour vous laisser passer."* He saluted the deputy director and walked back to his patrol car.

Nick spat out his displeasure to the car's other occupants. "Shit, we didn't need that loss of time."

Alain quickly responded to Nick's outburst. "Yes, my friend, but at least we now know that we won't be stopped again—unless, of course, you run us into a tree."

Nick sped off onto the highway, leaving an explosion of dust and gravel in the car's wake.

ψ

Nick drove slowly around Square Mèro until he spotted Lucy's car then quietly pulled in behind it. Gabriela exited the vehicle first, quickly followed by the men in the front seat. She rushed up to the locked driver's side door. "Lucy, are you okay? How's Luc?" Her panicked voice reverberated throughout the car's interior.

Lucy opened the door and rushed into Gabriela's arms. "Yes, Gabi, we're fine—but what do we do now?" Nick and Alain also hugged the frightened young woman then leaned into the car's open door to confront Luc.

Nick roughly grabbed Luc's shoulder. "What in hell's name did you think you were doing?"

Luc looked defiantly at Nick, then quickly regretted his quarrelsome behavior and apologized. *"Je suis tellement désolé. J'ai tout gâché."*

Nick tried to soothe the young man. "It's okay. Nothing to apologize about. You haven't ruined everything. We'll still figure out a way to get the bastard."

Alain silently wished that what Nick had just said was, in fact, true.

ψ

"We've got to get off the street." Nick turned toward his daughter. "This is your neck of the woods. Any idea where we can find a cheap hotel where they won't ask any questions?"

"Daddy! What kind of woman do you think I am?"

Nick immediately tried to backtrack. "I'm sorry, honey, that didn't come out right. But there must be a hotel nearby that we can check into."

Lucy went online and found a small hotel just three blocks away from where they were parked. She dialed the number. "*Bonjour, monsieur. Pardonnez l'heure tardive, mais avez-vous trois chambres disponibles pour ce soir et demain soir également?*"

The hotel's desk clerk was delighted to receive this unexpected late-night windfall and immediately confirmed Lucy's request for three rooms for two nights starting tonight. Lucy would bunk with Gabriela, Nick and Luc would share a room, and Alain would have his own room. They drove to the hotel and checked in. Alain took the car to a public parking lot four blocks from the hotel and strode back to join the others in Nick and Luc's room.

CHAPTER THIRTY-SEVEN

After the last of his guests had disembarked and his army of servants had begun the arduous task of cleaning up from the party, Rodriguez called Levi into his cabin. "I don't know whether to thank you or fucking fire you. You saved my life by shoving the kid to the ground, but you hired the fucking idiot in the first place." He paused, giving Levi time to ponder his uncertain future. "But you know what? The first outweighs the second, so I'm going to keep you on." He waved his security chief from his office. "But watch your back, Heifetz. Next time, I won't be so lenient."

Levi smiled at the man's arrogance. *Your time is coming, asshole, but you won't see it until it's too late.*

Levi went ashore, found a quiet table at an all-night bistro, ordered a double espresso from the tired-looking server, and called Sierra.

ψ

The following morning, the attempted assassination of Philippe Rodriguez was front-page news in all the area's newspapers. Press, paparazzi, and onlookers reported that they saw a young man accompanied by a female security guard get into a car and drive away. Police officers manning the barricades that surrounded the yacht's red-carpeted gangplank corroborated their story. The city's chief of police desperately wanted to know the felon's whereabouts, but none of the so-called prime witnesses could effectively describe the female security guard, the young suspect, or even the make of vehicle that she and the boy had driven away in. The chief was furious at his inability to get answers, so he summoned one of his detectives to drive him to Philippe Rodriguez's yacht. *J'ai besoin de putains de réponses.* Perhaps Rodriguez himself can help us get an arrest, he thought.

ψ

Sierra saw who was calling and answered on the first ring, she sounded desperate. "Levi, what the hell do we do now?"

Levi, for once in his life, didn't have a backup plan. "I don't know Sierra. Let's play it out and see where it goes."

"I spoke to Lucy. She and Luc are with Lucy's parents. Maybe they'll be able to figure something out."

Levi wasn't convinced. "Okay, we'll wait to hear from them. Worst case scenario is that I'll have more time to think." He hung up.

Sierra slipped out of her dress, pulled on a pair of jeans, struggled into one of her friend's form-fitting T-shirts, and stood in front of a mirror to straighten the creases around her shoulders. The ethereal image of Henri Deneuve morphed into the reflective surface of the mirror.

Sierra stepped back in surprise, but soon recovered her composure. "Professor, thank goodness you're here. What should I do now? Please help me figure a way out of this mess."

Henri smiled, but the deeply etched lines that covered his face exhibited a profound concern. "You must do what Heifetz suggests. Let it play out. Rodriguez knows that you and he are related, and that you know you are brother and sister. He will be in contact with you to try to charm you, try to twist your mind into believing that the cult of evil he leads is the only true path to eternal salvation."

The elderly professor lowered his eyes. "It will take all your will, courage, and inner strength to resist the temptations that he will offer. So, tread very carefully, *ma jolie fleur*, tread very carefully. Henri paused. "Remember, this is a man who ordered the horrific murder of his own mother." Henri Deneuve's image slowly faded, then vanished completely.

Sierra was shaking. The realization of what lay ahead was daunting and terrifying. *Why me? What the hell did I do except get born into this twisted nightmare? God help me—help me please.*

Still shaking, she picked up her cell phone and speed-dialed Lucy.

ψ

Officers at Police Nationale headquarters in Marseille had finally been handed a lead in the grisly murder of Claire Rodriguez. A dim-witted thug, known to be in the lower echelon of one of the city's most violent gangs, wanted to make a deal. The man, who liked to be called Le Serpent, was apprehended during a botched robbery attempt. The victim in his bungled break-in suffered a violent blow to her head resulting in her being hospitalized with life-threatening injuries. If the woman died from the wounds inflicted on her by the suspect, he'd be charged with murder and face a lifetime sentence in one of France's most notorious prisons.

Le Serpent was terrified. He was sweating profusely, and his bone-thin body shuddered violently with every question being thrown at him by the detective conducting the interrogation. He knew that he was stuck between a rock and a hard place: between the police and the gang of ruthless criminals he ran with, between death or prison. He finally broke down and began answering the barrage of questions being hurled at him.

Le Serpent knew, one way or the other, that the detective's final question could put the last nail in his coffin.

"Why did you kill and dismember Madame Rodriguez?"

"It wasn't me, but I know who butchered that *enforcer la chine de Rodriguez*."

The detective in charge of the case called Deputy Director Alain Moreau. When the call came in, Alain was ensconced with Nick, Gabriela, and the two young fugitives from Rodriguez's party.

"*Pardonnez-moi, l'inspecteur adjoint . . .*" The officer in Marseille went on, bringing Alain up to date on their recent breakthrough.

After he'd hung up, Alain turned toward his friends. "*Je suis désolé, mes amis*, but I must return to Marseille. There's been a development in the Claire Rodriguez murder case that requires my immediate attention."

He glared directly at Lucy and Luc. "You two stay put. Don't even think of going anywhere until you hear from me." Then he turned his attention toward Nick and Gabriela. "And you two make sure that they do as I told them."

He left the hotel to catch the next train to the Gare de Marseille-Saint-Charles in the southern city.

ψ

Marie, Philippe's harried assistant, knocked and entered the man's inner sanctum. "*Pardonnez-moi, monsieur*, the chief of police is on the phone and wishes to speak to you."

Philippe shrugged. *What the fuck does he want?* He picked up his phone. "This is Philippe Rodriguez speaking. How may I be of assistance?"

The beleaguered policeman explained the reason for his call. "I've heard numerous rumors that an attempt on your life may have occurred during your party last evening. Would you care to corroborate the story?"

"I too have heard these rumors, *monsieur*, but the truth of the matter is simple, a clumsy waiter dropped a tray of hors d'oeuvres and rushed over to wipe some of the mess from off my blazer. Nothing more, nothing less. There were a lot of people and a lot of drinking, which I'm sure could have resulted in mistaken assumptions."

The chief of police offered apologies for disturbing the wealthy businessman and hung up. Philippe scowled. "*Stupides bâtatrds lâches, je ne peux faire confiance à aucun d'eux.*"

ψ

"Get me Heifetz on the phone."

The order from Rodriguez to Marie sent the woman scurrying to her desk. "He's on the line, *monsieur*."

Rodriguez directed his attention to Levi. "I want you to dispose of the idiot kid who tried to kill me, then bring me back proof that he's dead."

Levi rubbed his forehead. *How the hell am I supposed to do that?* "I'm on it, *monsieur*. May take a couple of days though."

"I don't fucking care how long it takes. Just get it done."

Levi hung up and called Sierra. "Can you please give me Lucy's cell number? There's something that I need to talk to her about."

CHAPTER THIRTY-EIGHT

Alain strode into the imposing headquarters building of le Commissariat de Police on La Canebière in Marseille and flashed his identity card to the officer manning the reception desk. "*Détective Aubert, et dépêchez-vous, s'il vous plaît.*" His order to see the detective in charge of Claire Rodriguez's murder case precipitated a flurry of activity from the policewoman, and within minutes, a tall, fashionably dressed, slimly built man with a ruddy complexion and reddish-blond hair entered the room.

"*Bonjour,* Deputy Director Moreau. My name is Pierre Aubert." He extended his right hand. "I'm delighted that you could join us on this worrisome investigation." They shook hands, and the detective from Marseille led his Parisian colleague into the busy inner sanctum of the police station.

"I've arranged to have Monsieur Le Serpent taken to an interrogation room." Pierre shrugged his shoulders and smiled. "The guy's real name is Bernard Blanc. He's in custody for an offence that may lead to a charge of murder being laid against him. He wants to make a deal regarding the Madame Rodriguez case: it's the old story, leniency for information." Pierre spread his hands in feigned exasperation and led the way to a heavily guarded door. He was greeted by the officer standing watch, and he and Alain walked through.

Alain and Pierre Aubert made their way down a long corridor and finally entered an inhospitable windowless room whose only furnishing were a worn pale gray metal table and three equally well-used metal chairs. The man, who allegedly had information about the brutal killing and dismemberment of Madame Rodriguez, sat alone in the room. Alain and Pierre entered through a heavy metal door and sat uncomfortably in chairs facing Le Serpent.

"*Bonjour,* Monsieur Blanc," Pierre began. "Today we have a special visitor from Paris." He motioned toward Alain. "Deputy Director Moreau would like to ask you a few questions and, of course, he would be delighted if you answered them truthfully." The prisoner placed his handcuffed hands on the table and stared defiantly at Alain. The officer returned the man's gaze. "*Si la femme que t'as essayé de coller meurt, il n'y a pass de marché* . . . but if the woman you tried to rob lives, I'll see what I can do to ease your sentence."

The accused man lowered his head and spoke in an almost inaudible voice. "If Jean finds out that I squealed, I'm a dead man anyway."

Pierre Aubert turned to his visitor from Paris. "Jean Durand is the head of one of Marseille's deadliest gangs."

"Either way, I'm a dead man." Le Serpent shrugged and talked. "Two men were ordered to kill Madame Rodriguez—Marcel Fournier and Pascal Gagnon."

Pierre once again turned to Alain. "We know them both. They are two of Jean Durand's top lieutenants."

"Did Durand order the assassination?"

"*Oui,* Monsieur Moreau, but he received his orders from someone else."

"Do you know the identity of this 'someone else'?"

"I've only heard rumors, *monsieur.*" The fear in the man's face made him almost unrecognizable. "It is said that the man who ordered *madame*'s death was her son, Philippe Rodriguez."

The two policemen stood and left the room. Both were thinking the unthinkable. *What kind of depraved individual would order the death of the woman who gave birth to him?*

Alain broke the silence. "We have no case without evidence. Any fucking *avocat* would tear him apart. Who'd take Blanc's word for anything, especially when he's accusing someone like Rodriguez?"

Alain lowered himself onto a well-worn wooden bench, the only piece of furniture in the otherwise stark corridor. He took off his eyeglasses and rubbed his temples, pressing hard with the tips of his fingers until it hurt. "*Merde, merde, merde. Et maintenant?*"

ψ

Levi was on the phone speaking to Sierra. "Is Luc there with you?"

"No, he's with Lucy and her father."

"Do you know where they are?"

"No idea. She only said that they're in a safe place."

Levi took a deep breath, unsure whether he should tell her what he'd been ordered to do. Then he spoke. "Rodriguez wants me to kill Luc."

Sierra steadied herself against a table. "What? You're kidding me. Right?"

"Don't worry. I have a plan, but I'll need his waiter's jacket—the one he was wearing at the party."

Levi gave Sierra a quick rundown, telling her exactly what he was planning.

"Are you sure that it will work?" Sierra's tone conveyed her doubt and anxiety.

Levi shrugged. "Nothing's for sure but, right now, I can't think of anything better."

Sierra was dubious, but reluctantly agreed to Levi's plan. "Okay, I'll call her and get her to send the jacket to me."

ψ

A little later, Levi called Sierra again, wanting to confirm that she had received the garment from Lucy.

"Yes, Emilie just dropped it off," Sierra responded. "Are you sure that this plan of yours is going to work?"

He replied, "no, but with any luck, just maybe it will."

Levi stopped by Lucy's apartment and Sierra handed him a white server's jacket bearing the distinctive gold-embroidered logo of Rodriguez's yacht.

"I hope that Luc's not expecting to get this back." Levi shrugged, smiled, and left for the city's disreputable docklands area.

He found a deserted wharf, positioned the jacket on a rotted wooden piling, removed, a Beretta M9A3 9mm handgun from beneath his jacket, and screwed a suppressor to the weapon's nozzle. He stepped back ten feet and fired three rounds into the front of the garment, then sat on a crate and waited for the gloom of darkness to slide over the eerily silent scene.

It didn't take long. The scurrying sound of dock rats broke the ominous silence. Levi leveled his pistol, shot one of the larger rodents, then scooped up the vermin's body, squeezed its blood over the front of the jacket, and hurled the rat's body into the harbor's filthy black water.

He filled a large burlap sack with castoffs he'd stolen from the back alley of a butcher's shop, dragged the sack down the wharf, and threw it into a boat he'd rented. He started the vessel's small outboard motor, piloted the vessel through the harbor, and drove it out into the Mediterranean. He dumped the weighted sack of butcher castoffs overboard into the sea's choppy waters and returned to the harbor.

Levi's mind turned to the only loose end in his plan—a detail that he had absolutely no control over. *I hope that someone in the harbor master's security staff is keeping track of the comings and goings of boat traffic tonight.*

Levi needn't have worried. A sharp-eyed officer noticed and recorded the departure time of Levi's small craft and the time that it returned several hours later.

ψ

Levi knocked on the door of Rodriguez's cabin and strode in. He dumped the blood-stained jacket onto the man's desk. "It's done, and here's your proof."

"Just a fucking jacket? I thought that you'd at least bring me his head, or hand, or an ear." His mouth contorted into a twisted smile.

"I may be a killer, but I'm not a butcher." He was thinking about the brutal murder and dismemberment of Claire Rodriguez.

"Where's the prick's body?"

"I dumped it into the Med. Last I saw, it was sinking in a couple hundred feet of seawater."

Rodriguez pointed to Luc's bloody jacket. "Take this fucking thing with you."

After his head of security had left, Rodriguez picked up his cell and called the Cannes harbor control. He needed to corroborate his security man's story. "Did anyone there see a small boat leave the harbor last night?"

"*Oui, monsieur*, just one. It was a very quiet night. It returned three hours later. I can give you the exact times if you wish." The harbor man paused. "I think someone wanted to try their luck fishing."

Rodriguez stood, ambled over to one of the cabin's large windows, and peered out at the seemingly endless display of floating affluence. *It seems that I might be able to trust the fucking Israeli after all—gets the job done, cleans up the mess when he's finished, and leaves me in the clear.*

He smiled at the thought.

CHAPTER THIRTY-NINE

The men who murdered and mutilated Claire Rodriguez had made one fatal mistake: when they were hacking through the woman's femur bone, the twenty-two-inch blade of their butcher saw had shattered. The men quickly replaced the offending blade but left two broken pieces of the saw next to the remains of her leg. The remnants of the broken blade held bloody fingerprints of the murderers that corroborated Bernard Blanc's testimony that identified the killers.

Arrest warrants were issued for Marcel Fournier and Pascal Gagnon, and both thugs were apprehended in a seedy gang hangout on Felix Pyat in the city's 3rd arrondissement.

News of his men's arrests reached their boss, Jean Durand, and he issued an order for their immediate execution. The following morning, prison guards found the two men hanging from exposed ceiling pipes in their cells. Hastily scrawled suicide notes were found in the pockets of their prison uniforms.

ψ

Alain and Pierre Aubert were sitting in a café near the police headquarters.

Pierre sipped his tea. "*Et maintenant?*"

Alain was deep in thought, and it at first seemed that he hadn't heard his colleague's question. After a moment, however, he responded. "I'll tell you what's next—all steps are leading us to the summit. I think it's time that we paid a visit to Monsieur Durand."

ψ

"Marie, get me Sierra Petersen's number. It's on the party's guest list."

Marie scrolled through the list on her computer and passed the model's cell number to her boss. Philippe posted the number to his private contact list and then called.

"*Bonjour,* Sister."

Sierra recoiled at the sound of his voice. "*Bonjour*, Monsieur Rodriguez. *Que puis-je faire pour vous?*" She didn't understand why she replied in French, for some unfathomable reason the words just popped out of her mouth. *What the hell was that all about?* she thought.

"Are you available to join me for dinner on my yacht this evening? A family reunion, so to speak: just the two of us with excellent food, wine, and hopefully interesting conversation." He stopped for a moment. "Oh, and so that we're not disturbed, I will arrange to have Levi Heifetz, my chief of security, on guard outside the dining room door."

Upon hearing that her ally would be close at hand, Sierra agreed to Rodriguez's invitation. "Don't worry about sending a car to pick me up Philippe, I'll have my driver drop me off at the dock. What time would you like me there?"

"Does seven this evening work?"

"Seven it is. I'll see you then."

Sierra hung up and buried her head in her hands. *God, I hope I'm doing the right thing.*

She rifled through her suitcase and found something suitable to wear for dinner then quickly showered and dressed for her date. She thought about texting or calling Lucy but didn't want to get into a long-winded conversation about her decision to go to dinner with Rodriguez. Instead, she scribbled a short note to her friend:

Hi, you. Gone to Rodriguez's yacht for dinner. Will call you when I get back. It was signed with a doodle of a heart.

ψ

Jean Durand operated his various commercial operations from a centuries-old warehouse near Marseille's busy port. His legitimate business specialized in repairing mechanical and electrical equipment for large merchant vessels docked in the city's always-busy harbor. This enterprise generated huge profits for the man but was proportionally insignificant to the fortune he made from his other, less-public, businesses.

One of Durand's associates announced the arrival of Alain Moreau and Pierre Aubert. "*Hé, patron. Les flics sont ici pour vous voir.*"

Visits from the police were not an unusual occurrence for the crime boss, so he had no concerns about inviting the two men into his cluttered office. "*Que puis-je faire pour vous, messieurs?*"

Alain looked straight into the man's eyes and answered his question. "What you can do for us, Monsieur Durand, is explain why two of your men brutally murdered Madame Claire Rodriguez."

Durand looked surprised. "*Messieurs,* I have absolutely no idea what you're talking about."

Pierre told Durand about the evidence they had against his two henchmen—bloody fingerprints on saw blades found next to body parts of the deceased woman. "Sooner or later," he warned, "one of your stupid thugs will hand us information implicating you in the woman's murder."

Durand strolled over to his credenza, removed a large Cuban cigar from his humidor, and lit it. Alain secretly wished that the man would offer one to him. *Merde, I haven't enjoyed a good cigar since I left Paris, and the Cuban that Durand's smoking certainly smells good.*

Alain momentarily thought about the only time he'd ever enjoyed such an expensive smoke. *When my first kid was born, I think.*

Durand returned to his desk and spoke directly to the man eyeing his cigar. "We'll see, *monsieur*, we'll see." He pointed toward the door. "Now, *messieurs*, if you have no further questions, please excuse me. I have pressing business that needs my immediate attention."

As soon as the officers left, Durand picked up his cell phone and called Philippe Rodriguez.

"Philippe, my dear friend, it seems that we may have a small problem. Call me when you have a moment."

ψ

Luc was sitting in front of Lucy's laptop. From it, he remotely logged into his own computer, typed in a series of cryptic passcodes, and downloaded all his files and programs onto Lucy's computer. Five minutes later, by using unauthorized, possibly illegal, backdoor programs, he managed to hack into Rodriguez's cell.

"Nick, I think I've got something—listen to this." He replayed Durand's curt message to Philippe Rodriguez.

ψ

Sierra's driver picked her up at the front door of Lucy's apartment building. Her voice quavered. "I'm going to Philippe Rodriguez's yacht at the Yacht Club de Monaco."

Her mind was in hyperdrive. *God, what the hell am I doing? What if everything goes terribly wrong? Remember, that he's a monster who needs to be dealt with. Phew, I'm glad Levi will be close by.* Her mental turmoil continued until the car stopped and the driver leaned over the front seat. "*Nous sommes arrivés*, Mademoiselle Petersen."

Levi was waiting for Sierra at the foot of the red-carpeted companionway. He didn't give any sign of recognizing her. "Right this way, *mademoiselle, s'il vous plaît.*" He indicated that she should follow him up the gangway.

When they reached Rodriguez's cabin door, Levi knocked and entered the private domain. Rodriguez was on the phone speaking to Jean Durand. He looked up then held his hand over the mouthpiece. Levi announced his guest.

"Mademoiselle Petersen is here. Shall I show her in?"

"Make her comfortable on the aft deck. Offer her a glass of champagne and apologize for my delay."

Sierra heard every word of his instructions.

ψ

The conversation between Rodriguez and the crime boss was overheard and recorded in the hotel room occupied by Luc, Nick, Gabriela, and Lucy. Emilie, who'd been picked up by Gabriela following the Rodriguez party, was also there. Luc let out a jubilant cry and shut down the laptop.

Luc's exuberance was premature, because moments after Rodriguez had hung up from Durant, he placed another call, this time to the pilot of his private jet. "File a flight plan. We're leaving tonight for Mexico City."

Rodriguez checked himself in the full-length mirror that covered the doors of his wardrobe closet, straightened his jacket, and strolled out to welcome his glamorous dinner guest.

ψ

Nick called Alain in Marseille. He could hardly contain the excitement in his voice. "We've got them!" He went on to tell the policeman about the recorded conversation between Rodriguez and Durand that implicated both men in the murder of Claire Rodriguez.

Pierre Aubert was listening in on Alain's call. "It'll take me a couple of hours to process a warrant for their arrests."

As he was rushing from the room, he stopped and turned toward Alain. His smile spoke volumes. "*Merci*, my friend. We've been trying to get something on Jean Durand for many, many years."

Alain wasn't quite as jubilant. He was thinking about some of his earlier cases. *It's a long journey between arrest and a conviction. I hope that this one's going to be a smooth ride.*

ψ

An intimate table for two was set in a corner of the *Angelina*'s sumptuous dining room. Highly polished sterling silver flatware and exquisitely cut crystal stemware sparkled with the dazzling reflections from long-tapered candles. Tiny arrangements of perfectly cut white roses completed the elegant tablescape. Rodriguez had pulled out all the stops for his special dinner guest.

Imported Iranian caviar, perfectly prepared Wagyu beef from the Tajima strain of Japanese black cattle, and a feather-light île flottante topped with a delicate nest of spun sugar comprised the evening's menu.

Rodriguez was his most charming and attentive self throughout the whole meal, and Sierra was almost lulled into believing that everything she'd heard about the man's dark reputation was a lie fabricated by his enemies. Her only anchors to reality were her friends' convictions of his guilt and the unseen presence of Levi Heifetz standing outside the dining room's massive double doors.

"I think that we should take a trip together—call it a family vacation." Rodriguez filled Sierra's glass with champagne, then raised his own glass and made a toast. "To next of kin."

Sierra hesitated momentarily then lifted the glass to her lips and sipped the bubbly wine. The unusually bitter taste of the champagne was the last thing that she remembered.

ψ

Levi and one of the yacht's crew members gently lifted Sierra's unconscious body into the rear seat of a waiting limousine.

Rodriguez barked an order to the driver. "Get us to the airport and make it fast."

Levi was seated in the passenger seat next to the driver. He turned and questioned his employer. "What did you give her? How long before it wears off?"

Rodriguez smirked. "She'll be wide awake, and I'm guessing mad as hell, in about twenty-four hours."

Traffic at that time of night was light, and the trip to Rodriguez's private aircraft took less time than expected. The limousine pulled up next to the jet's boarding steps and, once again, Sierra's still body was moved—this time from the car to the aircraft.

Levi's job as chief of security mandated that he accompanies and act as bodyguard for Rodriguez wherever and whenever he was wanted, but he had never been asked to travel with the man aboard his private jet. "Do you want me to come along?" Levi asked, but he already knew the answer.

"Yes, for fuck's sake. We're flying to Mexico, and I don't want any problems with the *mademoiselle* here." He pointed to the still form of Sierra.

"I don't have my passport with me."

Rodriguez burst out laughing and pointed toward the girl. "Neither does she, but take my word for it, you won't need one." He spoke to the pilot. "Let's get the hell out of here."

The woman quickly responded. "Wheels up sir, as soon as I get clearance from the tower."

The aircraft rolled slowly onto the runway. The pilot heard air traffic control give them the all-clear, and then, with a thunderous roar from its powerful Rolls-Royce engines, the jet moved with ever-increasing speed down the runway and up into the night sky. It banked over the glittering coastline of Côte d'Azur and headed southwest towards their destination in Mexico.

Rodriguez removed his shoes and leaned back into his plush leather seat. He turned to Levi. "Do you want anything to drink?"

Rodriguez saw Levi look over toward the unconscious woman. "Don't worry, my friend. Nothing will be added to your glass."

"In that case, I'll have a black coffee."

CHAPTER FORTY

Three patrol cars from le Sûreté Publique de Monaco roared into Monaco's famed marina and a contingent of heavily armed officers ran up the companionway of the *Angelina*.

"Where's Philippe Rodriguez?"

The terse order, given by the force's senior officer, was met with defiance by the lone crewman. "He's not here, and I have no fucking idea where he is."

"*Aucun problème*, you might find that your memory will improve in jail."

The crewman considered his limited options and stammered out a response. "I believe that they went to the airport: Monsieur Rodriguez, Monsieur Heifetz, and Mademoiselle Petersen."

The officer in charge called Alain Moreau and Pierre Aubert and broke the bad news to them.

"*Merde et maintenant?*" Alain's question was aimed at no one in particular.

ψ

Following an uneventful trans-Atlantic flight, Rodriguez's jet touched down at a private airstrip. The runway and surrounding outbuildings were built in a valley high in the Sierra Madre mountains by one of

Mexico's most notorious criminals. The tarmac was painted with a camouflage pattern, and the surrounding buildings were covered with netting intertwined with lush jungle foliage. If viewed from the air, the airstrip would be virtually impossible to detect.

Levi and the still-unconscious form of Sierra Petersen were quickly moved from the aircraft's sleek cabin, and within minutes, the jet, still carrying Philippe Rodriguez, took off and was back on route to Mexico City's International Airport.

Heavily armed men ushered Levi into a waiting four-wheeler and carried the limp body of Sierra into a second vehicle. The two-car convoy drove through the area's dense jungle until it finally came to rest in front of a majestic Spanish-style hacienda.

Waiting for their arrival was an imposing, bear-like man with a large gray beard. He was dressed in white linen slacks and a white-on-white patterned shirt that emphasized his muscular arms and deep tan. *"Buenos Dias, mi amigo. For favour ven y acompáñame a alsorzar."*

Levi welcomed the man's invitation to join him for lunch. He couldn't remember the last time he'd eaten. "Where are you taking Señorita Petersen?"

"Don't worry, my friend. I have provided her with a beautiful room where she can sleep off her malady—and when she wakes, she'll have a spectacular view of her namesake mountains," he gestured to their surroundings with a wide arc of his arm.

Levi ate like a ravenous hyena: chicken avocado soup, plump shrimp quesadillas, and mounds of freshly harvested fruit. *"Gracias Señor, set uvo delicioso."*

"Ah, you speak Spanish."

"Just a little. Not enough for a full conversation."

"Then we shall speak English." He waved to one of the heavily armed men standing on the periphery of the terrace. "Saul here will show you to your room and we shall discuss plans for your immediate future following dinner." His remark sounded more friendly than ominous.

Levi was escorted to a stunningly beautiful room. He walked over to the window, pulled back the blue velvet curtains, and saw heavy metal bars covering every inch of glass.

A trapped bird in a gilded cage, he thought.

ψ

Luc rebooted Lucy's computer and hacked into the tower at Marseille Provence airport. The friendly banter between a man and a woman was all that he heard, but it was enough to make him shout out to the others. "*Merde, le jet de Rodriguez est parti il y a des heures.*"

"Can you find out where it's headed?" The question from Nick precipitated a flurry of activity from Luc. His fingers moved quickly across the keyboard until he let out a despairing cry. "They're going to Mexico City and should be landing any moment now."

Nick felt a nauseating sense of panic. He immediately picked up his cell phone and called Alain. "Rodriguez is on his way to Mexico. His jet left Marseille hours ago."

"Not just Rodriguez, *mon ami.* Apparently, Sierra and Heifetz are with him too."

The news hit Nick like a hard punch to the gut. *What in hell's name is Sierra doing with Rodriguez?* He turned to the others. "Rodriguez has Sierra."

The last time Gabriela had seen Nick so distressed was almost twenty years earlier, in Spain, when their friend Henri Deneuve was murdered by an ungodly nun.

She knew immediately what they should do and didn't waste a second in saying it. "Let's head back to Paris, get our passports, and fly to Mexico."

Lucy, Luc, and Emilie weren't going to be left out. "We're going with you. Sierra's our friend too, maybe we can help." The plaintive words, spoken by Luc, didn't go unnoticed by Gabriela. "Okay, go and get your stuff together."

Lucy took a taxi to her apartment so that she could pack—she noticed Sierra's note as soon as she entered the door. She read it, dropped the scrap of paper onto the floor, and cried. *Why Sierra? Why? What the hell were you thinking?* Lucy felt as if she'd lost her friend forever and couldn't understand why Sierra would do something so foolhardy.

ψ

Pierre Aubert and an elite squad of GIGN police officers screeched up in front of the warehouse that doubled as Jean Durand's headquarters. The force of highly trained tactical officers leaped from their cars and took up offensive positions in the building's grimy courtyard. Gunfire erupted almost immediately, and a bullet from a second-floor window hit Aubert in the upper chest. It felt as if a battering ram had slammed into his body. He grabbed at his chest, collapsed, and landed heavily on the hard-packed gravel. With great difficulty, he managed to slowly crawl and push himself behind one of the squad cars. "*Je vais bien!*"

After hearing that the detective was alive, GIGN officers surrounded the building and began systematically closing in on the gang boss and his cadre of ruthless thugs.

The ensuing battle became a scene of total devastation. Police vehicles were shattered by gunfire; glass shards and pieces of shrapnel split the air like deadly, unstoppable razors; and anguished men, who had been wounded by the seemingly endless barrage of firepower, screamed and moaned in unfathomably agony.

When it was all over, twisted bodies lying in pools of blood were scattered across the filthy courtyard. The acrid stench of gunfire and the plaintive screams and repugnant death rattles emanating from the throats of dying men made even the most hardened members of the GIGN team sick to their stomachs.

The battle was one of the city's most brutal takedowns, and before

Durand and two of his henchmen were taken into custody, nine of his gang members were dead and two police officers seriously wounded.

Pierre Aubert carefully removed his bullet-proof vest. The garment, made from tightly woven aramid fibers, had saved his life, but the impact that the bullet had made to his chest still hurt like hell.

The detective clutched at his bruised chest and limped over to where Durand was being manhandled into one of the squad's large black SUVs. *"Nous t'avons enfin eu, salaud."*

The crime boss spat at the detective. "You think you've got me, but just wait until my lawyers gets through with you." Then he laughed.

It took every ounce of restraint for the wounded officer not to punch Durand in his ugly, contorted face. He turned to the group of officers that surrounded him. *"Sortez ce connard de ma vue."*

ψ

Gabriela booked five premier class seats on a direct Air France flight from Charles de Gaulle Airport in Paris, to Mexico City International Airport. The big jet was scheduled to depart at eleven that night, and if everything went according to plan, they would be touching down in Mexico City at three-thirty the following afternoon.

"C'mon guys, if we're going to get back home in time to catch our flight we'd better get going." Nick's impassioned coaxing did little to speed up the process, and his patience was soon at the breaking point. "Ready or not, we're leaving in five minutes—the train isn't going to wait for us." he yelled.

ψ

The disparate little group of travelers arrived in Paris and immediately rushed to the apartment on Île Saint-Louis to pack for the next leg of their journey; the long flight across the Atlantic to Mexico City.

On their ride to the airport, Nick called Francisca Ramirez Flores, the Mexican police officer who, years earlier, had helped him and Gabriela shut down Hector Rodriguez and the heinous disciples of the Mexican cult he had headed. "*Hola*, Francisca. It's Nick Palmer. We're on our way to Mexico City and I believe that I might need your assistance once again." He went on to summarize what had recently transpired to warrant his call.

"Ah Nicholas, so the vile serpent has, once again, reared its ugly head." Her voice softened. "I spoke to Alain earlier—he told me to expect a call from you."

Nick laughed. "He must be psychic. By the way, we'll be staying at the Four Seasons in Polanco."

"Call me after you check in," the Mexican cop hung up. *Fuck, it'll take them hours to get through the airport. I'll just surprise them and pick them up when they land.* She smiled.

ψ

Nick, Gabriela, and their entourage of young friends checked their luggage, passed through security, and boarded a huge Boeing 787. The courteous flight attendant offered refreshments, and they settled back into the cabin's plush leather seats. Luc and Emilie were overwhelmed, it was the first time that either of them had traveled in such luxury.

The aircraft taxied onto the runway, the roar from its powerful engines increased, and it lumbered down the tarmac, slowly picking up speed until it took off into the night sky.

Lights from the French capital twinkled below them, then finally vanished beneath a canopy of thick, black clouds. It was as if every lamp in the city had suddenly become sympathetic to the dark thoughts inhabiting their minds.

CHAPTER FORTY-ONE

When Sierra woke, her head felt like it had been hit, repeatedly, with a large hammer. *What happened? Where the hell am I?* The last thing she remembered was sipping a glass of champagne on Philippe Rodriguez's yacht.

She stood, staggered over to the window and pulled aside the curtains. It was evening and her reflection in the darkened glass confirmed that she was still wearing the clothes that she'd worn at Rodriguez's shipboard dinner. She shook her head for what seemed like the tenth time. *Bars? Why the hell are iron bars covering the window?*

There was a quiet knock on the door, and a woman entered the room. She was middle-aged, attractively slim, and her thick black hair was pulled back into a severe bun that perched perilously on the back of her head. The woman was dressed in a white maid's uniform that looked as if it had been starched to within an inch of its life. Her face was beautiful but stern and radiated a look of constant fear. *"Buenas noches, señorita. Me han indicado que le informe que la cena servirá en una hora."* She stopped speaking and pointed toward an ornate antique armoire. *"Encentrará ropa adecuada en el armario."*

Sierra opened the doors of the armoire. It was filled with an array of beautiful dresses, blouses, and slacks, all of which were her size. The maid opened a dresser drawer filled with delicate lingerie, also in

Sierra's size. For some inexplicable reason that she didn't understand, Sierra didn't experience any feelings of fear or apprehension.

The bathroom in her gilded prison was beautiful beyond words and contained every conceivable toiletry that a woman could ever want. Sierra stopped in front of the marble-clad shower, dropped her clothing into an untidy pile at her ankles, and stepped in.

She lingered in the shower for a full twenty-five minutes. The hot water soothed the throbbing ache in her head and managed to relieve the pain that she felt in every other part of her body. The shower also gave her time to think about her predicament. *I'll bet that prick Rodriguez spiked the champagne and moved me to somewhere where I wouldn't be a problem for him.* She thought about the jungle and mountaintops that she'd seen through the window in her room. *Fuck, I bet the asshole flew me to Mexico.*

She still didn't have any idea how long she'd been unconscious. *Dinner's in less than an hour? I'd better get dressed and find out what the hell this is all about.* She stepped from the shower, picked out a white linen sundress, and pulled it over her head. After adding a touch of makeup and a simple silver necklace, she left the room. Two heavily armed men escorted her to a vast dining room. Every wall in the room was covered with a disgustingly abhorrent display of wild animal heads, obviously hunting trophies much prized by the owner of the hacienda.

There were three place settings at one end of the long oak table. The man sitting at the head of the table stood when Sierra entered the room. The seat to his right was occupied by Levi Heifetz, who also stood.

Sierra's mind was whirling. *What the fuck is Levi doing here? We're supposed to be on the same team.*

"*Buenas noches,* Señorita Petersen. Welcome to my humble home." The large man speaking gestured for her to take the seat to his left. "My name is Enrique Ortega, but my friends call me Rickie, and my other guest is Levi Heifetz, who I believe you know."

Levi nodded an acknowledgment.

Ortega sat and continued speaking. "You both will be my honored guests for the next two days, and then, with much regret on my part, you will be required to continue on the next leg of your journey."

The maid who had earlier delivered the dinner invitation to Sierra entered the room with the first course: ice-cold gazpacho garnished with sour cream and a sprig of fresh mint.

Ortega looked first at the maid, and then to his guests. "*Gracias, Sonya. Buen apetito.*"

Sierra started to ask a question. "Where . . .?"

Ortega lifted his hand and stopped her from asking her question. "Later, *señorita*. Following dinner, I will attempt to reveal all that you wish to know." He smiled. "Within reason, of course."

ψ

The big jet carrying Nick, Gabriela, and their three traveling companions was on its final approach to Mexico City's sprawling international airport. Nick turned and faced the others. "As soon as we land, grab your things. I want to get out of here as soon as we can—the airport's going to be crazy busy, and I don't want to be stuck at the end of the line going through the arrival's gates."

There was a bump, screech of tires, and a thunderous roar as the engines reversed their thrust to slow the aircraft down. Next came the long, slow taxi to the arrivals jetway.

As Nick had wanted, they were first off, and almost first in line at customs and immigration.

"Nicholas! Gabriela! Come this way." Standing behind the barrier was Francisca Ramirez Flores, their old friend in the Policía Ciudad de México, Mexico City's army-size police force.

Francisca stepped into the arrival hall and hugged both Gabriela and Nick. She was quickly introduced to Lucy, Luc and Emilie, and the disparate little group from France were quickly escorted through the customs and immigration lineups by the Mexican police officer—no questions were asked by federal airport officials, and no answers were given by the amiable police inspector.

Gabriella scanned the crowds surrounding them, then put her arm over the Mexican woman's shoulder. "Thanks for picking us, Francisca, it clipped hours off our time at the airport."

A large black SUV with police insignia boldly displayed on the car's side doors waited curbside at the arrivals level. They loaded their bags into the car's rear compartment and piled into the vehicle's three rows of seats. Francisca instructed the driver to take them to their hotel in Polanco.

Nick couldn't hold back. He leaned across the front seat and spoke to Francisca. "Has Rodriguez's jet landed yet?"

"*Si,* he landed a couple of hours ago, cleared customs and immigration, refueled, then immediately took off again."

Nick was puzzled that Francisca didn't mention Sierra or Levi Heifetz. "What about the other two passengers?"

"There were no others. Just Rodriguez, the pilot, co-pilot, and a flight attendant."

"That's impossible. There were three passengers on board when they left Marseille."

Francisca picked up her cell and called one of her subordinates at the police station. "Louis, call the airport's control tower and have the person in charge call me. I need to find out details about the arrival of a particular private jet."

Nick was deep in thought. *How in hell do two passengers just vanish from a jet on a transatlantic flight?*

ψ

When Jean Durant and his lawyer were confronted with the incriminating phone conversation between Rodriguez and him that Luc had recorded, the crime boss went ballistic. "*Merde,* that's just pure unadulterated bullshit. It could be anyone talking to anyone else. It's not enough evidence to keep me here." He stood, intending to walk out of the interrogation room, but he'd forgotten that he was handcuffed to the metal table in front of him. He sat back down and scowled at the police officers facing him. "You fucking bastards. You'll pay for this."

The lawyer put his hand on the man's broad shoulder and whispered in his ear. "Not so fast, Jean. With today's technology, *les flics* can easily identify both your and Philippe's voices."

Durand slumped in the chair, his indignation lessened, but inside he was still seething. *If I go down, so does that fucking Rodriguez.*

Pierre Aubert turned to the other officer in the room. "Take him away. I'm already sick of the sight of him."

ψ

Philippe Rodriguez was midflight on route to Puerto Vallarta when he was informed that Jean Durand had been arrested. Ava Rojas, the elderly woman on the other end of the call, gave Rodriguez complete details of the charges against the crime boss and told him about the recorded evidence held by the police.

Rodriguez's response was immediate. "Ava don't let the prick get out of prison. Hire someone to deal with him."

"No need for the added expense, Señor Rodriguez. I have contacts within the prison system who will be delighted to fulfill your order. All part of the service that you pay me so handsomely for."

ψ

Jean Durand's body was discovered by prison guards on the morning following his arrest and interrogation. The front of his prison uniform was drenched with blood from a fatal stab wound. The long-serrated knife that inflicted the gory murder was still protruding from the man's chest.

Pierre Aubert, along with a cluster of other police officers and guards, stood over the body while a pathologist examined the grisly remains of the crime boss.

"Did anyone come to see him last night? What guards were on duty?"

Pierre's questions went unanswered.

"*Jésus-Christ, personne ne sait rien?*"

There was still no response from the assembled group.

"*Merde*. Get me the names of all visitors and guards who were in the prison last night, *et dépêchez-vous*." The anger in the policeman's voice was palpable.

A short, heavily built guard raised his hand.

"*Monsieur*, one of the guards, a new guy, didn't show up for duty today."

"Who is he? What's his name?" snapped the detective.

"*Désolé monsieur, je ne sais pas*. Yesterday was his first day."

Pierre was about to order the senior guard to bring him the man's employment file but was interrupted by the ring of his cell phone. He held the device to his ear, listened, then hung up. The color of his normally ruddy face had turned a sickly shade of gray.

"*Merde*, they've just found the body of a man in a prison guard's uniform. They discovered him in an alley not far from here—his throat was slashed."

CHAPTER FORTY-TWO

Francisca's cell phone rang. She saw that it was the callback that she was expecting from the airport authorities.

"*Hola*, Police Inspector Francisca Ramirez Flores here. I'm inquiring about a private jet that arrived yesterday from Marseille, cleared customs, and departed almost immediately afterward for Puerto Vallarta."

"*Si*, Inspector, I remember it well. The aircraft is owned by a corporation controlled by Señor Philippe Rodriguez. They reported a minor instrument problem over the Sierra Madre mountains, causing the pilot to fly below our radar to remedy the issue. The jet was back on course and in contact with the tower within twenty minutes."

Francisca thanked the air traffic controller, hung up, and relayed what the woman had said to Nick and the others.

Nick looked dubious, then stated the obvious. "Would that be enough time to land, deplane some passengers, and get airborne again?"

Francisca answered. "Sorry Nick, I really don't know. Let me check back with the airport and see what she says." She dialed the number that she'd recently hung up from and once again spoke to the traffic control supervisor. Francisca asked the question posed by Nick, and after hearing the woman's answer, turned to face the vehicle's other passengers. "The short answer is yes, but it would have to be a very well-coordinated operation."

"The kind of highly efficient drop-off maneuver that drug smugglers might do?" asked Nick.

"That would be my guess, and if you're right, we have no idea where they'd be. It's very rough territory in the Sierra Madres."

Luc, who'd been listening intently to the whole conversation from the rear seat, chimed in. "There's a pretty common app that tracks every flight and every aircraft everywhere in the world. Let me pull it up and see what I can find out."

He flipped open his laptop and searched for the app. "Here, I've got it, but it's just showing me real time, not what's happened in the last few days."

His fingers began a ritualistic dance across the device's keyboard. It was as if he was silently playing Beethoven's *Symphony No. 9*. "Here, I've got it." He passed the laptop over to Nick. Francisca and Gabriela looked at the screen and saw literally thousands of tiny icons floating around a map of North America. Nick passed the computer back to Luc. "This is your game Luc; you figure it out for us."

Luc smiled at the man's feigned lack of computer knowledge, knowing full well that Nick was handing him the assignment to make him feel like he was an important part of the team. Luc took the device and zoomed into the map of Mexico, then zoomed even closer into the area surrounding Mexico City. He clicked onto one of the aircraft icons and an image of the type of plane appeared on the screen.

He turned and smiled. "Now all that we have to do is find Rodriguez's jet among all of the others."

ψ

The police SUV pulled up at the front entrance to the Four Seasons Hotel, and in a matter of minutes they were shown to their rooms by one of the hotel's courteous staff.

Nick and Gabriela had a luxurious suite with a large living room, a decadent ensuite bathroom, and a bedroom which could easily pass for a modern equivalent of one found in Château de Versailles—the former palace of King Louis XIV of France.

Gabriela sat on the edge of the downy-soft king-size bed then flopped onto her back. "It's too bad that we're not on holiday, I could easily get used to this." She smiled: not the happy-to-see-you kind of smile, but the seductive come-here-big-boy-I-want-to-make-love-to-you kind of smile. Nick lay down beside the beautiful woman, wrapped his arms around her, and kissed her. "God, I love you."

Their moment of ardor was interrupted by a loud knock on the door to their suite. "Hey guys, can we come in? I think that Em and I have just figured out where Rodriguez's jet landed."

Nick untangled himself from Gabriela's embrace, shrugged, and yelled toward the door. "C'mon in Luc."

The sibling's excitement was over the top.. They rushed into the suite carrying Luc's laptop and plopped down at the end of the bed between Nick and Gabriela.

"Here guys, take a look at this." Luc flipped open the screen, opened the newly found app and zoomed in on an icon high in the Sierra Madre Mountain range. Then he clicked onto an aerial view of what the map was showing.

Nick and Gabriela peered at the image. "There's nothing there but jungle."

"Take a closer look." Luc zoomed in on the image. "Look right there, in the top left-hand corner of the image." He pointed to a spot on the computer's screen. "See, there's a big black SUV and two men standing next to it." Nick looked again, and sure enough, half hidden by the canopy of trees, was the car.

Gabriela saw it too. "I think we'd better call Francisca," she said.

ψ

Sierra was famished, and following what she thought may have been the best gazpacho soup that she'd ever tasted, four courses of equally excellent Mexican delicacies were served and enjoyed. Levi and Enrique Ortega ate their dinner with a similar level of pleasure and appreciation.

After the remains of the meal had been removed, Ortega lit a huge Cuban cigar and leaned back in his chair. "Now, you mentioned that you have questions."

Sierra jumped right in. "Where am I? Why am I here? What do you plan to do with me?"

"First, you are at my private villa in Mexico's beautiful Sierra Madre mountains." He made another sweeping gesture with both arms. "You're here at the request of a great friend of mine—Señor Philippe Rodriguez. And, as to your last question, you and Señor Heifetz will sadly be my guests for only one more night. Tomorrow morning you'll be taken on a car ride through the jungle to the coast, where my men will deliver you to Philippe." He took a long drag on his cigar, exhaled a plume of pale blue smoke, and called for the maid. "*Sonya, hemos terminado aquí, por favor acompaña a nuestros invitados a sus habitaciones.*"

The maid bowed to her employer and indicated to Sierra and Levi that they should follow her. They stood and walked out of the room—followed closely by two of Ortega's men.

Sierra turned toward Levi. "Why so quiet? Didn't you have any questions for that fat asshole?"

"He didn't tell us anything that I didn't already know, and besides, he's going to deliver us to Rodriguez." He paused. "And isn't that what this whole thing is all about?"

They were ushered back to their respective rooms.

The only sound that Sierra heard, other than the cacophony of jungle noise through her open windows, was the ominous click of the door to her room being locked.

ψ

Pierre Aubert placed a call to his colleague in Paris. Alain saw who was calling and answered immediately. "*Bonjour*, Pierre. What can I do for you?"

Pierre recounted the story of Durand's death and the subsequent murder of his assumed killer.

"*Merde*, Pierre. What about Rodriguez—any news about his whereabouts?"

"He's somewhere in Mexico. I have spoken to your friend Francisca Ramirez Flores. She picked up Nicholas, Gabriela, and the three young people at the airport and delivered them to their hotel in the capital."

"*Merci*, Pierre. Please keep me informed of any further news—and good luck with your murder cases." Alain hung up, but his mind was firing on all cylinders. *God only knows where this is going, but at least some very nasty people are off the streets—and out of the game.*

ψ

Nick met Francisca and told her what Luc and Emilie had worked out.

"Our resident computer whiz-kids have been able to locate the exact location of where Sierra and Levi are being held. I'll get them to send you the exact longitude and latitude in the mountains as soon as we hang up."

This information, which Luc sent to Francisca, set in motion a series of law enforcement maneuvers which, in scale, resembled an all-out wartime initiative against a hostile enemy state.

The following morning, a squadron of five H225 Super Puma military helicopters took off from the Mexican capital, each one occupied by heavily armed combat troops and members of the police department's elite special services division.

When the airborne tactical forces were close to their targets, the helicopters split into two divisions. Francisca was in the lead helicopter racing toward Enrique Ortega's sumptuous villa. The other two choppers were on route to the gang leader's secretive landing strip.

The policewoman yelled into the microphone in her helmet. Her message, heard above the scream of the aircraft's big turbine engines, was understood by all the aircraft's occupants. "*Amigos*, our mission today is to apprehend Ortega and his henchmen, and safely secure *Señorita Petersen y Señor Heifetz*." She was unaware of the bloodbath they were about to fly into.

ψ

Sierra and Levi were woken before sunrise, handed neat cardboard boxes containing food for their journey, and loaded into a waiting SUV. A second identical car stood behind the first.

Enrique Ortega stood on the front steps of his villa and waved. "*Adios, mis amigos. Saludos cordialmente a Philippe.*"

The cars transporting Sierra and Levi were two hours into their trip when the heavily armed helicopters carrying the strike force of police and military personnel landed on the drug lord's immaculately manicured front lawn.

CHAPTER FORTY-THREE

Philippe Rodriguez's jet touched down at Puerto Vallarta's international airport, and because he'd gone through the rituals of customs and immigration in Mexico City, his passage into the dazzling sunshine of the city was quick and painless.

A black SUV was waiting for him: the very same car driven by the very same men who had picked up and driven Jacqueline Blanchet, Claire Rodriguez's unfortunate maid, to her final destination and subsequent murder in the dusty hills south of the city.

The silence inside the vehicle was as stifling as the temperature outside. There was no joyful Mexican music blasting from the car's radio and no conversation between Rodriguez and the car's other occupants. The cartel men knew all about Rodriguez's remorseless reputation and didn't want to say anything that might result in serious repercussions to their health.

The SUV left the airport and drove north on Highway 200 to the exclusive enclave of Punta Mita, where they were swiftly ushered through the enclave's impressive wooden gates. The man guarding the entry didn't even look up, he too had heard of the new passenger's unmerciful reputation. The car continued along a series of winding, immaculately landscaped roads to a sumptuous villa owned by Rodriguez.

Ronaldo Ortiz, one of the country's most notorious gang leaders, had arrived at the villa several days earlier and was on hand to meet Rodriguez, his spiritual leader and factual head of his criminal organization. The Mexican gang leader was also a senior apostle of the council of La Orden de las Serpientes de Cristo, but even with his exalted position within the Order, he bowed in respect to the man who'd just recently arrived.

"*Bienvenido a casa, amigo mio, ha pasado demasiado tiempo desde la última pesque nos vimos.*" The tall, wiry man spread his arms to welcome his patron and ushered Rodriguez into the cool interior of the lavish hacienda.

Rodriguez loved this place. After many, often difficult, negotiations, he'd managed to purchase the land and build his oceanfront palace. The location was important to him because it was close to one of the vortices of Ley lines, the invisible network of linear energy bands that circumnavigate the globe. These lines of unseen energy are claimed to connect significant historic landmarks such as the Great Pyramid of Giza, Chichén Itzá, Stonehenge, and the like. Persons staying, or living, near Ley line vortices are said to enjoy spiritual vivacity and lucidity. Most importantly for Rodriguez, though, was that these undetectable lines of energy connected his home to the ancient Templo de Quetzalcóatl, Temple of the Feathered Serpent, in Teotihuacán near Mexico City, the most sacred of all places for the followers of the Order that he headed. Rodriguez took a deep breath. The jasmine-scented air immediately relieved the tightness in his neck and shoulders.

The driver from the SUV trod silently past them carrying Rodriguez's luggage. The man walked up the foyer's grand staircase and vanished into one of the second-floor corridors.

Ortiz placed his arm across Rodriguez's shoulders and escorted him to a spacious inner courtyard where, beneath a lush canopy of trees, a table was set with refreshments.

The men sat opposite each other, and Rodriguez spoke. "It's wonderful to see you again, Ronaldo. So much has happened since our last meeting." Rodriguez told his friend about Sierra Petersen, his half-sister, his lavish party, the attempt on his life, and his narrow escape from police officials in Monaco and France. "The woman has my bloodline and may possibly take my place as the next leader of La Orden de la Serpientes de Cristo."

"Don't think that way, El Cardinal. You have many, many years left to lead and guide our Order."

"I do hope so, Ronaldo. I really do hope so, but I've had this feeling, deep within my being, that my time may be limited." Rodriguez rubbed his eyes. "It's been a long journey, and I'm very tired. Would you take offense if I excused myself to take a small siesta?"

Ortiz stood and beckoned for one of his men to escort Rodriguez to his room. "Sleep soundly, El Cardinal. We'll talk more over dinner." He watched in concern as Rodriguez wound his way upstairs to his suite.

ψ

Enrique Ortega was in bed with his maid Sonya when the maelstrom struck. The woman was trying, unsuccessfully, to elude the thug's amorous advances, when suddenly the incessant *chop, chop, chop* sound of helicopters and loud staccato gunfire from his gang member's automatic weapons shattered the hacienda's normally tranquil atmosphere.

Ortega leaped from the bed and quickly pulled on a pair of jeans. He grabbed his handgun from the bedside table and rushed from the room, leaving the woman he tried to force himself upon cowering under the bed sheets. It took the drug lord less than five seconds to realize that he was under attack. He froze. Never in his wildest dreams did he ever believe that his home could or would be invaded. His men were ill-prepared for the onslaught of well-trained police officers and militiamen and were scattering from the barrage of hellfire being violently launched toward them in retaliation for their pre-emptive gunfire.

Ortega saw one of his most trusted lieutenants explode into a cloud of blood, flesh, and bone fragments when a fusillade of bullets hit him in the chest. Another of his thugs peered around one of the hacienda's ornate stone pillars only to have his head blown away like it was an overripe watermelon. Bodies were strewn in twisted contortions throughout the whole main floor and a grisly carpet of ever-spreading blood was quickly being absorbed by the room's priceless Persian rugs. Manuel Perez, Ortega's second-in-command, shot and hit a militia man. He was rewarded for his keen marksmanship by having his head blown away by the fallen man's comrades.

Ortega was crouched behind one of the second-floor balustrades, peering down at the bloodshed and devastation playing out below him, when a woman dressed in full battle fatigues ran through the double front doors. He raised his weapon and fired. Three bullets found their mark before he was cut in two by a hail of gunfire fired by officers of the combined strike force. Ortega tumbled and slid down the stairs. The blood, pouring from his many bullet wounds, was spreading through the hair on his naked chest, leaving a trail, like a red river of blood, that followed his descent down the steps.

Upon seeing that their leader was dead, the skirmish quickly ended. Ortega's remaining men quietly relinquished their weapons and were herded into small groups by the cadre of armed militiamen.

All that there was left to do was conduct a body count.

The lightning helicopter strike on the drug lord's airstrip resulted in a similar conclusion. Dead bodies, lakes of blood, with fires and explosions from burning fuel spewing ugly thick black clouds of smoke into the pristine tropical sky.

Francisca Ramirez Flores was dead, lying face down in a pool of her own blood. One of the bullets from Ortega's last stand had hit the woman in her neck, severing her carotid artery. She was one of just two fatalities suffered by the combined police and military force.

A sixth helicopter, a multi-use Sikorsky UH-60L Black Hawk

carrying paramedical personnel, was quickly dispatched from Mexico City. The helicopter landed, the medics carefully loaded the bodies and wounded officers into the aircraft's large cabin and the chopper took off. The remaining force gathered into small groups, quietly mourning their fallen comrades.

The squad's leader called into police headquarters. "Ortega and eighteen of his gang members are dead and we've apprehended fourteen other gang members. We suffered four casualties, two wounded, and two dead—Inspector Francisca Ramirez Flores and Sergeant Mateo Hernandez. We searched for Señorita Petersen and Señor Heifetz, neither of them was found."

The woman on the receiving end of the call, a good friend of the fallen policewoman, dropped the phone into her lap, let out an audible gasp, and silently prayed for her fallen colleague.

ψ

The car carrying Sierra and Levi bounced along the rough, brutally rutted jungle roads of the Sierra Madre Mountain range, until finally reaching a paved road that would take them to Puerto Vallarta. None of the car's occupants were aware of the bloody insurrection at Ortega's hacienda and airstrip.

"Where are you taking us?"

Sierra's question fell upon deaf ears. The only sound she heard was the constant hum of the SUV's huge tires as it raced toward its destination.

She slumped back into her seat and whispered to Levi. "Got any ideas yet?"

Levi smiled. He could easily take out the two thugs in the front seats, but that wouldn't help them get to Rodriguez. "Patience, Sierra, patience. These things have a way of working themselves out," he whispered.

CHAPTER FORTY-FOUR

Nick grabbed his cell and answered it on the second ring. As he listened, Gabriela watched his countenance turn noticeable darker. "Not Francisca! There's got to be a mistake! Tell me there's been a mistake!" His shoulders dropped, his voice sounded hollow, and the anguish that he was obviously feeling was fraught with unfathomable grief. He clicked the end call button then turned to Gabriela and broke the news of their friend's death.

"What about Sierra? Were they able to rescue her?" Tears were streaming down Gabriela's cheeks. Her despair at hearing of their friend's sudden death and her concern about the fate of Sierra was indelible written across her face.

Nick wrapped his arms around the distraught woman. "No, there was no sign of her or Levi." He paused to regain his composure. "So, who the hell knows where they are?"

ψ

News about the insurgence at Enrique Ortega's compound was conveyed to Rodriguez well before the story hit the media. Details of the insurrection were delivered to him by one of Ortiz's gunmen.

"*Senõr* Ortega is dead, as are many of his men. Those who survived the attack have been taken into custody by the *policía*."

The anger in Rodriguez's gut was like all the fires in hell igniting into one huge blast of brimstone.

"What about the woman and my fucking head of security? Any news of them?" Rodriguez screamed at the unfortunate man who was sent to deliver the news to him.

"*Nada, senõr.* They were both not there." The terrified man scurried from the room, desperately trying to distance himself from the man they called El Cardinal.

"Wait! Get back here." The messenger turned, and Rodriguez continued. "Tell Ortiz that I need to see him—right now!"

Rodriguez realized that he was pacing the room like a caged tiger. *Calm down*, he thought to himself. *Don't show anyone any sign of weakness.* He sat in one of the room's magnificent baroque armchairs, stretched his legs out in front of him, and waited for Ronaldo Ortiz. His fingers dug deeply into the chairs heavily padded arms.

ψ

The SUV carrying Sierra and Levi Heifetz pulled off the highway onto a dusty, rutted side road. The escort car in the two-vehicle convoy followed behind them. Several hundred yards later, and well-hidden from any inquisitive eyes, they stopped and the men in the front seats of the lead vehicle got out and opened the car's rear doors. The driver barked out an order to his passengers. "*Es hora de salir.*" Sierra and Levi were manhandled out onto the road.

"I need to go to the washroom." Sierra held out her arms, indicating the task would be difficult with her wrists bound with zip ties.

The driver pulled a gun from his jacket, pointed it toward her head, snipped the ties with a wire cutter, and led her toward a clump of scruffy bushes.

"You don't have to stand here and watch." The man guarding her didn't move but did turn his eyes away from Sierra.

When they returned to the car, Sierra saw that Levi was back in his seat with a black hood covering his head. The driver re-secured her wrists, placed a black hood over her head, and guided her back into her seat. Within minutes, the two-vehicle cavalcade was back on the highway racing toward their unknown destination.

ψ

In her native country of Mexico, and throughout many of the world's law enforcement jurisdictions, Police Inspector Francisca Ramirez Flores was a legend. This unassailable reputation was due, in large part, to her crucial involvement in the case nineteen years earlier, when she was instrumental in bringing down Hector Rodriguez.

Her legend grew and she was now considered to be a national hero by many of her country's citizens. Her determined courage and seeming invincibility in numerous dangerous operations in the years following the La Orden de las Serpientes de Cristo case had enshrined her enviable stature. Now she was gone, and law enforcement entities in her country, and throughout the world, remembered her bravery and dedication—and mourned her untimely death.

Francisca's funeral, held at the Catedral Metropolitana in Mexico City's Zócalo district, was attended by thousands of mourners, including a massive contingent of police officers from around the world, all wearing their finest pressed-and-polished full-dress uniforms.

Nick, Gabriela, and Lucy were seated on a well-worn wooden pew in the first row, directly in front of the impressive church's sanctuary. With them, in the same row, was the slain officer's family. Police officers who had helped Nick and Gabriela shut down Hector Rodriguez and his evil cult so many years ago were also in attendance: Deputy Director Alain Moreau flew in from Paris for the funeral, as did Javier Ruiz from Madrid and Silvio Bianchi from Rome. Even Josh Nicholson, Nick and Gabriela's old boss from Chicago, was in attendance to pay his respects to their fallen comrade.

Francisca's ornate coffin was positioned in front of the main altar.

It, and much of the church's interior, was festooned with flowers and notes of condolences from well-wishers throughout the globe.

Nick was asked by the slain officer's family to deliver the eulogy. The honor was a task he was reticent about. He wanted, even felt obligated, to speak about Francisca's life and death, but the thought of delivering a second tribute so soon after doing so for his other fallen friends weighed heavily on his psyche. *First it was Louis and Natalie Faucher's funeral, and now it's this. I pray to God that this is the last one I'm asked to perform*, he thought.

The ceremony seemed to last forever. The accolades, from many of Francisca's colleagues, seemed to last even longer. Finally, it was Nick's turn to speak. He stood at the lectern, looked around at the congregation, cleared his throat, and began to speak.

"Francisca was a dear friend and esteemed colleague. Although it has been many years since we worked together on the case that catapulted her into the global spotlight, she retained a humility that spoke to her self-effacing character and professional dignity." He paused and wiped away the beginning of tears that were welling in his eyes. "Those who knew her well understood that her toughness was underscored by compassion, and her bravery by an unflinching passion to do the right thing—no matter what the cost."

He paused again and looked toward Gabriela as if to receive moral support. "Francisca and I met again recently. Once more, I needed to enlist her and her police colleagues to assist in eradicating the heinous cult we believed to have been destroyed so many years ago. It was, during this undertaking, that she paid the ultimate sacrifice." Nick gave up all hope of containing his grief, and as he spoke, his voice choked, and tears began trickling down his cheeks. "In many ways, I bear some of the responsibility for her death, and it is a burden that will stay with me for the rest of my life." Nick lowered his eyes. "Francisca will always be fondly remembered for her unimpeachable dedication to duty, her remarkable bravery, her love of family, country, humanity, and her devotion to the police force that she was such an integral part of."

Nick looked up toward the assembled crowd. "I will miss her, and I know that all of you here, and others throughout the world, will miss her." He stopped speaking. It was as if words alone were not enough to communicate his overwhelming despair. "Unfortunately, criminals and other miscreants are very probably partying at the news of her demise."

He looked down at the coffin. "Goodbye, Francisca. I promise to devote my life to finishing the task that we embarked upon."

Nick stepped down from the chancel and returned to his seat next to Gabriela. If the flow of tears from the assembled congregation could be harnessed into hydroelectricity, it could have powered every light in the massive city.

ψ

The reception following the funeral ceremony was held across the Plaza de la Constitución in one of the ornate formal reception rooms of the Palacio Nacional, seat of the country's government, and official residence of the Mexican president.

Nick and Gabriela circulated among the crowd of guests who had gathered to honor Francisca. They chatted and reminisced with colleagues from many of the world's police jurisdictions and gratefully accepted sincere condolences from numerous others who were in attendance at the somber event.

It was a difficult day for Nick and Gabriela, and all that they wanted to do was escape the melee of mourners and return to their hotel. As they tried to make their getaway, Josh Nicholson caught up to them near the room's main door. "Hey, you two, you're not going to get away that easily." The bear of a man hugged Gabriela and vigorously shook Nick's hand before also engulfing him in his massive arms.

The last time that Nick and Gabriela had seen Josh was five

years earlier when he and Mary, his wife of some fifty years, had visited them in Paris. The couple were on a holiday celebrating both their wedding anniversary and Josh's retirement from the Chicago police force.

Josh threw Nick a pointed question. "Are you still seeing these angel ghosts of yours?"

Nick smiled. The man's direct-to-the-point manner hadn't changed. "Yeah, boss, they've come back, as has the Serpents of Christ cult—and the evil bastards are still sacrificing young women."

Josh frowned and shook his head. "Is there anything that I can do to help? I've decided to hang around Mexico City for a week or so and do the tourist thing. I'm pretty sure that it will bore the shit out of me in no time."

Nick rested his hand on the big man's shoulder. "Thanks, Josh. Give me a day or two to think it over. I'll call you day after tomorrow, okay?"

As the couple left the noisy gathering, Gabriela turned toward Nick. "Y'know, honey, Josh has more experience than almost everyone in the room. He could be a great asset."

ψ

The vehicle carrying Sierra and Levi drove for what Sierra thought was about an hour before it slowed down and stopped. She heard a muffled exchange between their driver and another man through the hood covering her head and rightly assumed that they'd almost reached their destination. She heard the distinctive sound of heavy gates creaking open and the big SUV moved forward at a much slower pace. Levi leaned over to her and whispered, "Prepare yourself, Sierra. We're getting very close to the endgame."

CHAPTER FORTY-FIVE

Rodriguez and Ortiz were discussing the raid on Enrique Ortega's hidden hacienda and airstrip in the Sierra Madre mountains. Their conversation was anything but deferential and often became intense and heated. Rodriguez was pacing around the room, screaming profanities, and pounding his fists into just about everything that he happened to pass.

"That fucking cop from Chicago is behind all of this. The prick destroyed my father and now he's out to destroy me." He turned toward Ortiz and barked out an order. "I want him dealt with once and for all, I want him and his whole fucking family dead." He slammed his fist into a wall, causing a rare eighteenth-century portrait of a prominent Spanish nobleman to crash onto the floor. "And get it done now . . . *Lo entiendes?*"

A soft knock on the door interrupted the vitriolic onslaught. "*Adelante!*" Rodriguez barked.

The angry order to enter the room terrified the man on the other side of the door, and he hesitated for a few seconds too long. Rodriguez strode over to the door and ripped it open. "Didn't you fucking hear me? What the hell do you want?"

The man cowered and delivered his message. "*Disculpe, señor, han llegado la señorita Petersen y el señor Heifetz.*"

News of the arrival of Sierra and Levi had an immediate calming effect on Rodriguez, and he ordered the man who delivered the message to escort his newly arrived guests to the villa's lush poolside terrace. "Make them comfortable, serve them some of Juanita's delicious lemonade, and inform them that I will join them shortly." His request was delivered in the messenger's native Spanish.

Rodriguez watched him leave then turned toward Ortiz. "Call Ava and tell her that I'm offering a million dollars to the person who kills Palmer, and I'll pay half a million each for all the others in his family, including the fucking Faucher kids. Now, *amigo,* get the fuck out of here. I've got to freshen up to greet my guests."

ψ

Sierra and Levi were sitting in the shade of a gigantic parota tree in Rodriguez's lushly landscaped terrace. The azure-colored infinity pool, located halfway down a slight grade in the garden's topography, was fed by a waterfall emanating from a rocky outcrop on the pool's southern edge. The sound of waves rushing onto the beach, the happy gurgling of the waterfall, and the constant song of tropical birds was a far cry from the busy, bustling, built-up environments of Monaco and the French Riviera—and vastly different from the neighborhood in Manhattan that the young model called home. Sierra sipped her drink and looked around. "Wow, who says that crime doesn't pay?"

Levi wasn't impressed with her casual remark. All that he could think of was the suffering, pain, and death that had paid, and was probably still being paid, for the opulence of Rodriguez's Mexican retreat. "Don't say things like that. It offends every fiber of my being." Sierra immediately regretted her thoughtless remark. "I'm sorry, Levi. You're right, that was unforgivable of me."

Rodriguez strode onto the terrace. "*Buenas noches,* sister. I do hope that your trip wasn't too uncomfortable." His movie-star good looks belied the evil creature that both Sierra and Levi knew lay beneath the charismatic facade.

"Our trip, dear brother, was unpleasant, uncomfortable, and unnecessary. Your men are repugnant hoodlums who should be hung up by their disgusting—"

Rodriguez abruptly cut her off. "But look around you, dear sister." he spread his arms, indicating the tropical paradise surrounding them. "Don't you think a that a small amount of discomfort at the beginning of your journey was well-worth the destination at its end?"

Levi knew that behind Rodriguez's wide smile lay the fangs and forked tongue of a deadly viper.

ψ

Jules Cadieux, a lieutenant in the defunct Marseilles gang once headed by Jean Durand, had been contacted by a woman who offered generous fees to men like him to eliminate people. Cadieux knew the woman by reputation only. He knew that she was a legendary assassin who detested hearing the word "no." He'd also heard that the woman always paid promptly after the kill had been confirmed. Whoever this Nick Palmer was, killing him would be worth the generous reward.

With visions of easy riches dancing in his head, he took the first available flight to the Mexican capital, where he enlisted the help of a local computer hacker. He paid the rail-thin woman, referred to him by one of his criminal associates in Marseille, to locate the hotel where Nick and his traveling companions were registered. Then he purchased a big .357 magnum Ruger GP100 handgun and lingered outside the hotel for his targets to appear. It didn't take long.

Cadieux's intended victim exited the hotel, paused, and looked around. The would-be killer raised his weapon and fired. Simultaneously, his intended target dropped to the pavement and the bullet slammed harmlessly into one of the building's impressive stone columns. It was as if the killer's intended victim had been warned.

Jules Cadieux was quickly tackled and pinned to the ground by a heavyset Mexican cop who was on duty near the hotel's front entrance. Nick leaped to his feet and rushed over to where the shooter was being held.

"Who the fuck are you, and why are you trying to kill me?"

The man twisted his head upward and stared defiantly at Nick. "Fuck you."

Before Nick could respond, the ear-piercing sound of sirens shattered the rarefied air of the city's exclusive Polanco district and a squad of police cars screeched to a halt at the hotel's front entrance.

A detective leaped out of the lead car, pushed her way through the small crowd of onlookers, and strode over to where Nick was standing. "Señor Palmer, very nice to see you again." She glanced over to where the would-be assassin was being led away by her colleagues. "Now, what the hell is this all about? Why did this *hombre* want to kill you?"

Nick shrugged. "I have no idea." He stopped talking and stared at the attractive detective. "Have we met before?"

The woman smiled. "*Si señor*, at Francisca's funeral—my name is Isabella Moreno. My mother was Francisca's sister."

ψ

Gabriela was in their room when she heard the gunshot. She ran downstairs, pushed her way through the small crowd of curious onlookers, ran out of the hotel, and rushed over to where Nick and Francisca's niece were standing. "Nick, what the hell's going on? Are you okay?" She turned toward the detective. "*Hola,* Isabella, lovely to see you again." She shook her head in feigned exasperation. "Perhaps you can tell me what's going on. My husband seems to be tongue-tied." Both women laughed at Nick's obvious discomfort.

"It is very serious, *señora*. A man attempted to kill your husband—fortunately for the *señor*, he stumbled. If he had remained on his feet, he would now be a dead man."

Gabriela spun around and faced Nick. "Rodriguez?"

"I think that's a real possibility," he replied.

ψ

"I didn't stumble. Henri yelled for me to get down just moments before I heard the shot." Nick and Gabriela were sitting next to each other on their suite's plush sofa. She had her arm draped over his shoulders. It had been almost twenty years since someone had tried to kill either of them, and this attack brought back memories that they both would prefer to forget.

Gabriela turned her eyes skyward and smiled. "Thank you, Henri, thank you for saving this hapless creature who I call my husband." The quiet moment was interrupted by the shrill sound of Nick's cell phone. He picked it up. "Nick Palmer here."

Gabriela watched as her husband's face contorted into a desolate mask of vulnerability. "What's happening, Nick?" The concern in her voice was palpable. Nick waved her away and continued listening to the woman on the other end of the call.

The words Nick that was listening to struck him like a thunderbolt, blasting every ounce of vitality from his body. His hands were shaking uncontrollably, his head felt as if a nail had been driven into his forehead, and a cold, clammy sweat enveloped his entire body. He leaped to his feet, hurled the phone against the wall, and strode around the room trying desperately to calm his frayed nerves.

He sat back down, reached over and pulled his wife closer. Gabriela pushed him away. "Who called? What's happening? Answer me, goddamn it!" Gabriela's nerves were nearly shot.

Nick was breathing heavily; it was if he'd just run a marathon. "That was Isabella on the phone." He took a deep breath, then slowly exhaled. "The police have interrogated the prick who took a shot at me and apparently it didn't take much coaxing to uncover his motive." He didn't tell Gabriela details about the harsh methodology the police had used to obtain the man's quick cooperation. "There's a bounty on our heads—a million bucks for me and a half million each for everyone in or close to our family, including Emilie and Luc."

Gabriela gasped. "That's Lucy, Madeline, Henri Jr., and me—he's painted a target on each of our backs. Oh my god, Nick, what are we going to do?" She began violently shaking, devastated with the possibility of losing her entire family—losing everything that she'd ever loved.

Nick held Gabriela tightly until her immediate terror had dissipated.

"You, me, Lucy, Luc, and Emilie are to stay put here in the hotel. That's a direct order from Isabella." Nick gently massaged the back of her neck. "She's providing round-the-clock police protection for us."

Gabriela pushed away. "But what about Madeline and Henri? She's in California and he's at university in Lyon."

Nick's mind was operating on steroids. "I've got an idea. I'll call Josh Nicholson." He stood and retrieved his cell from the floor, where it had landed—thankfully unbroken after he had thrown it. He called his former boss.

"Josh, it's Nick. You offered your help and now I really need it. What I'm asking you to do for me and Gabi is the biggest favor I've ever asked from anyone." Nick went on to describe everything that had transpired. "Would you take Madeline and Henri Jr. to Chicago and make sure that they're safe?"

Josh sounded dumbstruck. "Those goddamned bastards—sure I'll take them. The kids can stay with me and Mary until this whole shit show is over."

Nick breathed a huge sigh of relief and gave a thumbs up sign to Gabriela.

Josh immediately assumed the role of the police boss he once was. "You give Madeline the heads up, and I'll personally pick her up on my way back home. Then get hold of Henri Jr. and get him out of France—the sooner the better. Yesterday would have been best." Josh calmed down. "Y'know Nick, you, Gabi, and I still have a lot of friends in the Chicago force. They'll cover your kids like an iron blanket, so once we get them there, you guys can rest easy."

Nick hung up and told Gabriela to call their daughter in California. They needed to tell her about the danger that she was facing and coordinate arrangements for Josh to pick her up. Gabriela's call to their daughter elicited a response that was typical of the strong-willed young woman.

"But mom, the class is going on a scuba trip to Catalina tomorrow. It's part of the syllabus that I need to complete my term."

Gabriela had calmed down. "Being dead is permanent, Madi. If you stay alive, you'll have a thousand opportunities to go scuba diving, and complete your course. Expect a call from Josh Nicholson and get packed right now. You're going to Chicago with him."

Finding their son wasn't as easy. He wasn't answering his cell, and after several tries to reach him, Nick called Alain Moreau.

Alain had recently returned to the French capital after attending Francisca's funeral. "Alain, it's Nick. Can you call your contacts in the Lyon police department and have them find Henri Jr.?" He went on to explain the reason behind his urgent request.

"*Merde*, Nicholas. I'm on it. I'll have the boy call you as soon as we locate him."

Four hours later, the call that Nick and Gabriela were anxiously waiting for came in. "Hey, dad. What's happening? What's the panic? I was visiting Musée des Beaux-Arts with some friends when I was picked up by the police."

"Where are you now? And why weren't you answering your cell?"

The young man sounded exasperated. "For God's sake, dad, I'm at the police station, I turned off my phone earlier because I was in a museum."

Nick apologized and explained the situation to his son. Then he gave Henri Jr. explicit instructions. "Get packed and get on a flight to Chicago right now."

Josh Nicholson called Nick at the hotel in Mexico City. His call was put on speaker so that Gabriela could hear it too. "Rest easy, you two. Your brood is safe and secure at my house in Chicago, and Mary is hovering over them like a mother hen." Then his tone got more serious. "The place is surrounded with cops. Not even a fly could get in. Take care of yourselves. We'll talk soon." Relief filled the room like a warm cashmere blanket, and the distraught parents collapsed onto the sofa with relief. Gabriela buried her head against Nick's shoulder. "Wow, Josh is really something else, I don't think I know of anyone else who could have pulled off that retrieval job any faster."

Nick stood and looked down towards his wife. "The only problem now is that Sierra and Levi will have to go it alone. We can't risk going out to help them."

"We always have Henri and the angels on our side though," Gabriela said hopefully. "And Isabella Moreno too. If she's anything like her aunt, she's a force to be reckoned with."

CHAPTER FORTY-SIX

CCTV footage from surveillance cameras installed both inside and outside of Enrique Ortega's opulent mountainside hacienda were reviewed by an elite group of specialists at Mexico City's police department. The carnage that these men and women were witnessing was more horrific than any action film and infinitely more violent than many of the skirmishes' the officers viewing the screens had ever been involved in—the blood-splattered lenses on some of the cameras brought home, in nauseating detail, sickening evidence of the deadly assault.

An officer, in his mid-twenties, called over to one of his colleagues to see something on his computer screen. *"Ven aquí y echa un vistazo a esto. Qué piensas de esto?"*

His colleague leaned in to take a closer look then asked the man to blow up the image. It showed a beautiful woman and a thin man with a dark complexion being herded into the rear seat of the first of two black SUVs. The men were armed, and the passengers seemed reluctant to enter the vehicle. The footage was obviously taken before the surprise attack on the drug lord's compound.

"Deberíamos informar al Detective Moreno," the man's colleague said as she grabbed her cell phone.

ψ

Isabella Moreno was at her desk filling out paperwork on the attempted assassination of Nick Palmer when a call from the officers reviewing the security footage came in. She listened to what they had to say, grabbed her jacket from the back of her chair, and rushed downstairs to where footage from the hacienda was being reviewed and analyzed.

"Show me the footage." Her tone of voice was kind but authoritative. She leaned into the screen and pointed to the two seemingly reluctant passengers being herded into the cars. "That, I believe, is the famous model Sierra Petersen, and the other person fits the description of the Israeli guy that Nicholas Palmer told me about."

She had a second request. "Blow up the image so that I can see the license plate." The young officer did as the detective requested. "Those idiots." She shot her two junior colleagues a look of pure contempt. "Don't they know that plate numbers mean that we can easily track them down?"

Isabella hastily jotted the license numbers in her notebook. *"Gracias chicos, due un gran trabajo."*

Isabella returned to her desk and called her contact at the city's licensing division. *"Buenos dias, señorita.* Detective Isabella Moreno here. Can you quickly find out who's the registered owner for this plate number?" She slowly read out the number. "They're Jalisco plates—will that be a problem?" She was referring to the Mexican state on the country's Pacific coast.

The woman answered, *"No hay problema detective,"* and less than two minutes later, copies of the SUV's registration documents appeared on Isabella's computer screen.

The detective swore under her breath. *"Maldita sea,* there're no names, just numbered companies." Her next calls were to the Registro Publico dela Propiedad y de Comercio office in Mexico City, and because some companies are oftentimes registered in one, or more, of country's many states, she called the corresponding government office in Jalisco.

ψ

When Levi woke, it was 3:20 a.m., and he was sweating profusely. The covers on his bed were scattered over the floor—positive proof of his restless sleep. The nightmares he'd been experiencing since the wanton shooting and death of his friends at the café in Palestine were getting worse—worse to the point of being unbearable. The staccato sounds of gunfire, the blood, the devastation, the twisted, mutilated bodies of his fallen comrades, and his many long months of agonizing recuperation and recovery filled his dreams. *It'll soon be over*, he thought. *Once Rodriguez and his rabid congregation of followers are destroyed, it will all be over.*

He got up, opened the curtains, and looked out through the window. The moonlight was as bright as the midday sun, and long shadows of Rodriguez's heavily armed guards crisscrossed the gardens like silent sentinels of impending death.

He picked the blankets from off the floor and climbed back into bed, hoping his horrific dreams would fail to continue, and that finally he'd be able to capture the sleep that he so desperately needed.

ψ

The alfresco breakfast at Rodriguez's hacienda was as abundant as the greenery surrounding the terrace: huevos rancheros, papas con chorizo, breakfast burritos, baskets of freshly picked fruit, crystal jugs of juice, and sweet pillowy sapodillas filled the buffet table to overflowing. Sierra was famished and filled her plate with every delicious morsel. Rodriguez and Ortiz sat opposite her at the shaded table, quietly sipping coffee.

Levi strolled onto the terrace, picked out a burrito and a glass of pineapple juice from the buffet, and joined them.

Rodriguez looked at both of his captives in turn. "I do hope that your accommodations were satisfactory, and that you both enjoyed a good night's sleep." He raised his cup and took another sip. "We're going to be staying here for two or three days—to relax and refresh ourselves from our travels. Then we'll be flying to Mexico City." Both Sierra and Levi shot him a questioning look. He smiled. "I have an important meeting to attend, a meeting requiring both of your participation." He stood. "Now, if you'll please excuse me, I have some pressing business to take care of." The man turned. "I will fill you in on all of the details before we take off." Ortiz followed Rodriguez into his private office.

Sierra leaned into her companion and whispered, "Do you think that he's taking us to the conclave of apostles?"

Levi replied, "Possibly, but how do we contact Nick and the others to tell them what's happening? This place is as secure as a bank vault."

ψ

Nick had never felt so helpless. The room felt more like a prison than an elegant suite in one of the world's most famous hotels, his only consolation was the knowledge that his two youngest children were safely ensconced in Chicago with Josh and Mary Nicholson.

He turned toward the others. "Goddamn it, nothing's getting done. We're wasting precious time being here, locked up in the hotel like privileged criminals." Gabriela, Lucy, and the Faucher siblings felt the same way but were more reserved in expressing their frustration.

Emilie was nervously shaking her knee as she sat. "I wish that we knew what's happened to Sierra and Levi. Are they still alive? Or has Rodriguez murdered them?"

Gabriela put her arms around the distraught young woman. "I'm sure they're fine, but I agree with Nick. We've got to get out of here and get on with it." The problem was that none of them knew what the "it" was, or even what they'd do if they did know.

ψ

Isabella Moreno's call to Jalisco's corporate registration offices got the results that she was looking for. The numbered corporate entity named on the vehicles' registration documents was Kukulkan Investment Corporation, a financial services company based in Mexico City. The detective had heard the name before; either from her aunt, or possibly from her grandfather. She opened her computer and searched the name—two results flashed onto her screen. The first was a corporation's website, which needed a password for her to gain access. The second listing took her breath away. "Kukulkan is the name of a Mesoamerican serpent deity worshipped by the Yucatec Mayan people before the Spanish conquest of their homeland. The depiction of the feathered serpent is closely related to the Aztec deity that worshipped the snake god Quetzalcoatl."

The correlation between the name of the financial services company and the organization of evil headed by Philippe Rodriguez was irrefutable—she grabbed her jacket, told the desk officer that she was going to see Nick and Gabriela at their hotel, and rushed out of the station.

CHAPTER FORTY-SEVEN

Sierra was lounging on one of the terrace's beautiful handwoven hammocks flipping through a Spanish fashion magazine from the large stack of periodicals on the library's round table.

"Are you enjoying your second day in paradise?" Rodriguez's seemingly innocuous question caught her by surprise. "We'll be leaving for Mexico City the day after tomorrow, and there's a lot we need to discuss before we depart."

He pulled up a chair. "As my half-sister and only relative, your birthright is preordained and as such you will be seated to the right of me during the meeting that we'll be attending." Sierra dropped the magazine and stared at Rodriguez, who continued his dialogue as if it was a normal conversation between two friends—or two family members.

"It's a meeting of the apostles of La Orden de las Serpientes de Cristo, a religious order founded many centuries ago by our ancestors."

Her half-brother appeared to be choosing his words more carefully. "The order is the bedrock of our power and the fountain from which many of our other business enterprises have sprung." He waved for an attendant to bring lemonade for them both. "Some of these ventures may, at first, seem repugnant to you, but as you will soon discover, they also fund many of the charities that I'm associated with."

Sierra couldn't believe his justification for the heinous crimes that he was said to have committed.

Rodriguez crossed his legs. "The apostles—call them the board of directors if you wish—are comprised of experts in each of the fields they represent. Each apostle runs a separate division of the Order, and each of them reports directly to me." He paused again. "Ronaldo Ortiz, who you've recently met, is one of the Order's most senior apostles. You'll meet all the others at the meeting."

Their lemonades arrived and were placed on a table by a solemn, immaculately dressed attendant. Taking a sip, Rodriguez continued. "Levi Heifetz will stand guard inside the doors of the meeting room. Other formidable followers of the order will be positioned outside the doors and throughout the building." He stood and smiled down at the woman. "There's much more that I have to tell you, but that must wait for another time."

Sierra watched her half-brother walk away. *Jesus Christ. Because we have this crazy, tenuous relationship, he believes that he can trust me.*

Rodriguez found Ortiz berating a groundskeeper. "Ronaldo, do me a favor and keep a close eye on our guests for me. I'd like to know, minute-by-minute, exactly what they're up to."

ψ

The cordon of police officers surrounding the famous hotel's front entrance, and sentinels guarding the building's other doors, didn't deter a small group of reporters from lingering, paparazzi-like, within viewing range of the hotel. Among them, acting as if she was intrigued by what was happening, was a sharpshooter from Canada.

The woman, who registered with a false passport, was known as Mrs. Abigale Rose. She looked to be in her mid-sixties, she had a cheerful disposition, and a slight limp necessitating her using a cane. When she checked into the hotel, her luggage was thoroughly searched by the police and, satisfied that it contained nothing dangerous or concerning, she was handed the key card to her room and directed to the bank of elevators.

Over the ensuing days, Mrs. Rose spent her time visiting art galleries and museums, and shopping in the area's many designer shops. She always returned to the hotel with shopping bags, which were duly removed from her taxi and searched by the police. Nothing suspicious was ever found, and as the days wore on the ritual of searching the elderly woman's bags lessened to a point of being neglected altogether—this was exactly what the killer knew would happen. Earned trust, she'd learned, was an integral part of everyone's DNA, and wide smiles, coupled with generous tips, always helped speed the way in which trust was attained.

Piece by piece, over the following several days, various components of her custom, state-of-the-art sniper rifle were successfully smuggled into her room in the shopping bags she always carried when returning to the hotel.

During the evenings, Mrs. Rose did her due diligence. Through casual conversations with staff and by carefully observing the comings and goings of various police and security personnel, she soon discovered the location of the suite housing Nicholas Palmer and his wife, and the adjacent rooms occupied by his daughter and her two young friends. The rest, she believed, would be easy. She'd already selected her shooting position on the roof opposite the Palmer's room, which had a direct line of sight into both their living room and bedroom.

The seemingly innocent elderly woman sat on the bed and assembled her deadly weapon. First, she dismantled her cane. She carefully slid the rifle's barrel out of the hollow shaft, then shook four high-velocity bullets from the cane's handle. Next, she expertly pieced together the remaining components, and finally, attached the scope and sound suppressor. She lifted the rifle to her shoulder and checked to confirm that the weapon's scope was aligned. Satisfied that all was as it should be, she laid the weapon on the bed and anticipated her next move.

ψ

Isabella Moreno knocked on the door to Nick and Gabriela's hotel suite and was quickly ushered into the luxurious accommodations. "Pack your bags. We're moving you guys out of here."

"Why? Aren't we safe here?" asked Nick.

"Just standard procedure here in Mexico." She was lying, but the detective's little fib got the desired results, and soon the three of them were packed and ready to leave the comfort and safety of the hotel.

"So, where are you taking us? And what about Luc and Emilie?" Lucy asked.

"We've already taken Luc and Emilie to a hotel in Centro. Don't worry, they're under twenty-four-hour guard, both inside and outside of their suite."

"Why in hell's name didn't you tell me sooner. I've been worried sick that I hadn't heard from them." Nick was jabbing his finger at the detective.

"Sorry Nick. I felt it was better for their safety that we separate you, and I instructed them not to contact you until after I'd spoken to you."

Nick was about to yell at Isabella, but Gabriela held him back.

"Thank you, Isabella. Now please tell us where we're going." Gabriela's voice was much more consolatory than her husbands.

"Not far—and I think that you'll like it." Said the officer wearily.

ψ

A tight circle of combat-trained police surrounded them as they left the hotel's front entrance and covered them as they got into the two black SUVs. The driver of their vehicle tapped the window with his knuckle. "*A prueba de balas.*"

Isabella smiled. "He's letting us know that the car is bulletproof."

The two-car convey pulled away from the hotel's front entrance and drove away in the direction of the city's historic district.

Abigale Rose witnessed their departure and shrugged. *Oh well, I guess I'll have to make alternate arrangements.*

She went back into the hotel, slipped the doorman a generous tip, and went up to her room to dismantle her weapon and pack. She smiled to herself. *I don't believe that I'll have to smuggle these things out of here. I'm sure they won't be checking the luggage of departing guests.*

ψ

The bulletproof SUVs carrying Nick and Gabriela, Lucy, and Isabella pulled into the courtyard of the Palacio Nacional on the east side of the Zócalo. They were transferred into two innocuous sedans which drove out of the massive building's main door and turned back in the direction that the group had just recently left.

While they were being driven to their next destination, Isabella Moreno took the opportunity to appraise Nick about what she'd unearthed. "Kukulkan Investment Corporation is a global financial services company headquartered here in Mexico City. I believe that with a little more digging we'll find out that it's headed by Philippe Rodriguez."

"What the hell does 'Kukulkan' mean?" questioned Nick.

Isabella described the word's meaning.

"So," Lucy responded, "Kukulkan and Quetzalcoatl could be interchangeable—both are Mesoamerican snake gods."

Isabella nodded. "*Si*, and I believe that the coincidence is far too obvious to ignore."

"Do you know where their offices are located?"

"*Si*. Not far from where you'll be staying next."

The balance of their ride to the new hotel, on Paseo de la Reforma, was spent in silence.

ψ

Abigale Rose's taxi pulled up in front of the hotel she'd booked for the remainder of her stay in the Mexican capital. She was standing at the reception desk when she was distracted by the arrival of new guests. The newcomers were whisked directly into a waiting elevator. It was Nicholas Palmer, his wife, and Lucy, his daughter. She raised her eyes to the ceiling and thanked God for giving her a second chance at winning the multi-million-dollar jackpot.

CHAPTER FORTY-EIGHT

"We're leaving for Mexico City tomorrow."

Sierra was in Rodriguez's sumptuous living room, flipping through the same Spanish fashion magazine that she was looking at earlier. One of the photographs taken of her on an earlier shoot graced the front cover, and there was also a six-page spread of other pictures of her on the inside pages. She wondered if photographs from the shoot she had just completed in Paris would get the same amount of exposure, and whether she'd even be around to see them.

Rodriguez took the periodical from out of her hands and gazed at the image. "*Muy hermosa hermana*." His acknowledgment that she was beautiful did little to change her opinion about her half-brother.

"What other tidbits do I need to know about the meeting?" Her tone was ambivalent.

"Well, little sister, I guess that this is as good a time as any to tell you about some of the order's other businesses." He sat next to her and took a moment before speaking again. It was as if he was carefully considering what his next words should be.

"As I mentioned earlier, some of what I'm about to tell you may seem repugnant, but it is necessary that you understand the full extent of our business operations so that you, in case of my demise, can carry on the family business." He stopped speaking and stared at Sierra. His dark eyes seared into her inner being and touched the very core of her pride, her ego, and her conviction of what is right and what is wrong. It was like an inquisition, a test of her loyalty to him and to the depraved organization that he headed.

Then he smiled. "I'm very old fashioned. I believe that family comes first, and loyalty to family is a bond that cannot be broken." His thoughts flashed back to his mother. *But sometimes it is necessary to cut one's losses, no matter what the cost.*

He continued. "I trust you, because you are family by birthright, and I trust Heifetz because he saved my life." *But I don't trust him unconditionally*, he thought.

"The disagreeable parts of our business are mostly illegal, and our partners and associates in these businesses are what you'd call scum of the earth." He let his words sink in. "The family firm has very lucrative ventures in extortion, drug smuggling, slavery, arms dealing, money laundering, online pornography, and such." He looked toward Sierra, as if trying to gauge her reaction. "The more acceptable sides of our enterprises include real estate, financial services, insurance, shipping, energy, hotels, and hospitality."

Rodriguez's mood darkened. "However, if you tell anyone about what you've just heard, or what you will hear at the conclave, family or not, famous or not, beautiful or not, you will be dead." The threat was delivered through the man's clenched white teeth.

He stood to leave but had one more request. "You know, Sierra. It is customary that before the conclave, we must share a bed." A lascivious smile momentarily flashed across his handsome face.

ψ

Nick had unpacked his suitcase and was checking out every nook and cranny in their new suite. Gabriela and Lucy were still consumed with unpacking and hanging up their clothes. Nick's cell rang. He checked the display and saw Luc's name on the screen. "Hi, Luc. How are you and Emilie doing? Is everything okay?"

"*Nous sommes très bien,* Nick. Isabella booked us into an amazing hotel in Centro. Our rooms are fantastic and overlook the Zócalo, that's the huge square in front of the cathedral." Luc continued talking; his excitement growing with every spoken word. "This morning we watched the Mexican military raise the biggest damn flag you've ever seen and then, later in the evening, they did the same maneuver in reverse."

Nick inhaled deeply, then smiled. He'd been worried about the Faucher siblings. "So, what else have you guys been up to?"

Emilie answered. "We took a sightseeing tour on a double-decker bus, visited the Museo Nacional de Antropologia, then went to the Frida Kahlo Museum, and also saw Leon Trotsky's former house."

Luc interrupted his sister. "I've also been online, keeping track of Rodriguez."

"Any news on that front?" Nick said hopefully.

"Not too much. Only one thing. Rodriguez's pilot just filed a flight plan—Puerto Vallarta to Mexico City. They're taking off tomorrow." Luc burst out laughing.

Nick playfully admonished the young man. "You little bugger, I'll get you for that one day. Stay safe and stay in touch."

Gabriela and Lucy entered the room. "Who called?" they asked in unison.

Nick filled them in on his conversation with Luc, then he called Isabella.

ψ

"That's one fucking thing that's definitely never going to happen." Sierra was telling Levi about the last thing Rodriguez had said to her. "No goddamned way that I'm going to share a bed with that prick."

"And how do you propose to tell him?"

"Easy. I'll tell him the truth."

Levi looked confused.

"I'll just tell him that I'm gay. That women turn me on, not men."

"You and Lucy Palmer?"

"No, Lucy and I are just good friends. No sex involved." *Although sometimes I wish there was*, she thought.

"I hope that he believes you," Levi replied.

ψ

Flights from all four corners of the earth began arriving at Mexico City's sprawling international airport. Ten of these flights carried apostles of La Orden de las Serpientes de Cristo. Nick's call to Isabella Moreno about Rodriguez's flight plan spurred her into action, and within the hour, she had members of the city's impressive police force watching passengers disembark. They were looking, to no avail, for any suspicious-looking travelers.

Isabella called Nick to break the news to him. "*Lo siento*, Nick. We've got nothing."

"These people are affluent, and they'll only be staying in town for a day or two," Nick replied. "Perhaps you should check who's registering at the city's luxury hotels, and also keep an eye on the building where Kukulkan Investment Corporation offices are located." He hung up and turned toward Gabriela and Lucy. "Goddamn it, I wish I knew what's happened to Sierra and Levi."

ψ

Sierra was alone in her bedroom when she was disturbed by a knock on the door. Rodriguez strode in uninvited. He was wearing a bathrobe and nothing else. "Tomorrow the conclave begins. Tonight, we'll consummate our bond." He slipped off his bathrobe and let it pool around his ankles.

"Sorry to disappoint you, Brother, but I'm gay. All men, even men as handsome as you, don't turn me on."

Rodriguez stopped in his tracks, then smiled. "Don't worry, Sister, that doesn't bother me one little bit. He strode over to the bed, forcibly shoved Sierra down onto her back, and began tearing at her clothes.

Sierra had years of practice dealing with the unwanted advances of men. She reached down, grabbed Rodriguez's testicles then pulled, squeezed, and twisted. When her fingernails tore into the skin of his scrotum, her depraved half-brother let out an agonized scream. He lifted his fist and tried to hit her, but his feeble response resulted in a brutal head butt from his would-be victim. The blow broke Rodriguez's nose, triggering a cascade of blood from both nostrils.

He jumped up and screamed, "You fucking evil bitch."

Sierra released her grip on his swollen manhood. "Then I guess we're very much alike—you fucking evil bastard."

Rodriguez stomped from the room, one hand holding his groin and the other clutching his robe, which he held to his nose. "Get me a fucking doctor," he screamed at Levi. Levi smiled at the man's obvious discomfort and did as he was instructed.

Sierra went to her bathroom, slid into the shower, and washed the blood and anger from her mind and body. When she stepped out, she wiped the steam from the mirror, and watched as her reflection morphed into the face of Jessica Devlin, the young American girl who was sacrificed in Paris. "*Merci*, Mademoiselle Petersen. You did to Hector Rodriguez's son what we all wished we could have done." The girl's smiling image faded and vanished.

CHAPTER FORTY-NINE

Abigale Rose settled into her new room. Because she had registered prior to Nick and his family's arrival, the usual police security protocols weren't in place at the hotel's entrances. The elderly killer carefully unpacked the components of her sniper rifle, dismantled her cane, screwed the barrel onto the weapon's assembled parts, attached the skeleton-like stock, and finally secured the scope to the top of the rifle's action. She lifted the rifle to her shoulder, peered through the scope, and visualized her target, Nicholas Palmer, in the weapon's crosshairs. Next, she hid the gun underneath the room's king-size bed and removed a breakaway travel cane from her luggage. She left her room and limped convincingly to the lobby to chat with some of the hotel's staff. She hoped that her lucky streak would hold and that she'd be able to garner information regarding the location of the Palmer family's hotel suite.

ψ

Intelligence officers from Mexico City's army-sized police force were contacting the city's most luxurious hotels. Their efforts were oftentimes thwarted because the influx of tourists checking in to enjoy the capital's many attractions made isolating members of La Orden de las Serpientes de Cristo virtually impossible.

Additional officers were taking up discrete positions outside the contemporary high-rise office tower on Paseo de la Reforma where the corporate headquarters of Kukulkan Investment Corporation were said to be located. They conducted random checks of visitors to the huge building, but they too had to admit defeat.

Isabella Moreno had also dispatched officers to Licenciado Adolfo Mateos International Airport in Toluca. Located just forty kilometers west of the city, it was the preferred facility for private jets flying in and out of Mexico City. Her hope was that Philippe Rodriguez's jet would land and that her police colleagues would be able to identify the deplaning passengers. This tactic was a long shot. Because it was a domestic flight, emanating from Puerto Vallarta, normal customs and immigration procedures were virtually nonexistent, and it wouldn't be unheard of for deplaning passengers to pass through the executive terminal unnoticed.

ψ

Because of the injuries inflicted upon him by Sierra, Rodriguez's flight was delayed. His broken nose was treated with a continual application of ice packs, but his two black eyes and injured scrotum were said to require no treatment. "The swelling and coloration of your eyes and testicles will take time to heal, it could be a week or two, or perhaps even a little longer," the doctor had said.

The doctor's prognosis did little to soothe Rodriguez's pent-up anger. Then he smiled. *The bitch is tough. She'll be perfect for our organization.*

Rodriguez sought out his head of security. "Levi, call the pilot and tell her that we'll be taking off in a couple of hours. Then tell my fucking sister to get ready to leave."

ψ

NEXT OF KIN

The flight from Puerto Vallarta to Mexico City took a little over an hour. Rodriguez had already been notified that all the apostles had arrived in Mexico City. Each of them was registered under a false name in different luxury hotels throughout the city. He'd informed each of them that the conclave would take place on the evening of the following day. He'd yet to share the location of his meeting with the cadre of evil. *I do hope they'll like my little surprise*, he thought to himself.

One hour before wheels up, Rodriguez, Sierra, Levi, and Ortiz were picked up by two black SUV's and driven to Puerto Vallarta's international airport. The disparate little group was escorted through the airport's VIP Lounge and taken onto the tarmac to Rodriguez's waiting jet.

The pilot expressed concern when she saw her injured employer. "*Señor Rodríguez, ¿que passó? ¿Estás bien?*"

Rodriguez waved the woman away. "*Estoy bien, solo un pequeño accidente.*" Then he took his normal seat, up front on the left-hand side, directly facing the bulkhead.

Sierra sat in the second row across the aisle from Levi, and Ortiz sat in the row behind them.

The pilot received clearance from the tower and the aircraft taxied onto the runway. The jet accelerated, took off into the clear blue Mexican sky, banked over Banderas Bay, and headed southeast toward their destination.

ψ

Abigale Rose had carefully selected her *nest*, the term commonly used by military personnel to describe a location offering the best line of sight for a sniper to accomplish their mission.

She'd learned from her conversations with some of the hotel's staff that the Palmer family usually took breakfast on the terrace next to the swimming pool. Her shooting position, on the third floor directly opposite the terrace, was where she waited on the day before the conclave was scheduled to occur.

As if on cue, Nick, Gabriela, and Lucy, accompanied by two plainclothes police officers charged with protecting them, strolled out onto the terrace—they were totally unaware of the danger facing them. An attractive hostess seated them at a poolside table and a server stood by to take their breakfasts orders.

Abigale lifted the rifle to her shoulder and was about to shoot when a bus boy delivering coffee to the table obstructed her view of Nick, her prime target. She lowered the weapon and waited for the boy to leave.

Then something strange happened. She heard a loud, authoritative voice.

"Put the weapon down. Put it down NOW!"

She spun around, expecting to see a police officer, but no one was there. *What the hell? My mind must be playing tricks with me.* She once again raised the rifle to her shoulder.

Simultaneously, a third officer, also charged with protecting Nick and his family, heard a similar ethereal voice. "The killer is on the third floor overlooking the terrace."

The officer looked up and saw the glint of light reflecting off the weapon's barrel. He pushed Nick to the ground and screamed *"Refugiarse!"* at Gabi and Lucy, telling them to take cover. Then he made a mad dash up the stairs to assist his colleague who had already tackled the startled woman. Before Abigale Rose hit the ground, her finger squeezed the weapon's trigger. Her shot went wide and hit the officer standing next to Nick. The bullet slammed into the woman's chest, sending a spray of blood and fragments of flesh over a group of terrified guests who, until that moment, were enjoying their meal of breakfast burritos, fresh juice, and coffee in the warm, sun-dappled paradise.

The officer who tackled the killer called for reinforcements, and within minutes the elderly woman was dragged, kicking and screaming profanities, into a waiting police vehicle.

Gabriela and Lucy were crouched under the table with Nick, who was trying to cover them with his body. The screams of guests and hotel staff filled the air, and women at an adjacent table were clawing at their faces and clothing, trying desperately to scrape off the gory fragments of the slain cop.

Nick and his family were hustled back to their suite and told to lock the door. Lucy burst into tears and began to shake. Nick and Gabriela tried to comfort their daughter, but nothing they said, or did, could consoled her.

ψ

Later that morning, the officer who'd tackled the killer reported to Isabella Moreno, he didn't tell his superior that his hunch was an unearthly voice instructing him what to do. She might think that the pressure of his job had finally pushed him to the edge of insanity.

It wasn't until later that Nick thought about the thwarted attempt on his life. *Strange. I didn't get any kind of warning from Henri or from any of the other ghosts of angels.*

ψ

Rodriguez's jet touched down at the airport in Toluca and glided effortlessly to the private terminal. Two dark gray SUVs were waiting in front of the terminal's arrival doors, ready to whisk them to Rodriguez's gated residence in Polanco, Mexico City's most exclusive neighborhood.

"Relax, we'll be there in an hour or so." Rodriguez was speaking to Sierra, the only other passenger in the lead vehicle. Levi Heifetz and Ortiz followed closely behind in a second, identical car.

"Won't the apostles wonder what happened to your face?" Sierra asked.

"Not if they want to live," was the man's terse reply. Secretly, he knew that the gold snake mask he wore at every conclave would cover his facial injuries.

Exactly ninety minutes from the time they deplaned, the two-car convoy pulled up to the iron gates of Rodriguez's home, a starkly modern hacienda comprised of imposing multicolored angular walls. The lead driver punched in the code, the massive gate swung open, and the cars pulled up in front of a home comparable to what Sierra had only seen in high-end decor books and magazines.

Rodriguez smiled at Sierra's look of absolute wonderment. *"Mi casa, su casa."*

CHAPTER FIFTY

An unmarked police car carrying Isabella Moreno and two other officers had followed the SUVs from the airport and watched as they vanished inside the gates of Rodriguez's home. The detective pulled her cell from her purse and called Nick. "Rodriguez, Sierra, Heifetz, and a thug called Ronaldo Ortiz have just pulled into a house in Polanco." She paused. "I ran a check to find out who the owns the place, and big surprise, I discovered that the house's owner is a registered a numbered company in Bermuda."

"I'll you bet dollars to donuts that it's owned by Rodriguez," Nick replied. "Is there any way you can get in for a closer look?"

"No, I don't think so. The place, as far as I can see, is crawling with armed guards. I've requested a revolving stakeout, so they won't be able to make a move without us knowing it." Isabella ended the call.

ψ

The luxury condominium building located directly behind Rodriguez's villa was built many years earlier by a development company owned, indirectly, by Hector Rodriguez and La Orden de las Serpientes de Cristo. During its construction, a secret tunnel was built between the two buildings. This subterranean passage emanated in the villa's basement and exited into one of the condominium's lower parking garages. It was a well-planned escape hatch built by Hector Rodriguez in the event he needed to elude any unwanted intrusion into the main house. Only his son Philippe, his daughter Angelina, and a few trusted colleagues, most of whom were now deceased or incarcerated, knew of its existence.

"Are the cops still outside the gates?" Rodriguez's question was directed toward Ronaldo Ortiz.

"*Si, patrón*, they're still there."

"If they're still there tomorrow, we'll use the tunnel."

Ortiz had heard rumors about the underground passage, but until that very second, didn't know of its existence.

"We'll leave at exactly seven tomorrow evening. Make sure that our guests are ready." He motioned for Ortiz to leave him.

Rodriguez went to his office, pulled his laptop from its bag, and sent an encrypted message to the group of apostles waiting in various locations throughout the Mexican capital. The secret message revealed the location where the conclave would be held. *I'll bet that will be a big surprise for them,* he smiled at the thought.

ψ

Sierra was in her room. There seemed to be a hundred scenarios racing through her head. *I wonder how this is all going to play out.*

There was a gentle tap on her door. "Sierra, it's Levi. Can I come in?"

She unlocked and opened the door.

Levi put his finger to his lips, indicating that she shouldn't speak. Then he searched the suite for any hidden microphones or cameras. "Would you like to go for a predinner walk? The gardens are amazing, and I know that you haven't seen them yet."

The pair left the room, passed several guards, and wandered out into Rodriguez's tropical paradise. One of the guards followed them.

As per his instructions, he kept a discrete distance between himself and his spiritual leader's guests.

The hacienda's central courtyard boasted an enormous fountain. The sound of splashing and gurgling water pouring from a horizontal spigot in the pale blue palisade provided Levi with the cover he needed to speak to Sierra. They sat, close to each other, on a bench carved from one gigantic piece of pink granite.

Levi leaned in and whispered, "Both of our rooms have cameras and microphones, so be very careful about what you say or do."

"Jesus, Levi. I'm scared. The conclave is tomorrow, and I have no idea how we're going to take down Rodriguez—and I'm not even sure that I can do it."

Levi saw the look of terror and apprehension in Sierra's eyes.

He placed his hand on her shoulder. "Don't worry. I wish I had a plan, but with all of Rodriguez's bloody secrecy, it's been impossible to predict his moves."

Sierra turned and looked directly into Levi's dark eyes. She had questions that needed answers.

Levi saw her apprehension. He gently squeezed her shoulder to reassure her, then continued, "But, based on all that I've experienced, an opportunity will always reveal itself."

A guard walked over. "*Pardon señor, señorita.* I've been asked to inform you that dinner will be served in forty-five minutes."

The two friends walked back to their rooms to change for what might very well be their last supper.

ψ

A selection of Mexican-inspired canapés was passed around by a white-jacketed member of Rodriguez's household staff. Tall glasses of champagne were poured, and the host proposed a toast. "To my honored guests, particularly my newly found sister, and to tomorrow's special conclave." He was about to continue, but a gentle chime calling them to dinner interrupted whatever he'd planned to say next. Rodriguez shrugged. "We'll finish our conversation after we've enjoyed our dinner." He stood and led them into the house.

ψ

The dining room in Rodriguez's house was dazzling. The walls were brightly painted in homage, Sierra believed, to Luis Barragán, but unlike the eminent Mexican architect's minimalist aesthetic, the walls featured original paintings by some of the country's most revered artists: Frida Kahlo, Jose Clemente Orozco, Rufino Tamayo, and two particularly disturbing works; one by David Alfaro Siqueiros, and the second by José Guadalupe Posada. A huge, marble-topped table, which could easily seat at least twenty guests, occupied place-of-pride at the center of the room.

Sierra strolled from one painting to another, admiring each masterpiece. Before she'd switched her major from art history to economics, she had planned on entering the world of art galleries, museums, and auction houses. Rodriguez joined her. "Beautiful, are they not? Art has been a passion of our family for generations, and I'm delighted that you share our obsession."

There were four place settings at one end of the long table. Reflections from a dazzling array of candles danced off crystal stemware, fine porcelain tableware, and gleaming silver cutlery.

The first course, posole, was described by the host as a pre-Hispanic dish once used as part of ritual sacrifices—the analogy wasn't lost on his guests.

What followed were five additional courses, each more delicious than its predecessor. Finally, dessert, strong coffee, and port. Cuban cigars were offered to each of the guests. Only Rodriguez and Ortiz picked one from the ornate rosewood humidor.

The diners moved back onto the terrace. Rodriguez turned toward his guests. "Tomorrow is going to be a very special day for all of us.

I suggest that we retire early, get lots of rest, and gather again for breakfast in the morning. Good night. Sleep well." He stood, left the remnants of his still-glowing cigar in an ashtray, and walked into the house. The others quickly followed.

ψ

Outside the gates, the shift had changed. Now two new police officers sat in an unmarked car, waiting for something, anything, to happen. It would be a painfully long and boring night for the two young detectives.

CHAPTER FIFTY-ONE

Abigale Rose was interrogated by senior members of Mexico City's homicide division. She lied, saying the bounty that had been placed on the heads of Nick and Gabriela's family was extended by an unknown person. She said that she was told about the opportunity by someone in Toronto. "I don't know the person's name. I never met them. I don't even know if it was a man or woman." Rose paused and took a long drink from a water bottle. "The deal was brokered on the dark web, and I received details of the assignment by courier."

"Can you give us the name of the courier?"

She laughed. "Sure, it was John Doe. I didn't see him drop the package at my door and didn't see what kind of car he came in. If you haven't got any more questions, I'd like to go back to my cell."

"Just one more—if you were successful in killing Señor Palmer, how were you going to get the money?"

"Easy. The cash would have been delivered, just like the instructions for the assignment were." Her expression changed to one of cruel annoyance. "Less, of course, because of the middleman's forty percent fee. Now can I go?"

After the woman left, the two cops looked at each other. "*Lástima que suspendieron la pina de muerte.*"

After the interview with Abigale Rose, Isabella met the officers who had conducted the interrogation at their desks in the station's bullpen. "Any luck?"

The man and woman just shook their heads. "*Nada*, Isabella," the female officer said, "but before we questioned her, we sent her prints to the cops in Toronto to see if they could help us identify the woman."

Isabella had a conflicted look of frustration and dogged determination on her face. "And?"

"We just got a response." The female officer turned her computer so that Isabella could see the screen. "Her real name is Ava Rojas. She has a rap sheet stretching from Canada to Africa to South America and every country in Europe and the Far East. Lots of arrests but no convictions."

Isabella scratched her head. "*Rojas* is a Spanish name. Did the cops in Toronto find out if she had any connection to Rodriguez?"

"Not directly, but they believe that her brother worked for Hector Rodriguez."

"Ask them if they could find out when and where she traveled. Then let's see if her trips coincide with any unsolved murders." She turned to leave, then swiveled around. "*Gracias*. The Rojas woman will rot in jail for killing a cop, and I'm sure we'll unearth lots of other homicides."

Isabella walked toward her office. *Hopefully some of the murders that Rojas committed will allow us to get closure on some other very nasty murders here in Mexico.*

ψ

If the circumstances had been different, Nick, Gabriela, and Lucy would have enjoyed their stay in the warmth and sunshine of Mexico. As it was, they were all on tenterhooks, not knowing what was happening to Sierra and not knowing when someone else might try to kill them.

"I can't live like this." Lucy was in tears. Mascara was running down her flushed cheeks from her swollen red eyes. She ran into the bathroom to splash water on her face and clean off her smeared makeup.

The ghostly apparition of Henri Deneuve appeared in the mirror before her. "Do not worry, *chérie*, it will soon be over, and although harm will befall someone you care for, retribution will descend heavily upon the head of the serpent."

"Who? When? Where?" Lucy screamed at the mirror, but the countenance of the elderly scholar had already faded and vanished. She held tightly to the edges of the sink and tears, like tiny rivers, poured from her eyes.

"Lucy, are you okay?" This question, which came from her father, resulted in another round of uncontrollable sobbing.

Lucy finally opened the door and faced Nick and Gabriela. "Henri appeared in the mirror. He said that someone close is going to be hurt." She fell into Gabriela's arms. Gabriela tried to comfort the stricken young woman, but she couldn't stop Lucy's anguished sobbing. "Who do you think it will be? Sierra, daddy, you, or me?"

Nick felt the walls closing in around him—it was like his body was slowly being crushed by a vice.

He reached for his cell phone and called Isabella. When the call was answered, Nick's face reflected his iron will. "Enough is enough. I know that you want to protect us, but we just can't sit here doing nothing. We need something to make us feel useful—anything to make us feel like we're helping."

"Good, I was just about to call you." Isabella told Nick what they'd found out about the Canadian woman who'd tried to kill him. "Trouble is Nick, we're stretched tight, so if you guys can follow up on what the cops in Toronto are sending us about the Rojas woman, it would be a great help."

Nick knew exactly what she was saying. *Sit tight Nick, here's a little something you can do without leaving the hotel.* Nick responded in anger. "Fuck off, Isabella. Gabriela and I need to be in the field where the action is. Lucy's a lawyer. I'll get her to deal with the Canadian shit." He hung up without even saying *adios*.

ψ

Sierra got very little sleep that night. The anticipation of what might happen at the conclave played heavily on her mind. *What if I can't go through with it? What if Levi doesn't go through with his part? What if both of us die?* Thoughts of the unknown, the uncontrollable, and the unexpected filled her mind. *There's nothing that I can do except let the pieces fall as they may—like a massive row of dominos.*

There was a gentle knock on her door. "*Señorita*, breakfast is about to be served."

Sierra had already showered and dressed. She touched up her makeup and went downstairs to the terrace.

Rodriguez, Ortiz, and Levi were already at the table, and all three men stood when she approached.

"Good morning, sister, I do hope that you had a good sleep." There was a look in his eyes that immediately put her on guard.

"Thank you, Philippe. I slept like a baby."

The meal, as usual, was beyond reproach but none of them seemed to be hungry—instead, they picked hesitatingly at the bounty on the buffet. It was as if the anticipation of the night's conclave had dulled their appetites.

"We leave this evening, following an early dinner."

Rodriguez's words left Sierra feeling that their evening meal may just be her last.

He continued. "Today is time for preparation and relaxation." Rodriguez stood. "I will speak to each of you individually before we leave."

ψ

Sierra returned to her room and waited for her turn to be briefed. One, two, four, six hours passed, and Rodriguez didn't show up. *What the fuck is he up to?* she thought.

Just before dinner, there was another tentative knock. "*Señorita*, dinner will be served in twenty minutes."

Sierra was nervous. Was it Rodriguez's plan to leave her in the dark? Was he using the tactic of avoidance to unhinge her? Her mind was racing, and her hands were clammy with terror. She pulled her thoughts together and went downstairs for dinner.

Rodriguez greeted her as she entered the dining room. "I apologize for not being able to see some of you today. Sometimes, business takes precedence over good intentions." Rodriguez sat and invited the others to join him at the table.

ψ

Following dinner, Rodriguez led the group down into the hacienda's basement. He pushed aside a stack of boxes, opened a hidden door, and directed them to follow him through the dimly lit tunnel. The farther they went, the more the walls of the cramped space seemed to close in on them. Sierra felt an indescribable panic, a sense of foreboding that engulfed her whole being.

"We're almost there." Rodriguez stopped in front of another door, opened it with his key, and led them into a sparkling white, freshly painted underground parking garage.

The expanse contained fifty or so cars. Two nondescript sedans pulled out from where they were parked and pulled up in front of them.

Rodriguez smiled. "Please get in. This will be the final leg of our long journey."

CHAPTER FIFTY-TWO

Luc and Emilie were sitting next to the railing at a table on the rooftop restaurant of their hotel. They had an excellent view of the Zócalo, Mexico City's massive main square, and had just witnessed a smartly dressed contingent of Mexico's military men and women complete the ceremony of lowering and folding the country's huge flag.

As the crowds of tourists and *defeños* began leaving the area, Luc spotted a pair of familiar faces. "Em, isn't that Sierra and Levi down there?" He pointed to a couple: the woman was tall and beautiful, and the man small and sinewy. The young woman squinted to see who her brother was pointing at. "*Oui*, Luc, that's definitely them. I wonder where they're going?"

Luc was already on his cell. "Hey, Nick, Em and I just saw Sierra and Levi. They're in the Zócalo with Rodriguez and some other dude, and it looks like they're heading toward the cathedral."

Nick was thunderstruck. Isabella had officers covering Rodriguez's home. How in hell's name did they manage to slip past the cops? Nick's mind was running on hyperdrive.

He thanked Luc and hung up his phone. "Gabi, quick, get your jacket. We're getting out of here. Luc just called—he saw Sierra, Levi, and Rodriguez in the Zócalo heading toward the cathedral. Lucy, call Isabella and tell her that we'll meet her there."

"I'm coming too, and don't try to stop me." Lucy grabbed her jacket and followed them through the door.

ψ

The Catedral Metropolitana officially closed at 5:30 p.m. It was now after 8:00 p.m. Nevertheless, as Luc and Emilie watched, Sierra and Levi, along with a dozen or so other visitors, were being ushered into a side door of the magnificent building. "*Merde*, I think that the conclave is being held inside the cathedral." Luc placed another call to Nick.

ψ

Isabella Marino hung up from her call with the breathless Lucy and rushed to her superior's office. She apprised her boss about the situation in the Zócalo and within minutes was on her way, leading a small convoy of tactical police vehicles in a race toward the cathedral.

She arrived at the same time as Nick and Gabriela. "I can't fucking believe it. Rodriguez is holding the conclave in the very same place where we took down his father." Nick was about to run towards the huge church.

Isabella grabbed Nick's shoulder. "Stay back. I know that you want to be in on the action, but it's a police matter now, and I don't have the time or desire to babysit you and your family."

Nick pushed her away. "You don't know where the secret chamber is, and I do."

Isabella nodded, then handed him a bulletproof vest and handgun. "Okay, but if there's any shooting, stay well back."

The force of Mexican special unit police officers was like a small army. They entered the church one by one. Each officer had switched off the safety catch on their fully loaded automatic weapons and were on high alert for any real or perceived threats. They passed by the magnificent display of gold adornments and silently made their way down into the very bowels of the cathedral's basement.

Nick stopped in front of the hidden room where he, Francisca, and long-forgotten members of the Mexican police department had crushed Hector Rodriguez and the leadership of La Orden de las Serpientes de Cristo.

Nick's eyes widened. "It's not here. The entrance has been sealed." The anguish in his voice echoed off the basement's cold, stone walls.

Isabella's gloved fingers traced along the seams of cold damp cement that, many years ago, was used to cover and seal the dank chamber. "There's got to be another hidden room somewhere." She gave orders for her team to spread out and search the cathedral.

Gabriela was thinking. *What if the conclave isn't here? What if Rodriguez is playing us with a trail of breadcrumbs like in Hansel and Gretel?* She turned toward Nick and Isabella. "Is there any other way out of here?"

"There's another door on the opposite side of the cathedral," said Nick. "The last time I was here, several of the apostles tried to escape through it."

"Let's take a look. I've got a hunch that they're not in the cathedral at all." Gabriela, Isabella, Lucy, and several members of the tactical unit followed Nick back up to Altar Major, the huge cathedral's main sacristy.

"It's over here." Nick ran toward a side door and pushed it open. *Strange, it's not locked*, he thought.

Gabriela bent over and picked up a pale turquoise bead from off the pavement. "What's this?"

"There's another one here," said Lucy. She ran ahead and picked up another bead. "These are beads from Sierra's mother's rosary. I remember her showing it to me in Paris. I think that she's leaving us a trail."

Isabella spoke quietly into her walkie-talkie and called for her colleagues to join them.

"Let's hope that she doesn't run out of beads—or get found out," said Gabriela.

CHAPTER FIFTY-THREE

Museo del Templo Mayor is a strikingly modern building specifically designed to hold the priceless treasures and artifacts discovered during excavations of the adjacent ruins. The museum is located a short walk away from the Catedral Metropolitana and the Zócalo.

Rodriguez had previously arranged after-hours access to the museum for a special tour of foreign dignitaries. Extravagant donations to the museum, and individual stipends to selected guards, made the unprecedented request and subsequent visit possible.

One of the famous museum's most popular galleries features a wall of replica skulls, an eerie depiction of the skulls of martyred prisoners discovered by archaeologists when they were excavating ruins of the original temple.

At the request of the museum's generous patron, a round table, covered with flickering candles and surrounded by thirteen chairs, had been set up directly in front of the gruesome wall. These chairs were now occupied by Rodriguez, Sierra, and the apostles of La Orden de las Serpientes de Cristo. The room's only other occupant was Levi Heifetz, who stood in the shadows, guarding the assembly from any unwelcome intrusion.

Except for Levi, all those in attendance wore coarse black hooded robes that were tied at the waist with a thick multicolored rope. Rodriguez's face was concealed behind a twenty-four-karat gold mask shaped in the image of the ancient Aztec snake god. A stainless-steel likeness of a serpent's forked tongue was protruding menacingly from between its fangs.

Rodriguez stood and slowly walked around the table, touching the shoulder of each apostle with the gold serpent ring that he wore on the middle finger of his right hand.

As he walked, he spoke. "My dear and devoted companions. Since our last conclave, an event of momentous significance has occurred." He stopped directly behind the chair occupied by Sierra.

The young woman was terrified. Flickering flames from the candles amplified the shadows of apostles against the skull-filled wall of the room, casting ghostly highlights on their partially hidden faces. Sierra felt the soft touch of Rodriguez's hand on her shoulder. She recoiled slightly at the unexpected contact.

"This woman is my sister and, like me, is a direct descendant of the high priest Coatl and Christina de Delgado, the founders of our faith." He took a deep breath, the sound of which was terrifyingly amplified through the mask that he wore. "And like me, the holy blood of the snake god Quetzalcoatl flows through her veins."

Rodriguez took one step back from where Sierra was seated. "In the event of my demise, this beautiful young woman would assume leadership of our order. It is to her that you would pledge your devotion and total allegiance."

He calmly removed the colored rope from around his waist. "But that, my eminent friends, is not going to happen. Instead, my dear sister will be honored tonight by becoming a martyr—the ultimate offering to our great lord Quetzalcoatl."

He swung his rope over Sierra's head and pulled it tightly against her throat.

Levi leaped forward, and with lightning-fast speed, tackled the man in the mask and knocked him to the floor.

Rodriguez, Sierra, and Levi went down in a jumbled heap of limbs and robes, and in the melee, Rodriguez's mask flew from beneath his hood and clattered noisily along the floor. Levi grabbed it, lifted it high above Rodriguez's body, and plunged the snake's steel tongue into Rodriguez's chest. A rasping gasp of death emanated from Rodriguez. Blood gurgled out from his chest, spread across his coarse black raiment, and flowed out onto the floor beneath him.

A stunned silence followed. For a moment, nobody in the chamber moved. Suddenly there was an anguished scream from Ronaldo Ortiz. "No!" He pulled a gun from beneath his robe and fired at Levi. The bullet smashed into Levi's back, and he fell forward across Sierra's barely breathing form and Rodriguez's blood-soaked body.

Another sound distracted the shooter. The door behind him crashed open. Ortiz spun around to see who the unwelcome intruder was. He raised his weapon but didn't get a chance to fire it.

Two shots rang out in quick succession and Ortiz fell, face up, across the table. His body convulsed and blood began pumping out from both a large hole in his forehead and a second grisly opening in his throat. Isabella Moreno rushed in ahead of the elite squad of special forces officers. Nick, Gabriela, and Lucy followed closely behind her.

ψ

Lucy ran over to where Sierra was lying. She gently lifted Levi's bloody body from off her friend and removed the sash that was tightly wrapped around her throat. "Sierra! Sierra, can you hear me? Are you alright?" The young woman slowly lifted her head and nodded.

"Don't talk, you don't have to talk" Tears of joy streaked down Lucy's flushed cheeks. She was still on her knees hugging her friend when the paramedics arrived.

The first team to reach the scene, a man and woman, lifted Lucy off her friend and quickly checked Levi's vital signs. "*El hombre todavia está vivo!*"

News that Levi was alive elicited a weak smile from Sierra. "Levi saved my life. He saved my life."

The second team of first responders went to work assisting their colleagues. Sierra and Levi were gently lifted onto gurneys. Intravenous tubes delivering pain medication were inserted into both of their arms', medical monitoring equipment was hooked up, and the team's two patients were wheeled out to waiting ambulances. A third ambulance took the bloody bodies of both Philippe Rodriguez and Ronaldo Ortiz to one of the city's grossly overcrowded morgues.

The jarring sound of quickly departing sirens reverberated off the city's ancient walls, waking many of Centro's sleeping visitors and residents.

ψ

The police unceremoniously herded the black-robed cult leaders against the wall of skulls. Gabriela looked at them. "There's something disgustingly creepy and fitting about this image," She whispered to Isabella. The detective shrugged and agreed.

The apostles were searched, handcuffed, and then taken one-by-one to a squad of waiting police vehicles. Their notes and laptops were collected and transported to the police's cybercrimes division.

Nick, although overjoyed with the evening's successful takedown, looked despondent. "Now the real problem begins."

The others looked at him as if he was crazy. Only Gabriela understood his remark. "It's true. How are we going to deal with the thousands of Rodriguez's followers spread throughout the world? In a depraved way, they're just as guilty as Rodriguez."

CHAPTER FIFTY-FOUR

News of Philippe Rodriguez's death was the lead story online and in print and broadcast media throughout the world. The brutally truthful stories reported on almost every detail regarding his heinous criminal activities.

The resulting rush of underworld bosses, high society families, celebrities, global leaders, and high-profile business bigwigs attempting to deny any association with the man was described by one prominent media pundit as "an out-of-control three-ring circus."

ψ

The president of the Russian Federation was working at his desk in the Kremlin. He looked up, displeased that he was being disturbed. "Enter."

A woman dressed in the uniform of president's security detail softly entered his office, handed him a folded note, bowed, and backed silently out of the room.

The pasty-faced leader opened the note, and a thin smile crossed his face. He scrunched the paper into a tight ball and tossed it into his wastebasket. *Good, the bastard's dead, and for once I didn't have to arrange it. Now I can get back to business as usual.*

ψ

Luc and Emilie were enlisted by Mexico City's police cybercrimes unit to help them decipher the encrypted data contained on computers confiscated at the museum. Slowly, the team unearthed massive amounts of incriminating evidence. Each revelation resulted in a series of arrests by police jurisdictions throughout the world.

Because of her involvement in the operation, Isabella Moreno was promoted to first lieutenant in the Mexico City police force, and in her new role, took a lead position coordinating international investigations regarding Rodriguez's criminal associates and their illegal activities.

ψ

Sierra visited Levi daily. His condition was serious, but doctors and staff at the Hospital Angeles in Mexico City managed to save the man's life. He was in a private room surrounded by flowers and frequently checked on by a hand-picked team of concerned doctors and nurses.

Sierra brought more flowers into the room, and Levi laughed. "No more, Sierra, it's beginning to look like a goddamn greenhouse in here."

Ignoring him, Sierra arranged the flowers in a vase. "Nick and the others want to come and see you. Are you up for all that adulation?"

Levi smiled. "Perhaps in a few days. Right now, all that I want is to rest."

Sierra leaned over, kissed the man on his cheek, and silently left the room.

Except for his physical wounds, Levi couldn't remember the last time that he'd felt this good. The demons, terrors, and dark nightmares that had haunted him for what seemed like an eternity had all but vanished. *I wonder if the ghosts of angels that I've heard them talk about have anything to do with me feeling this good?*

ψ

In Washington, the House and Senate, in a rare moment of bipartisanship, unanimously passed a bill declaring that La Orden de las Serpientes de Cristo be designated an international terrorist organization. Membership in the order would invoke prosecution, resulting in serious fines and incarceration. Other nations throughout the western world passed similar legislation. For all intents and purposes, La Orden de la Serpientes de Cristo was dead—or forced to be even more deeply hidden.

ψ

Three weeks later, it seemed that everyone connected with the case was crowded into Levi's hospital room celebrating the demise of Philippe Rodriguez and the heinous Order that he controlled. Sierra and Lucy were there, alongside Nick and Gabriela, Luc and Emilie, Isabella Moreno, and on a zoom call, Alain Moreau and Pierre Aubert in France and Josh Nicholson with the two youngest Palmer siblings in Chicago.

Levi was sitting up in his bed with a wide smile on his tanned face. His chest was bandaged, and numerous intravenous tubes still dripped their life-saving medicine into his slim, tattooed arm.

Nick popped open a bottle of champagne, poured the bubbly liquid into delicately engraved flutes, and raised his glass in a toast. "Here's to all of you. Your sacrifice and unwavering dedication helped bring Rodriguez and his cult of evil to its end. Thank you." He raised his eyes skyward. "And here's to Francisca Ramirez Flores and all the other brave souls who made the ultimate sacrifice in the name of justice. You will always be remembered."

Gabriela took a sip, raised her glass, and made another toast. "And here's to the many young women who lost their lives—innocent martyrs, who didn't deserve to die." She paused and looked toward Luc and Emilie. "And to Natalie and Louis, whom I'm sure are in heaven, proudly looking down on their two wonderful children."

Luc and Emilie choked back tears. Thoughts of their loving parents, and the realization that all that remained of them were fond memories of their time together, was overwhelming to them. Gabriela noticed their heartache and rushed over to hug the two young heroes.

Nick looked around at the small group of friends. "I only wish that Henri could be here to join us in this celebration."

Nick heard an ethereal chuckle, and then, in a familiar voice meant only for him, came the words, "Who says that I'm not here, *mom ami*? Who says that I'm not here?"

Nick smiled, raised his glass of champagne to the elderly professor, and whispered softly, "*Merci,* my dear friend. Thank you for everything."

ABOUT THE AUTHOR

A.E. Lawrence is a pen name. The real person lives with Vickie, his wife of forty-plus years, and Stella, a small sometimes overly affectionate dog, in a restored century-old stone barn in a village slightly northwest of Toronto.

In a previous life, the author founded a successful marketing & design company in Toronto and has won numerous awards for writing ads, commercials, brochures, videos, and the like for a wide variety of clients.

When not writing or doing chores, you'll find him fly fishing at his club, travelling for fun and literary research, or simply enjoying the company of family and friends.

www.ingramcontent.com/pod-product-compliance
Lightning Source LLC
LaVergne TN
LVHW091811210525
811870LV00001B/136